Maker on the
High Road

Henry Melton

Maker on the High Road

Henry Melton

Wire Rim Books
Hutto, Texas

WRB

Maker on the High Road © 2023 by Henry Melton
All Rights Reserved

Printing History
First Edition: January 2023
ISBN 978-1-935236-90-0

ePub ISBN 978-1-935236-91-7
Kindle ISBN 978-1-935236-92-4

Website of Henry Melton
www.HenryMelton.com

Printed in the United States of America

Wire Rim Books
www.wirerimbooks.com

Acknowledgements

Sometimes it's hard to nail down where the idea of a story came from. The best I can do is recognize all the people who helped me work out the details.

I'm very grateful to Jeff Barnhart, CEO of the Hereford Regional Medical Center for the behind-the-scenes tour of the hospital and the details the Plant Operations crew; Vincent Gallegos, Israel Olivo and Johnny Zambrano shared with me.

Thanks also goes to Clay Phennicie who allowed me to look over his shoulder when he was building a Long-EZ plane and took me on a few touch-and-go exercises many long years ago.

Helpful advice came from Xantheus Lawrence of X Of All Trades for 3D printing issues.

And also, I'm thankful to Hatch, New Mexico. I hope to come back soon.

Recognizing my own defects in getting words down on the page, I'm very grateful to the people who tell me what I got wrong; Jim Dunn, Linda Elliott, Todd Hartman, Mike Lynch, Scott McNay and Tom Stock.

Contents

Hatch New Mexico Region

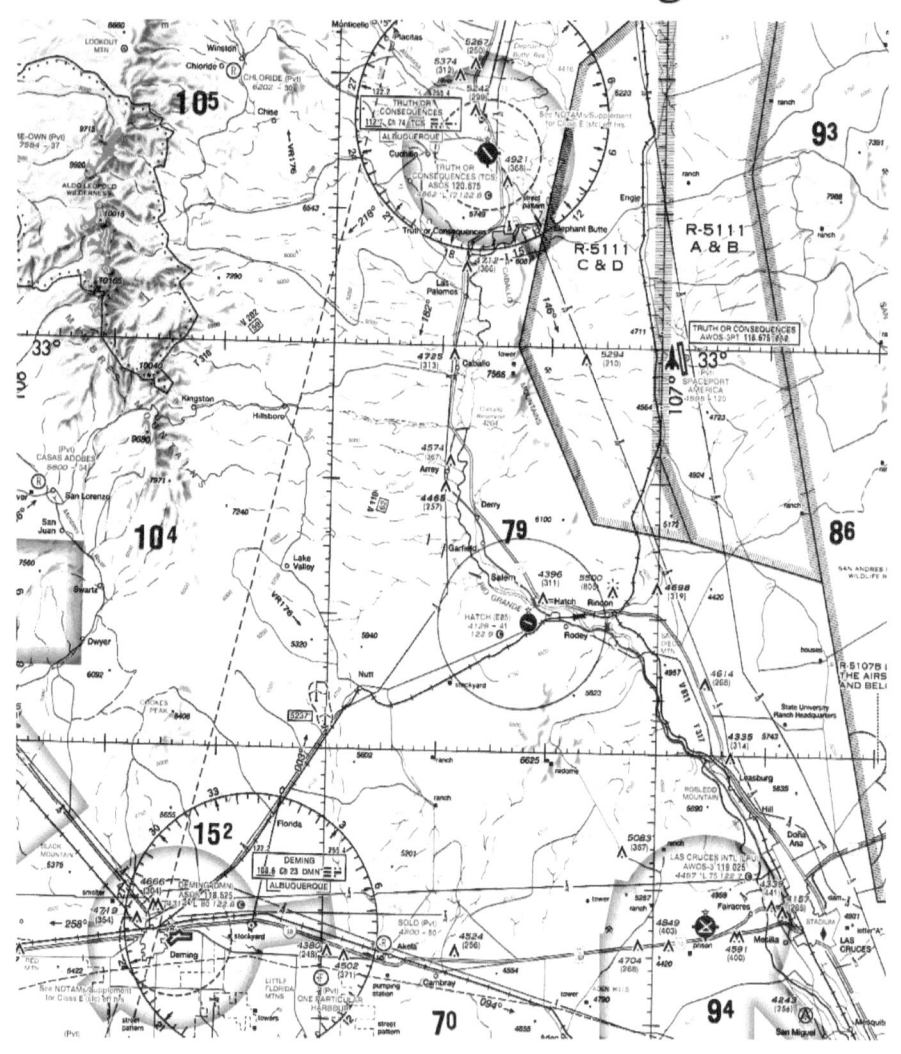

Leaving for Tucson

Luke glanced at the clock—3 AM. He sighed and rubbed his eyes.

Am I getting old? Twenty-four isn't old. But he'd had more resilience when he was a teen. He remembered staying up all night tweaking his slicer program to handle new and different source materials back then.

He stared at the code before him. *This isn't any different.*

But he knew it was. Hacking his 3D printer to work with a different kind of high temperature filament at smaller dimensions was just a bit different from focusing an ultraviolet laser to cut holes much smaller than he could see.

I'm just lucky I have access to all this stuff.

He looked around at his place. The equipment he'd bought at a bankruptcy sale was still mostly packed in crates along the south wall of the small warehouse building. On the north side was his bed, the microwave and the shower he'd jury-rigged from PVC pipe and vinyl sheeting. He was just lucky the warehouse already came with a decent toilet. He emptied his bank balance and gave up his apartment to come up with the cash to buy the equipment, and the rental on the abandoned warehouse was less than half what he'd been spending on that apartment.

I'll really regret it when the summer heat wave hits. A fan is just not going to be enough.

He closed his eyes and realized he was on the verge of dozing off in his chair. And he needed to go to work in the morning. He still needed that paycheck.

He made sure the file was saved and powered down the screen. The computer had its jobs to do in the background so it stayed on.

He staggered over to the bed and collapsed.

...

"Wait." Luke hurried into the examination room and turned the heart-rate monitor around. He wiggled the square insert on the back. The screen flashed and then went dead again. He nodded and reached for a paper clip that had fallen behind the instrument back before they went to using tablets to track the patient records. He bent it into a square U-shape and wedged it around the loose fuse holder. The monitor came back on.

The nurse blinked. "You fixed it?"

He shook his head. "No. I'll bring a replacement." He walked out.

He was barely back at the plant operations work room, checking out a working monitor from the stores when the phone rang.

"Luke Moore, Plant Operations."

It was Dr. Easton. "Good. I caught you. Nurse Jenkins said you fixed the monitor?"

"Oh, no. I just brought it temporarily back to life until I could pull a replacement. I'll have to open it up and replace the fuse block to fix it."

"But it's working."

"Yes, until someone bumps it the right way and then it'll go out again."

Dr. Easton sighed. Luke knew he was always worried about the budget. "So, is this an easy fix?"

"Oh, yes. I have the parts and everything. I'll have it checked out before long. We don't have to buy a replacement."

"That's good. It's not in the budget. But… you could have explained all that to Nurse Jenkins."

"Sorry. I wanted to get to work moving the replacement into service as soon as possible."

Luke knew it wasn't that. He just wasn't very glib when talking to women. *I'll need to work on that, or I'll never get a girlfriend.*

Dr. Easton asked, "Are you interested in working this weekend? You said there was a backlog of repair jobs."

Luke sighed. "Sorry. Normally I would, but I have a conflict. Carlos Smith is on call."

"Oh, right. Your convention. You told me about that. Where is it this time?"

"Tucson."

"That's a few hours drive. Well, enjoy the event."

Luke had his fingers crossed. He'd never attended the Tucson convention before and had no idea how his artwork would sell there. What with the motel room and travel cost, plus the charge for the table spot, he just had to hope he'd turn a profit.

...

Backing the van into the warehouse through the big doors let him load up out of the sun. *I really ought to put a bed in the van and save on the motel costs.* But he knew that he really needed a shower over the duration of the weekend-long event and there wasn't really space in the van to install any kind of shower stall, along with the water supply and drain.

Some day, when he had money, he'd investigate an electric RV with living space and enough storage room to carry all his gear. But it was obvious that such a luxury was far out of his reach.

As it was, gas was a big part of his expenses. The van didn't have great gas mileage. But... there was no way he could stack all his boxes on the back of a motorcycle and drive the hundreds of miles to the convention.

So he loaded his 3D-printed art, all shrouded in bubble-wrap, into large boxes, as well as a supply of smaller boxes he'd unfold as needed when a customer purchased something. He also loaded his little Ender 3D printer and a battery-run power generator strong enough to run it. The convention did have power available for the tables, but he couldn't afford the price. Some conventions charged $50 or more per day just to plug into a wall socket. His battery box was good enough for several hours usage.

Packed in a suitcase was his costume and soon enough, he was ready to hit the road.

...

The route from Hatch, New Mexico to Tucson was nearly all desert, but with the interstates, it was only a little over four hours. Luke enjoyed the drive. He settled in behind a big truck and cruised in the silence, mentally working out the details of one project or another.

I bet I can do without an igniter. Make a ring of needles around the entrance. He wasn't sure it would actually work, but it ought to. The only way was to fabricate one and test it out. The point of a needle ought to have the most intense electric field available, but would it be enough to ionize the air coming into the tube?

But how to grow the needles? They'd have to be connected to the aluminum substrate.

The miles passed by.

He arrived at the Tucson Convention Center and checked in, unloading his boxes with a hand trolley and beginning the set up at his table. Under the retractable banner that proclaimed Maker Products along with photos of dozens of his items, he set up his 3D printer and his most dramatic statues. On the other side of the table were shelves with some of the smaller and more affordable items that would probably make up the bulk of his sales.

In the center of the table was a big picture book of thousands of items he could print on demand. There was a limit to how many he could print during the con, but he could charge extra for them.

There were a dozen other vendors he recognized from other conventions. Many of them attended all the same events he did. Some of them had been doing this for decades and knew all the tricks.

But soon enough he had his table set up, ready for the tomorrow's crowd. He took a colorful table sheet decorated with blue robots and spread it out over his product. It was certainly not enough to stop a thief, but it would reduce general temptation. The event organizers were supposed to keep the area under lock and key.

It was time to check in at his motel.

Luke chose the cheapest motel available and just put up with the results. He had earplugs to soften the noises from other rooms and a mask to block out the light from the street lamps. He didn't expect anything from the free breakfast advertised—he had his own food bars and fruit to eat.

The worst recurring problem was the room key cards with magnetic stripes that never lasted more than a few hours for him. Was he unlucky, or just too magnetic?

If he could have counted driving to Tucson and setting up all on Saturday morning, he would have just stayed the one night. Unfortunately, he couldn't manage that.

Friday night supper was a chicken salad from a drive-thru Whataburger.

Special Orders

The scent of hot plastic was familiar as his 3D-printer was dancing around, building up a gold-colored tiara for the customer. Other customers were fascinated by the process and were happy enough to buy toys, models, and statues from his stock.

"Do you have this one in blue?" asked a customer.

Luke nodded, "Yes, let me find it."

"Does this work?" asked another costumed attendee a bit later, holding up a painted ophthalmoscope.

Luke smiled. "No, the original was corroded, so I gutted the wiring and painted it. I added a clip, so you could hang it on your costume." He showed it off. The button still clicked, but the light didn't come on.

Luke's own costume, an eclectic steam punk mishmash, was designed to show off some of his gadgets as well. He was quite prepared to sell items off his costume if anyone showed interest.

Steam punk and Ghostbuster themed costumed people were prime customers, since he had a lot of non-functional gadgets for sale. Some of them even had moving parts, but he wasn't in the business of selling real gadgets.

"Can you paint this?" asked a teenager, pointing to a bland white statue of a barbarian swinging a sword.

"Yes, it's designed to be painted. It's just that I'm not the guy to do it. It takes me five times the effort to paint a statue as it is to make it in the first place. Besides," Luke chuckled, "I wouldn't do a very good job of it."

The boy bought the figurine, nodding to himself, probably with grand plans for it. Table-top gamers were regular customers.

The woman standing next in line, with long blonde pigtails, dressed as Sailor Moon, had been listening. "So you can make custom statues?"

Luke felt his mouth close up. He nodded and pointed to the big books. "Anything in here. The larger ones I'll have to ship." He could manage the standard phrases.

She nodded and thumbed through the pictures. "I don't see what I'm looking for. I was hoping to get a Sailor Moon figurine."

Luke shook his head. "Copyright. I can only do public domain or special licenses."

"Oh," she sighed. "so these aren't your designs?"

"No. Not an artist."

She nodded. "But where did you get all these?"

"Websites. Some free, some pay. STL models."

She frowned. "But no anime figures?"

He shrugged. "Didn't look. Can't print everything."

She chuckled, and glanced at the man in the Ghostbuster costume waiting behind her. "Well, we'll talk later." She moved off into the crowd.

Luke wondered for an instant if he had met her at another con, but there were other customers who deserved his full attention.

...

Saturday was a good day, and Sunday wasn't bad. As usual, Luke was limited to what convention activities he could see, stuck as he was at his table. He barely managed a couple of bathroom breaks during the floor hours. Some vendors had multiple people attending the table, but he was on his own.

But, it was entertaining to watch the customers wander by, decked out in their costumes. Whether it was a toddler in Star Wars pjs or a dedicated cosplayer in elaborate jewelry and feathers, he appreciated the enthusiasm.

His steampunk costume was less authentic. Not that there was any official steampunk costume—that was part of the attraction. Most of the others had elaborate back stories to explain their choices. Luke's costume was just a walking billboard for his products.

The clock ticked down for the Sunday closing hours. As usual, the crowd dwindled away. And as usual, those people who had promised to return at the end of the day for their last minute purchases never showed.

Luke had a few idle minutes to add up his sales. It was going to be a profitable weekend, but hardly a record-breaker.

Then came the final announcement and he began to pack up.

...

He was home by ten, giving him just enough time to unload the van and get some sleep before he was due back at work in the morning.

The main reason Dr. Easton hired him was his ability to repair and calibrate the electronic equipment. Getting a piece of gear back up and running was only the first step. Carlos Smith, the other half of plant operations, was twice his age and excellent at most of the other tasks, like plumbing, carpentry and standard electrical. But Carlos had been in the habit of just shelving anything electronic. The hospital had been getting a mobile repair service in periodically to handle everything Carlos couldn't deal with.

Some medical devices had rigorous licensing requirements. It would be disastrous if a device gave the wrong measurements to the doctors who had to make life or death decisions based on those numbers. Some things were as simple as replacing a fuse or a battery. Others had critical devices that when changed had to be calibrated to national standards before the gadget could be released back into service. But having a tech in-house to do it was much cheaper than shipping the device to a lab in another state.

The process was often time-consuming, so he had a backlog. It was two in the afternoon before he took a lunch break. He got a sandwich from the lunch counter and sat down to relax.

One of the nurses glanced his way, picked up her tray and moved it to his table.

"So about the Sailor Moon figurine...."

Luke blinked, staring at her.

"A wig?"

She chuckled and tucked her short brown hair back behind her ear. "Well, of course. Hip-length pigtails is hardly a practical hair style for a nurse."

He sighed and shook his head. "Didn't recognize you."

She waved her hand. "No problem. I didn't recognize you at first either. For one thing, you were talkative. What's the deal? Do you need your steampunk hat on to loosen up, or what?"

He shook his head. He knew that wasn't the reason.

She sighed. "So you can make the figure if you have the right model, is that it?"

He nodded.

She pushed. "So it's just the licensing issues, right?"

He nodded. Then said, "Unpainted."

She nodded. "Right. I'll have to paint it. I suppose I could make a separate video of that."

He tilted his head, puzzled.

She smiled. "When I'm not being a nurse, I stream videos. That's what I was doing most of the weekend, being Sailor Moon at the convention, showing videos of all the attractions. I even took pictures of the vendors. You didn't notice me?"

He shook his head.

"Well, you were talking to a customer at the time. I hope you didn't mind the free advertising."

He shrugged.

She shook her head. "You really don't talk much, do you?

"Well, I've got to get back to work. When can you show me where to find these computer models you need?"

He frowned. He had everything set up on his computers at home, but it would be hard to coach her how to do it on her own computer.

"Um. My place. After seven?"

She considered. "Okay, I can do that. What's your address?"

I can't get the place clean by then, but it's a lost cause anyway. He pulled out one of his Maker Products business cards and circled the mailing address.

She peered at the card. "That's on the other side of the tracks, isn't it? You work out of your house? I'll see you then."

She picked up her tray and left. He concentrated on his sandwich.

Maybe I ought to watch the Sailor Moon shows. I never really got into that one. It's obviously designed for young girls. Still, there are a lot of women who cosplay as Sailor Moon and the other variants. They must have some reason for it.

He remembered a few years ago when he had the intent to catch up on it and started watching Sailor Moon Crystal, or something like that, but for some reason, he'd abandoned it halfway through the first episode. *I didn't last long enough to get involved with it.*

Which anime website had that been? He'd sampled several of the sites and dropped them because they were too expensive or lacked the variety he wanted.

I'll just ask … oops, I didn't get her name. What was the point of name tags if he didn't read them?

Well, he wasn't going to ask around to find out. People would talk.

He finished off the sandwich and headed back to the workshop. He needed to finish what he was doing before the end of the day. If he left early enough, maybe he could clean up the place before she arrived. *I should have said eight instead of seven.*

But it was too late. He didn't have her name or number. No way to call her to change the time.

Bracelet

Luke was sweeping dust out the warehouse door when he noticed an old Buick moving down the street, reaching the dead end of the dirt road, and then start creeping back.

He stepped out into the sun and waved. The Buick stopped in the middle of the street, and then pulled into his parking lot.

When she opened the car door, he said, "Not a house."

She shook her head. "I gathered. I thought the GPS was messed up when I pulled onto this street." She got out. "You have your own business place."

"Just a warehouse." He gestured to the door.

She frowned. "There's no sign."

"Not a storefront."

She went inside and looked around at the big open space. "And you live here?"

He nodded. The other buildings were mobile homes with nice large fenced yards, and as a dead-end road with no traffic, there were often kids playing out in the middle of what passed as a street.

She pulled out her phone. "Do you mind if I take some video?"

He frowned. "Go ahead."

She framed the image and began talking. "Today, I've come to visit Maker Products. The company's owner, Luke Moore, has a whole warehouse of devices at his disposal for producing his gadgets and artwork.

"Luke, could you explain what this device is?"

He nearly froze up, not expecting an interview show. He hoped she wasn't streaming it live.

Luckily, he didn't have to think much about it.

"That's a CNC laser cutter and engraver. It uses a computer-controlled laser to cut or engrave wood, tile, metal and such. It's something like a laser printer in the office, but with a much more powerful laser that can burn through most materials."

"What do you use it for?"

Luke shrugged. "I can make custom signs. For example, if I wished a sign for my warehouse, I could easily make it with this device."

She smiled. "And what's this device over here?"

"That's one of my 3D printers. It melts this monofilament plastic and deposits it to build up the model."

"You say *one* of your 3D printers? How many do you have?"

He blinked and looked around. "Um. Eight of them, I guess. That one over there is damaged and doesn't really count."

"Why do you have so many of them?"

He felt uneasy looking at her, so he focused on the lens of her cell phone camera. "Well, the technology has continually improved over time, so I kept getting the new, better version as they came out. But the older ones are still perfectly functional within their range of sizes and materials, so I like to keep them all up and running."

"Do you ever have them all working at once?"

"More often than you'd think. 3D printing isn't nearly as fast as printing a page on a laser printer. Some models take hours to complete. If there is a particularly popular model that people might buy at a convention, say when a new superhero movie comes out, then I might have several of the machines all running at one time, producing inventory I might need later."

She nodded, and turned off the camera. "You're starting to sweat. I didn't mean to put you on the spot like that."

He shrugged. "No AC."

She looked around at the warehouse and saw the big box fan turning. "Yes, I can see." She smiled. "But it was nice hearing you talk in more than monosyllables."

"Was that live?"

"Oh, no. It was just something I might use later if I wanted to produce some show about your stuff. I take a lot of small videos and edit them together into something more smooth."

He nodded. "I can make something for you. Something quick."

She nodded, "And I could video it."

He waved her over to the computer desk. He had three monitors connected, so it looked more elaborate than it really was. He waited for her to start up her video again.

Luke brought up the web browser. "This is one of the most popular websites for STL models for 3D printers." He downloaded the model of the bracelet and ran another program.

"The slicer program converts STL, which is stereolithography, the model expressed as triangles, into G-code, which is the code to drive the 3D printer.

"And now we move the file over to one of the printers." He held up a spool rack. "Choose a color."

She tapped a light blue. He took the spool and inserted it into the printer.

"The first step is to align the platform." He went through the process and with the model inserted, he tapped the buttons and the printer began working.

She had a small tripod in her bag and quickly set up her phone to video the whole process. "I'll speed up the playback in the final edit, but this is fascinating."

Watching the bracelet being slowly built up couldn't hold her attention very long. "So," she asked, "is this the way I could get the Sailor Moon figurine?"

He nodded. "Pretty much, although I won't be surprised if you have to purchase the file. You could probably get a commercial figurine for maybe $50 at the cons."

"I know. I've seen them, but I'm looking for something a little more ... special. So, show me how to find the model."

He gave her the bookmarks and turned her loose to search on her own.

It wasn't ten minutes later before she said, "I found one." But quickly she added. "It's not very good."

"Keep looking, there are probably a lot more."

As the scent of vaporized plastic perfumed the air, she worked, giving up on one website and starting on another.

"Um. Luke, come here."

He pulled up a stool so he could sit behind her and stare at the screen.

She pointed, "What are these things?"

There were photos of the model in various stages of production.

He nodded. "The printing process lays dots of molten plastic on top of the previous layer that has already hardened. It can't deposit a dot in mid air and expect it to hover there. So, like here on her pigtails, the model puts in an extra platform underneath the hair, so that there will be a place to deposit that first dot. It's the same over here on her skirt. Once the model is completed, then you have to carve away that extra platform and sand the surface smooth."

She frowned. "That looks like extra work."

"It is, but there's no help for it. I've actually seen models that flip the statue on its head with the feet and hands in the air to get around the problem, but that wasn't done on this one. There's danger that it wouldn't be stable."

She chuckled. "I can see that." She tapped at the license fee. "What happens if I buy this and it turns out that the model is faulty?"

He shrugged. "I suppose you could try to get a refund, but really, a lot of this is based on good and bad reviews. Look at the reviews yourself and see if you trust it."

She nodded. "I guess I'll look some more. I really only want to do this once. Do you mind if I come back again?"

"No."

"Good. I don't want to interrupt the video of the bracelet, and I'd like to video me looking for the model, too."

"It should be another fifteen minutes for the bracelet."

"Um. How much will Sailor Moon cost me?"

"Other than the license fee?"

"Yes, how much for the expense of getting it printed out, and this extra stuff carved off?"

He considered. "Many of the cons I attend want photos and promotional material from their vendors. I've been skimping on that. If you make me a good promo photo and a video, then I'll do the Sailor Moon figurine for free."

She grinned. "I was planning to do a promo anyway. That's great. Can I video the statue being created as well?"

"Yes, but it'll take a while. You'll have to plan for that."

She nodded. "When is your next convention?"

"Lubbock, Texas in three weeks."

"Okay. We'll need to check to see when we both have the same day off, but I can work with that."

The printer finished the bracelet and after he peeled it up from the platform, and made sure it was free of any excess drips, he handed it over to her.

"It expands."

She flexed the band and slipped it onto her wrist. "This is nice." She adjusted it. "It's amazing to see something real being created out of a database entry."

"Databases are real."

She shook her head. "Something physical. You're used to this. I'm not."

She took a snapshot of the bracelet on her arm. "What do I owe you for this?"

"Nothing."

"Then have you had dinner? I haven't eaten yet. I'll feed you."

Luke considered. "There's Sparky's. I'll let you buy me a burger."

She chuckled. "Don't tell anyone at work, but I do like a good burger from time to time, too. Let's go."

Bushnell

He rode in her Buick and they sat at one of the tables, munching on fries and burgers.

She asked, "What got you started in this maker business?"

He shrugged. "Legos. You can make nearly anything out of those plastic bricks, but as I grew older, I realized the really fancy models needed specialized parts that just connected to the bricks, but weren't really standard lego bricks. Sometimes I'd scavenge a Star Wars model or something, just to get the special pieces for a project of my own design.

"When I heard about 3D printers, where you could practically make anything you could model on the computer screen, I had to save up my nickels and get me one."

He shrugged. "After that it was just a big money-sink, and I had to find a way to make money to pay for my hobby."

She nodded. "Well, there's something that's been bothering me." She glanced around, but there was hardly anyone eating close to them.

She lowered her voice. "Some of those things you were selling at the con were medical devices, weren't they? Did they come from the hospital?"

He grinned and pulled out his cell phone. A few quick taps and he brought up a screen and handed it over to her.

She peered at the tiny PDF document. "So, you bought them for scrap?"

"Yes. Dr. Easton wanted me to trash them. There were boxes of old gear that were there long before I arrived. I made him an offer and made it clear I'd be selling them as artwork."

"I see that. He signed off on it." She handed him the phone back. "So you buy scrap and repurpose it."

"I had to promise I wouldn't sell any of the medical devices as functional. They're gutted and repainted. They're perfect for cosplay, but hardly anything else."

"Well, I'm just glad you weren't doing anything underhanded."

He shrugged. "I try to stick to the rules. Dr. Easton didn't care about the scrap, but I insisted on a document to cover the bases."

She chuckled. "Do you want a contract for the Sailor Moon project?"

He shook his head. "If we ever discuss money, then maybe."

"Well, I appreciate the idea of getting that statue. I've loved Sailor Moon forever."

"Why?"

She blinked and looked at him sideways. "You have something against Sailor Moon?"

"No. It's just that I've never gotten into the series. I tried Sailor Moon Crystal, but it never clicked for me. I'm just curious why it's so popular. You weren't the only one in that costume, and apparently there are others as well—different colors."

"Yes, there are guardians for other celestial bodies as well—Mars, Venus, Jupiter, et cetera."

"It's not science fiction, is it? There's magic and it sounds like mythological roots."

She chuckled. "I could talk about it for hours. But yes, more magic than science. But it's a prime example of the magical girl trope. An ordinary teen gets a magical something that allows her to transform into a powerful warrior."

"You want to be a warrior?"

She took a deep breath and thought. "Not really. I just never wanted to be the sidekick.

"When I first got into comics and anime, it seemed like the girls were always secondary characters. Sailor Moon was different. It was the guy who was the sidekick."

He nodded. "I guess I can understand that. I've seen teen girls in the same costume. It just didn't quite …."

"What?"

He shook his head. "Nothing."

She looked stern. "Don't leave me hanging like that. What were you going to say?"

He took a deep breath. "I'm no cosplay expert. You could probably tell that by what I was wearing."

He concentrated on his fries. "But it seems that there's a mismatch. Sailor Moon is cute and all, but she's hardly beautiful. And you…." He stalled out.

She asked, "Are you saying I'm not cute?"

He winced. "It's…." He really couldn't say much more.

She laughed and swatted his hand. "Sorry about that. I shouldn't be like that with you. You were doing so well, but once you started thinking about me as a girl again, you locked up. I'll stop, or else you'll never be able to talk in more than single syllables."

"If that." He nodded.

Not really meeting his eyes, she started explaining the various characters in the series. She overwhelmed him with the first quick rundown. He was pleased that there was even a Sailor Pluto. At least in anime, the planet hadn't been reclassified.

But when she started talking more in depth about some of the major characters, he asked, "Then why aren't you Sailor Mercury. Smart. Wants to be a doctor."

She shook her head. "The personality is all wrong. Besides, I like being the main character, didn't I say that?

"And I don't really want to be a doctor. Being a registered nurse is about right for me. I'm really in demand these days, didn't you know?"

Luke listened some more, comfortable to let her do almost all the talking.

But they finished their food, and their drinks were both refilled and drained again.

She sighed. "I guess I'd better get on home." She picked up her keys.

He nodded. "I'll just walk back. I need to stretch my legs. But…."

"What?"

"Could I get your name?"

She put her fingers to her lips. "You don't know?"

He shook his head. "I'm bad with names. If I read your name tag at work, I immediately forgot it."

She shook her head, amused. "Well, I've got your info from your card." She pulled out her phone and tapped. "Sending you my contact."

His phone vibrated. There was a message from her with contact information for Anna Bushnell, R.N. He tapped it and installed it on his phone.

"Anna. Thanks for the meal."

She raised her wrist. "And thanks for the bracelet. I guess I'll see you at work."

He nodded. "Yes, Anna." He forced himself the say her name. That was the only way he'd remember, by repeating it to himself several times.

She giggled and headed out. Her old Buick rumbled to a start and she left.

He went to her contact sheet and read all the information. She had several social media names listed, as well as her house address, her phone and even her work phone number and extension.

"Anna. Anna Bushnell. Like the binoculars."

That ought to be easy to remember. He couldn't remember people, but he was very familiar with equipment names.

He strolled out in the dark. There were some street lights, but just a block away from the main road, heading toward his warehouse, it got darker. He knew it was stupid to cut across the tracks, but home was a lot closer that way. The stars were out. He looked for planets.

There was Jupiter. Sailor Jupiter was supposedly strong, right?

And there was Mars. He shook his head. A Shinto priestess who attended a Catholic school—there was certainly a lot of back story to the series.

He could see why it had become popular. Lots of female heroes for the girls to look up to and the visuals had enough skin for the male fans. He doubted he'd ever be a fan, but he owed it to Anna, Anna Bushnell, to find out where it was streaming and watch a few more episodes.

When he reached the warehouse, he walked around to the back. Where most lot owners had built their homes on the lot, the original owner had built a place to repair large trucks. It was at the edge of town. Behind the building was open ground, hardly a field. It was just normal New Mexico rock and low brush. But, he had an outdoor lounge chair here. It was shaded during the day and on warm nights like this, he could stretch up under the stars and the building blocked most of the city light. Off in the distance, the mesas made a nice bottom frame for the sky.

He was confident there were animals out there in the dark. He'd seen antelope, coyote and others before. His warehouse property was inhospitable, but just a block away, there were watered lawns and tended plants that were probably tasty to the rabbits he'd seen. The closer to the river, the greener the city got.

Luke was content to be on the edges. He really had no inclination to garden and keep plants looking nice for the passers by.

I'll want to use the high-res printer for her statue. Maybe I need to finish my prototype before then.

But he could start that in the morning and let it run while he was at work.

He needed a good substrate before he started on the detail work.

Prototyping

Luke had his dawn schedule—pre-packaged protein shake and a banana for breakfast while he reviewed his RSS feeds. But this morning, he took a couple of minutes to start his plasma tube prototype. The 3D printer went to work, building a sample he could test.

The idea was simple. He wanted a cheap way to convert air into ionized plasma, guide it down a tube, accelerated with a big electrostatic field, and then bend the plasma stream with a magnet so that the carbon ions would hit the metal backstop at a different location from the other ions.

If he could cheaply separate carbon out of the air, then maybe he could make something useful.

It was all straightforward stuff, he just wanted to experiment to see if he could find ways to do it all with less energy cost than usual.

It was all old tech. Mass spectrometry was first invented in the late nineteenth century and refined over the years. Luke knew he wasn't likely to make any big new discoveries, but it was a logical thing to experiment with. Most of the commercially available gadgets were big and only concerned with detecting minute traces of chemicals. He wanted to do something very different. To extract carbon from the atmosphere in any great quantity, he'd need to do it cheaply and move large volumes of air.

Of course, his prototype was tiny and the tube could only move traces of gas, but if it worked, the 3D printing and other techniques he was using could be scaled up. Maybe one ion tube couldn't do much, but he could print a million of them in a block.

But if it didn't work, or if it used too much electricity to extract the carbon, then it would be better to discover that in a little prototype first.

That was how solar electricity was invented. They made a tiny little solar cell and experimented until it worked. Then they made millions, billions of them. Together, they produced a serious amount of electricity.

While he ate breakfast, he scanned his RSS feeds. He had hundreds of websites that were merged together into his feed. There were webcomics, news sites, and anything that had captured his attention over the years.

One of his favorites was ScienceDaily. It was an overview of all the scientific research articles that appeared—dozens per day. Of course many were in fields that didn't interest him, but often he would see something there that would make big news a few days later on the more prestigious news sites.

The articles were small, just a few paragraphs, but if it was something he was really interested in, then there were generally links or references he could follow.

This morning, there was another one that caught his interest. Materials scientists at the University of Texas had discovered a tin alloy that, when made into a one molecule thick 2D material, caused ions in close proximity to behave like polarized light.

That's interesting. Another metamaterial. I wonder what would happen if I coated the inside of my ion tube with that alloy?

He marked the article for later review. Metamaterials, where ordinary elements acquired totally different characteristics when made into ultra-thin versions, were being discovered all the time, and no one quite had a handle on all the different ways metamaterials could behave. He'd love to dig into it more but he still had to get off to work.

...

When he arrived at the hospital, he could see activity at the emergency entrance. He slowed to a crawl in the parking lot and watched as a doctor and nurses helped a very pregnant woman into a wheelchair. It wasn't unusual. The hospital was the best medical care around, especially for people off to the west.

He parked around the back with the other employees and entered with his keycard.

Jude Haskell, dressed in his scrubs, was poking at the shelves.

"Looking for something?"

"Oh, hi Luke. Yeah. The blood pressure cuff in room eight isn't working." He pointed over to the table.

Luke noted the model, pulled a replacement from its bag and handed it over.

"I'll log it."

"Thanks. It's getting hectic today."

Like nodded. "I saw a woman at the ER entrance."

"Yeah, the husband called ahead to warn us they were coming. They drove two hours to get here."

"Not a local, then."

Jude sighed. "Nope. The 'maternity desert' strikes again."

Luke had heard the term before. Rural hospitals were few and far between. For people living in small communities, getting good health care meant a long drive.

Jude rushed back to his duties. Luke took a quick look at the blood pressure cuff. The tube had a crack in it, which allowed the air pressure to leak out. He could fix that, but the inflatable cuff itself was also showing signs of wear. It was hardly an expensive item, as medical gear went. He logged the cuff as unrepairable and put a replacement on the list of items to be purchased.

The morning went as usual, catching up on the backlog of items to be repaired or recalibrated. Carlos showed up and went outside to tackle some of the yard work. Plant operations had to take care of everything.

He saw Anna in the hallway, but she was busy and they didn't normally eat at the same time.

She wanted to video the whole process, from purchasing the model to printing the statue, and then probably one of her painting it.

She said they needed a day off together, probably so that she could dedicate her cell phone to recording the hours-long process of printing the model.

He frowned. He did have an extra camera that he could dedicate to the process so that she wouldn't have to use her cell for everything. They could video her making the purchase after work and then he could handle the printing and capture that.

Of course, he wouldn't mind spending the whole day with her. Maybe he'd just make the offer and see what she said. He shouldn't read too much into her interest. She was just looking for material for her streaming videos.

They never really connected for the rest of the day. She'd already left by the time he finished his last project and she was probably tired from the long day. He wouldn't bother her.

. . .

Back at the warehouse, Luke took the long pencil-sized prototype ion tube and examined it under his microscope. While the hi-res printer had done a fine job making the tube smooth to the touch, under the scope he could see the texture left from the hardened droplets. The channel in the middle had been designed as a long funnel, with a centimeter diameter opening at the top narrowing down to nothing by the time it reached the bottom of the 50 cm tube. He'd hoped for a microscopic opening at the bottom, but the printer couldn't achieve that level of detail.

It was time for the next step. He clamped the tube on the workbench facing the UV laser. He'd been working on the adjustments for some time. He hoped the laser wouldn't turn his ion tube into a slab of molten plastic.

He'd acquired the laser when a small semiconductor firm went out of business. They had wanted to use the laser to create specialized radio-frequency integrated circuits. The laser was already built to carve nanometer-scale bits on elaborate microcircuits to tune radio spectra. The laser was quite expensive and he had been incredibly lucky to pick it up for salvage prices. If the salvage company had any clue what it was worth, they could have made a mint. Luke spent nearly all his money on the equipment and then had to find a place to store it. Just a bit of fate that stranded him in Hatch, New Mexico. It wasn't worth it to haul everything back home to California.

But if he was right about the laser, and his software changes did what he'd hoped, then he could make fine-detail changes that his 3D printers couldn't achieve.

The laser was pointed at the open end of the tube. Behind the tube was a cheap solar cell that would tell him in an instant if any of the laser made it all the way though the tube. That was his safety cut-off switch.

He put on his safety goggles to make sure none of the UV light could bounce into his eyes and fired the laser for a microsecond.

Other than the noise of the power supply fluctuating, there was no evidence anything happened. He hadn't expected anything dramatic, but it was better to make a trial run.

Next, he engaged the focuser. This elaborate system used electrostatic fields to manipulate the prisms and lenses used to focus and aim the laser light. When he fired a 100 microsecond burst, the laser light was steered around the inside of the tube.

And he could tell at once, by the scent of vaporized plastic in the air, that it was working. He eyeballed the ion tube, but he couldn't see anything different. He repeated the process ten times before powering down the laser and fishing a fiber optic probe into the tube.

It was difficult to see on his display, but the micro-texture left by 3D printer was definitely smoothed down. He pulled out the probe and tried it again.

After twenty-five of the 100 microsecond sweeps, he couldn't see any defects on the inside of the tube. On sweep twenty-eight, the laser punched through the end of the tube and shut it down. He had his process.

The exit hole was just barely visible to the naked eye. The microscope showed a perfectly round hole.

Now to test it. His theory was that a slowing narrowing tube might provide a substitute for electromagnetic focusing. If he could produce a narrow stream of ions without spending electricity for the confinement, then he could reduce the energy expense.

He fit an air tube over the wide opening end, and inserted the pinhole end into a vacuum chamber. He connected a tank of air with a pressure gauge at the supply end and cracked the valve.

Ten minutes later, he had the bad news. No matter how much he turned up the pressure, the pinhole could only pass a trickle of gas. Making it ionized would hardly increase that.

I'll have to rethink this.

· · ·

Luke was picking up a burrito at the drive-thru when his cell phone alerted him. He glanced at it. Anna had sent him a link.

He waited until he was back at the warehouse eating to move the link to his computer and brought it up on the big screen.

Anna appeared on the screen, framed by text and a photo of a Sailor Moon manga. This was her *Anna and the Fantastic* channel.

"Greetings again, this is Anna and I wanted to share with you a real life fantasy. It's new to me, although it may be old hat to some of you. Here's a glimpse of the Maker world."

She shifted into an edited video, storytelling how she encountered Maker Products at the Tucson convention. There were clips showing him selling his stuff at his table. She then followed up with her visit as he pointed out his machines and then followed up with the selection of the bracelet, him showing her his collection of colored filaments, and the high speed video of it being printed for her.

And then back to Anna sitting at her desk, wearing the bracelet.

"Now to me, this making of physical items directly from a picture on the computer is magical, and I'm thinking of manifesting something even more special in the future."

She made the usual pitch for subscriptions and then there was a link to his Maker Products website from the business card.

He checked, but there was no activity. Well, maybe the video had just come out, or maybe she had too few viewers that this little bit of advertising didn't really make any difference.

He shifted back to her site and subscribed.

There was a list of previous videos, so he sampled a few. It was a pleasant way to kill an hour or so, and he got his mind off his ion tube failure for a bit.

Looking at all her social media links, it was clear that she never mentioned her last name and there was no hint that she was a nurse. The image she presented was just a cosplay social performer who visited conventions and interviewed people she found interesting.

It was obvious that she had just added the Lubbock convention to her list.

He closed the site. He'd come back and view the rest of her videos eventually, but for now, maybe he should consider what to try next on the ion tube project. He couldn't allow one roadblock to stop him.

The Bus

Luke only worked a half day at the hospital, making sure that the logs were updated and the shelves were properly stocked. There were long term projects he could deal with, but he was more interested in researching how he could make his ion igniter and he couldn't in good conscience browse the internet while clocking hours at the hospital.

He caught Anna at lunch, but she was a bit distracted by her real work. She shook her head when he mentioned he had a spare camera.

"No, I've got my workflow down using my cell phone videos. I don't want to risk messing with a different video type. Maybe I'll experiment, but not for this video."

She sighed. "Besides I'm looking forward to a day off to relax. I love babies, but too many premies with jaundice in a row and it gets old. You know, I think these days come in surges. It's like the COVID days, people dying in the hallways, it calms down, and then comes another wave."

Luke shook his head. "I don't think childbirth comes in waves."

She chuckled. "You'd be surprised."

They made a tentative plan to video the printing of her statue before the Lubbock convention, but then she had to hurry back to her duties.

...

For twelve hours Luke was deep into the internet. He was frustrated at how many scientific papers were only available behind paywalls, but he'd been here before and some of his subscriptions were still valid.

What he wanted to achieve was a bunch of conductive needles with sharp points. If electrically charged, the electric field around the points should be strong enough to ionize the air.

The whole idea of strong electric fields around spikes had been discovered back in the Ben Franklin days—that was the whole idea behind lightning rods. Nobody could stop lightning, but maybe you could control where the strike happened. Some buildings had a whole series of spikes evenly spread around, under the idea that if the electric field was spread out, then the lighting would strike somewhere else where there was a single, stronger field.

He wanted to do something similar, only on the microscopic scale. He could plate parts of the ion tube with aluminum easily in his deposition chamber. On top of that, around the mouth, he needed to grow his needles. Once he charged the aluminum, and thus the needles, the air would be exposed to a disruptive electric field, hopefully enough to strip electrons from the nucleus.

By the time he quit for the night, he had three different processes to try. The silver crystals seemed the easiest, so he'd try that one first.

He shook his head. *Not tonight.* He needed some sleep.

...

The week followed the same pattern. Luke put in minimal hours at the hospital, making sure everything was covered, but spending long hours at the warehouse working on version two of the ion tube. He made the opening slightly larger and coated the interior with aluminum. When he grew the silver crystals at the mouth and connected a voltage supply, he was pleased that, in the dark, he could see the blue glow of ionized air in a tiny ring.

With an air tank connected to the mouth and the exit end inserted into a vacuum chamber, he tested the air flow, and again it was disappointing. Yes, there was evidence of ozone in the outflow, but it was hardly a beam of ions that he could feed through a magnetic separator.

It was obvious that the ions and the electrons were recombining early in the process and just bouncing against the walls of the tube, restricting the flow.

He sighed, and dreamed of the diagrams he'd seen of the big expensive mass spectrographs.

...

His phone's insistent ringtones dragged Luke out of sleep. It was still dark.

"Hello?" He fumbled the phone, but didn't drop it.

"Luke?" It was Dr. Easton. "We had a bus accident on the interstate. They're still bringing people in. I need you get get all available bed monitors up and running. We'll be staging people in the hallways again."

Luke was awake. "I'll get there as soon as I can."

"Hurry." The phone clicked.

He hurriedly dressed, choosing his scrubs this time. Normally he didn't care if he looked medical, and showed up in jeans and shirt since he barely ventured out of the workshop, but he sometimes needed to look like a medical professional just to make the patients comfortable.

When he pulled into the dark parking lot, an ambulance had unloaded and was racing off toward the interstate to pick up more injured with its lights flashing and the siren blaring.

Luke was pretty sure what was needed. The examination room beds had some of the gear—blood pressure meters and such—but they might need real time monitors. He needed to get all the spares out of storage and working. If they needed beds in the hallways, then he'd need to get creative.

Nurses and orderlies showed up for the next few hours, telling him what they needed and then hurrying off. His time was split between installing the gear and getting the idle machines ready to work.

...

"Are you a doctor?" asked the little boy with bandages on his face and one leg in a splint.

Luke shook his head. "No, I just plug in the machines." He grinned. "They wouldn't even let me wipe your snot."

He tapped the box of tissues and the boy chuckled and reached for them.

One of the nurses hurried in. "I can help you, Donny." She helped the boy blow his nose.

Luke made a conscious effort to look at her name tag. She was Mary.

"Nurse," the boy asked, "Is Daddy okay?"

"The doctors are still helping him, but he asked about you and I promised to watch over you. Your Aunt Patricia will be here soon to help you and your dad."

Donny frowned. "She lives in Oklahoma."

"I'm sure she will try to get here as quickly as she can."

Donny was just one of five children that had been injured. A tractor-trailer had a front tire blow which caused it to jack-knife, then it slammed into a bus, forcing it into the guard rails. Luke hadn't heard how many adults were hospitalized. Apparently the bus had rolled and skidded down a slope. Nobody was dead, but the urgent ones all came to their hospital. Others were sent to Sierra Vista Hospital in Truth-or-Consequences.

By mid-morning, the story was out and relatives, reporters, and local church workers were showing up in the parking lot.

I bet the personal injury lawyers will be out in force as well. Their billboards were hard to ignore.

When Luke caught up with the urgent repair work, he helped with the routine jobs—moving beds, setting up cones in the parking lot to keep order, and any job that didn't need a medical license.

He got a good look at the injuries while he was at it. When the bus rolled over, everyone went flying—there were no seat belts in the bus. Broken bones, scrapes and cuts were common. He was especially worried about the kids.

When he was eight, he'd broken his leg in a bicycle accident. He still remembered the hospital stay and then the long days at home. Even then, he had few close friends. There was nothing much to do except play with Legos.

Dr. Easton caught up with him in the corridor.

"Are all the beds fixed up?"

"Yes. Unless we get more patients, we should have enough."

Easton nodded. "Then go on home. I'd rather have you rested and available if there's a problem with the machines. We have people who can keep the floors swept."

"Okay. By the way, how long will the bus people be here?"

The administrator shook his head. "These are injuries, rather than diseases, so if they were local, I'd be sending them home as quickly as possible, but they were traveling. It'll be a juggling act for a while."

Luke went to his van and paused for a moment.

He pulled out his cell phone and texted Anna.

Luke: **Hey, Anna, I've got a question about the kids.**

Luke: **Those kids are stuck in the hospital and all their belongings are trash at the accident site. I know Donny is missing his toy cars, because I heard him talking.**

Luke: **I could make him some cars overnight, but I don't know what the other kids might want to replace their missing toys. If you get a chance, could you find out?**

Anna: **Busy now. I'll get back to you. Sounds like a plan.**

He started the van. He could get started on the toy cars at least.

. . .

There were a large number of toy car models out there for free use. He pulled a couple of cute ones with movable wheels that could be popped onto the axles and started them up on two different 3D printers with different colored plastics.

His phone popped up with new information over the next couple of hours. Darla was deeply into dragons. Joe had lost a Minion doll. Toby was a Dr. Who fan and loved saying "Exterminate!" in a distorted voice.

Anna: **And little Martha had a baby doll. But don't bother with that one. I have an old one of my own that I'll pass on to her. I doubt your machine can make the clothes.**

Luke: **Probably not, although I've heard of a machine that can. But that's not something I can do overnight. I'll get the machines running. What's your work schedule?**

It turned out that they could meet up mid-morning and hand out the toys. He had a deadline.

Darla was a mature eleven, so he chose the snake-like articulated dragon rather than the squeezable one.

For Joe, he found a set of various Minion characters. They were small, so he started a set of five different characters printing with the yellow plastic. Maybe he could paint the eyes if they finished fast enough.

Toby's TARDIS was started on a machine with blue plastic, and four

Daleks were printed in metallic gray.

With six of his printers working away making buzzing noises, he still had a couple of hours before bed, so he read the scientific paper about the 2D material that affected ions.

Maybe I can do this, but it'll take some experimentation to get the deposition thickness right. If the magic only happens with a single atomic layer, then it'll be tricky.

He took his latest pencil-sized ion tube and put it back in the deposition chamber and set it up for a very minimal coating with the tin alloy listed in the paper. He sighed. He'd have to test it tomorrow. For now, it had been a very long day and he needed some sleep.

Toy Delivery

Waking at dawn, he had toys ready to be finished.

He snapped the cars together and put them in a Maker Products box.

The dragon needed a little cleanup work before it could be put in its box. The snake-like body wound around a batch of cotton.

With some paint, he added eyes, goggles and overalls for the Minion characters and hoped they would dry fast enough.

He added some details on the TARDIS, and even colored the tips of the weapons on the Daleks.

I feel like a Santa Claus elf, getting ready for Christmas.

The warehouse had the pleasant scent of drying paint and freshly minted plastic. Maybe it was a stink to some, but making things was his pleasure.

With his boxes loaded and a stop by the Circle-K to get something that resembled breakfast, he made it to the hospital to meet Anna.

...

Luke was quietly pleased that the little kids forgot to thank him for the toys—they were too busy playing with them.

Toby was busily making a huge battle scene between the Daleks and the TARDIS. His father, with his arm in a sling and sitting in the chair nodded his thanks. Joe was giving each of the Minion characters their own speaking parts in squeaky voices as he played.

Darla thanked him for the dragon and positioned it carefully next to her pillow.

Luke said, "When you get home, model acrylic paint can be used to add more detail."

She nodded, and smiled. "This is great. Thank you. You make these for sale?"

"Yes, I generally sell them at science fiction conventions, but I made this one just for you."

She beamed.

Donny's aunt had just arrived from Oklahoma and was a little confused about the toy cars he was driving around the bedsheet.

Anna explained. "This was just Luke's idea. All the kids on the bus lost their toys and he's a toymaker, among other things."

When they went to Martha's room, Anna whispered to the little girl's mother and she nodded.

"Martha?"

The little girl was maybe four or five—Luke wasn't good at guessing ages. Her eyes grew wide when Anna presented the baby doll.

"I'd like you to meet little baby Suzy. She's been living at my house since I was your age, and she's been a little lonely since I've grown up. Would it be okay if she stayed with you now?"

Martha nodded eagerly. Anna turned the doll over with all the care she would have used with a real newborn. Anna showed off the little cradle and the two outfits Suzy could wear. There was even a miniature baby bottle Martha could feed Suzy with.

They said their goodbyes and hurried out.

Anna said, "That went well."

Luke nodded. "How long will they be here?"

She shook her head. "Some are already leaving, but who knows."

She hurried off to her duty station. Luke went back to the workroom.

...

Luke worked longer hours than usual, even as several of the bus patients checked out, either to continue their trip, stay with relatives or even in some cases—insurance-paid temporary housing.

Soon, his job would be putting all the extra equipment safely back into storage, ready for when it would be needed again.

He was tired enough that his ion tube stayed cold in the deposition chamber while he ate a quesadilla from the stand across the tracks and caught up on some of the web comics he'd been neglecting.

His phone vibrated.

Anna: **What's your schedule Thursday? Can we do the Sailor Moon then?**

Luke: **Maybe. I'll double-check tomorrow. Probably okay unless there's another bus.**

Anna: **Don't say that!**

He chuckled. He got up and checked his supplies. It would be uncomfortable if he ran out of the right color filament in the middle of making her statue.

The deposition chamber caught his eye and he pulled out the ion tube. Its color had changed slightly. The original plastic had been a dull white. When he coated it with aluminum, it looked like frosted metal. Now that he'd added the tin, he could see a hint of mottled discoloration added on top of that. Obviously, it hadn't been enough added to completely cover the surface, but he still needed to test his results.

He plugged it into the vacuum chamber and connected the air tube and the wires.

Once the vacuum was pumped down and the pressure gauge was stable, he turned on the air and charged the tube up to a hundred volts.

The vacuum pressure fluctuated. He quickly turned off the lamp. With nothing but the equipment lights, the chamber was hard to see in the darkness,

But yes, there was the glow of ions around the mouth of the ion tube, and maybe, just maybe, through the glass he could see a hint of glow coming from the exit hole.

He stopped everything and waited for the vacuum to pump down again. With just the air pressure, there was hardly any evidence that air was making it through the tube, but once he flipped the voltage on, he could see it.

It works. The 2D tin plating is confining the ions enough to keep them from hitting the inner walls of the tube.

That was what he'd imagined from reading the original paper, but it was exciting to see it actually happening. All the new materials science that was coming out about 2D materials was just magical to him.

But he really shouldn't be surprised. For the past few decades, the whole world had changed because people were learning how to harness microscopic materials. The cell phone in his pocket would be absolute witchcraft to people from a hundred years ago—maybe even fifty years ago.

It was just normal stuff to people today, but hardly anyone really understood what was going on inside those computer chips. 2D materials was just another layer of unknown that even the scientists were having trouble understanding.

Luke knew he didn't understand it at all. But that was okay. He was an engineer at heart. He didn't have to understand the deep physics of it. All he needed was an understanding of the rules of behavior. The real scientists said that the 2D tin alloy caused ions to align along the surface. If he coated the inside of a microscopic tube with that substance, then ions would be confined to the center of the tube, not impacting the surface at all, moving frictionless along the length of it. In some ways, it was like superconductivity, only for positive ions instead of electrons.

That was all he needed to know in order to make his ion tube work efficiently.

But now I need to know exactly how long to run the deposition to get the optimum coating. It was time to set up more experiments.

It was getting late, but he was too excited to sleep.

He went to his software and set up a new model. He duplicated the ion tube and created a model where he could print four of them at a time. Once he printed them and did the initial aluminum coating, he could snap them apart and apply four different tin coatings to narrow down the optimum settings.

It was past two when he dropped off to sleep, the bundle of four tubes growing on the printing platform.

...

There were a couple of thank you cards waiting for him at the hospital when he went to the workroom. Donny's aunt and Darla had taken the time to write him. Luke shook his head. He probably had never written a thank you note in his life, not unless his mother made him back when he was too little to know what was going on. He knew that was one of those proper etiquette thing people were supposed to do, but he'd never learned.

Still, he stuffed the cards in his logbook, like bookmarks. They were too nice to throw away, but he'd made the toys more for his own satisfaction than for the kids' gratitude.

The rest of the day was drudgery. Some equipment had to go back on the shelves, but each had to be checked and, in some cases, cleaned before they could go back to being proper spares.

He had a text mid-afternoon.

Dr. Easton: **Drop by my office when convenient.**

Luke finished his current task and sought him out.

Gossip said Dr. Easton was still a practicing surgeon, but it was rare he was called to mask up. Administrative tasks kept him busy full time. Small town hospitals were critically needed, but often on the brink, financially. He probably could use an administrative assistant, but the doctor was a hands-on kind of guy.

Luke knocked at the half-open door.

"Come on in."

Dr. Easton set down his pen and gestured to the chair.

"Luke, you've requested Thursday off?"

"Yes, is there a problem?"

"Not really. Will you be in town?"

"Yes. It's just a home project I need to work on."

Easton nodded. "That's fine. You're really working much more than your usual hours this week as it is."

"Aren't we all?"

The doctor leaned back in his chair. "It's times like this when I wish you were on full-time status. Have you given that any more thought since your last review?"

Luke considered. "A little. The job has peak times when there's never enough hours to get things done, and then it slacks off and I feel guilty about sitting in the workroom where there's little to do."

"And do you have a solution?"

He shrugged. "Maybe. But it would mean taking on a whole new task that is hardly urgent."

Easton looked interested. "What's that?"

"Well, part of the job is making sure that the building's network access is working properly. The IT people that came before me did a decent job of that, so I haven't had to do much, but there is a problem."

"Every room has a handful of devices that need network access. Some of them need to phone home for licensing issues or to download tables of data. Others have admin accounts that can be used to debug or update the computers inside. The problem is that so many of them are vulnerable to hacking. You know how often your computer or phone has to update its software?"

Dr. Easton nodded. "All the time, it seems."

"Well our heart rate monitors, and practically everything that has a digital display have computers too, and they're just as vulnerable to hacking, but there are billions of phones and just a handful of medical devices, relatively speaking. The companies that make them just can't afford to keep them patched.

"That means some joker halfway around the world could reach into the hospital's network and run a blood pressure cuff up to dangerously high levels, turn off alerts, or even fake the readings. Every device that is on the network, even security cameras and fire alarms could be messed with."

Easton frowned. "You say it's not urgent?"

Luke shook his head. "All this is possible. I just haven't heard of it happening yet. And, really, there are advantages of being a small hospital, with less of a budget to attract ransom seekers."

"I'll have to think about this."

Luke nodded. "As long as you know about it. It would be a big job to track down each device and find out what their vulnerabilities are and set up the appropriate firewall. It would take a long time."

Printing

Anna: **Are we still on for tomorrow?**

Luke: **Yes. You'll show up here?**

Anna: **Fine. How early?**

Luke: **I'm always up at dawn. We need to start early if you want your phone back the same day.**

Anna: **I got that. See you before breakfast then.**

Luke: **Looking forward to it.**

But I've got a lot of work to do before then.

He glanced over at his highest resolution printer. He wanted to use that for her statue, but it was still configured for his ion tubes.

After an hour, the printer was ready, but the laser was working on his latest set of experimental tubes, refining the inside of the tubes.

He'd run a lot of iterations over the past couple of days, experimenting with the thickness of the tin alloy and the aluminum substrate. He'd narrowed down just how long he had to deposit the tin, and now he was varying the aluminum below it.

He picked up one of the previous batch, checked the number he'd inked on the side, logged it, and hooked it up to the air and the vacuum. He pressed the switch charging the igniter and started the pressure recorder. The vacuum pump stopped and he tracked how quickly the pressure rose in the chamber, giving him a reading for how fast the ion tube pumped gas ions into it. He barely glanced at the glow of the igniter and went to check on the deposition chamber. Everything was on a timer and the test run would shut down on its own. He'd review the pressure chart plot and know instantly whether this ion tube was better or worse than the ones he'd run before.

But with a day-long visit with Anna coming up, he shook his head at just how cluttered and dirty the warehouse had become. He picked up the untested ion tubes and put them in an airtight plastic box and started dusting. With the remote, he started the robot vacuum cleaner. He'd probably have to empty it several times before he was done.

He was packing clothes into a laundry bag when the timer ended on the test. The igniter switched off, but if he had been watching, he might have noticed that the glow of ionized air at the mouth of the tube *didn't* extinguish. The valve to the air tank closed, but the tiny needle-like stream of ions streaming into the vacuum chamber *didn't* quit. Instead, the rubber tubing connecting the air tank to the ion tube began collapsing, squeezed down to a ribbon.

Only when all the air available to the tube was gone did the exit stream shrink and die.

...

He was up late, only taking time to finish depositing and labeling the ion tubes before quitting for the night.

He opened his eyes to first light, as usual. He hurriedly showered and dressed, not really sure when Anna would arrive.

He was considering breakfast when there was a knock on the door.

In a blue and white sailor costume, complete with her long blonde wig in pigtails, Anna smiled.

"Are you ready?" she asked.

"Well, yes. What do I do?"

She pulled up her cell phone. "First you'll show me the website where I can purchase the design for the figurine, just like you did the first time. Only, this time I'll be recording the video. You'll show me how you prepare it for the printer. Oh! And show me all the colors like you did before. I'll choose the white.

"I'll then set up my phone on my tripod to record the printer at time-lapse speed, and then we'll have breakfast and we can kill some time."

Since she had all the experience, he just let her call all the shots and talked into the lens when she focused on him.

Once she set up her tripod and camera, he started the printer.

"I still have my camera," he said. "Why don't I set it up over here so you can get an alternate view angle from time to time?"

She nodded. "What format?"

"It's a 4K video. MVI format. I don't know if that'll be useful to you or not, but it can probably be converted."

He set it up quickly, since the camera was already on a little tripod from the last time he used it. He made sure the camera card was empty and started it.

Anna nodded. "Now we can eat. And you'll have to keep me entertained because I'll be without my phone all day long."

He chuckled.

Anna had a bag with clothes. "I'm not going to be walking around all day as Sailor Moon. Do you have a place I can change?"

"I'll just wait outside."

He gave her some privacy and she came out looking normal a few minutes later. She shook her head. "I almost changed in view of the cameras, and then I worried whether you had any security cameras in the warehouse. I settled for the shower stall, but I got my feet wet."

He glanced down at her canvas shoes. "No security cameras, but that's probably a good idea. I just haven't had anything portable and valuable to worry about before now."

They went back inside to check on the printing. "This printer is reliable. We should be able to walk away for hours with no worry."

She nodded, watching the mechanism sweeping back and forth, laying down plastic droplets. She pointed. "What are those?"

He looked at the tray of untested ion tubes. "Don't touch those. I'm running an experiment." He picked up one of the old ones that had already been tested and handed it to her.

"This is an ion tube."

She frowned and tried to peer through the tube. "It's blocked. What's it for?"

He took it back. "There really is a tube that goes the full length, but one end is nearly microscopic." He went over to the vacuum chamber and frowned at the pressure plot that was left after last night's test. Either he'd gotten a very good sample, or more likely, there was a new leak in the tank. He decided to deal with it later.

She nodded. "You can tell me all about it over breakfast. Pancakes? Waffles?"

He nodded, suddenly hungry. "Pancakes."

She led the way. "I'll drive."

The old Buick was showing its age, but was still very comfortable. Anna went to a local restaurant on Hall Street. They ordered pancakes with sausage and eggs. Luke was very starved by the time they were served.

"I haven't eaten here before," he said.

"It's one of my favorite places. My parents would come here after church on Sunday every week. Dad died first, but Mom and I still made our pilgrimage."

"So you grew up here."

She smiled and waved at the town in general. "Oh yes, at least three generations here. Other than when I went off to school, I've lived here all my life. And even then, New Mexico State in Las Cruces isn't all that far away."

Luke caught the look on her face—some painful memory.

She caught his eyes and blushed. "Sorry. It's just one of those things. I was deep in a class studying the signs of cardiac distress at the very moment my mother had a heart attack and died alone at home."

He nodded. "Sorry. It must have been tough. You have other relatives here?"

She chuckled. "Yes, both by blood and the voluntary tía or two who won't stop checking up to see if I have a novio yet."

Luke tilted his head. "Novio?"

She laughed, "'Boyfriend.' So you aren't from around here?"

"No, but it must be nice to have home ties in a place like this."

"You were a military brat?"

He shook his head. "Worse. My father was a truck driver. We—my brother and I—had a reasonable home life in Barstow after my mother died, but just as soon as my brother left for college and I was capable of taking care of myself, Dad started taking long haul trips again. It was a mistake." He shook his head, remembering a particularly horrible time.

"The railroad settlement after Dad's accident paid off my brother's school loans and left me enough so that I didn't have to get a good job right away."

Anna nodded. "So what made you leave California?"

Luke looked embarrassed. "Will you laugh if I say I had friends on the internet?"

She shook her head. "I'm surprised. You appear to be social media ignorant."

"Well, pretty much. But I did have contacts and I followed blogs. Friends of friends. I didn't post much myself, but I followed their lives."

He crossed his silverwear on his plate to signal the waiter that he was done.

"And then the older brother of a classmate posted his job problems and wondered if anyone was interested in buying his 3D printer."

Luke shook his head, rethinking his life choices. "If I hadn't already been heavily into the maker vibe, I'd probably have moved anyway, probably seeking one of those high tech jobs. As it was, as soon as I heard the full story about the guy's troubles, I realized it was a rare opportunity for me. The whole company had collapsed and had to liquidate lots of high tech equipment for pennies on the dollar.

"I packed my father's van, terminated the lease on the apartment, and raced to New Mexico."

Anna frowned. "For some machines?"

He nodded. "Very expensive machines crated up and sitting idle. I had dreams of quickly finding a buyer and making millions on the transaction."

She smiled. "I gather that didn't happen?"

Luke sighed. "There really are high tech startups that need this stuff and would pay to get it, but I don't have those contacts. Instead, they're all focused on making their presentations to the venture capitalists who will buy them new equipment. I jumped in without doing my research." He shook his head.

"Craigslist?" she suggested.

"No, these are all so esoteric that there's no standard category to list them in. I'm belatedly doing some research. I read summaries of those people doing real work in the field. If I find someone I can contact, then I'll send out some feelers. No luck thus far. Cross your fingers I find a buyer before the technology shifts again and I need to send these to scrap."

She asked, "What were those ion things?"

He chuckled. "My ion tubes? It's just a little experiment. I'm trying to find a way to make a cheap stream of ions out of air."

"To clean the air?"

"In a way." He shook his head. "The grand scheme is to use mass spectrometer technology to strip carbon out of the air. Magnets would cause the ion stream to bend each element differently. I'd collect the carbon and let the oxygen, nitrogen and other elements go back into the air."

She frowned. "A climate thing? You couldn't make much progress with a microscopic hole in a little tube."

"Yes, but if it worked with one tube, then I could make a densely packed honeycomb of the things and process much more volume. Ideally, I'd make some kind of filter to process flue gas, or car exhaust, or anything that needs to be scrubbed of its carbon. But it'll only be useful it I can make it work cheaply. If it takes too much energy, then it's a losing proposition. That's why I'm exploring tiny chambers and surface effects."

Anna shrugged. "I don't understand, but I'm all in favor of a cleaner world."

When they went back out to the car, Luke checked an app on his cell phone. "It looks like the job is still only twenty to thirty percent done, but everything is working smoothly."

She peered at the screen. "Okay, then. We have more hours to kill. Since you're a stranger, let me show you around town."

The Tour

They cruised through an older part of town. An occasional house looked like it needed repair, but others on the same street were colorfully painted and well maintained.

Anna paused at the curb. "That's my house. I'm not showing you the inside because I haven't cleaned in ages."

Luke chuckled. "You didn't give me that excuse when you came to visit. You can never get a warehouse floor swept clean enough."

Her house and yard were in good shape. Luke asked, "Is that adobe?"

"Yes, it is. The walls are really thick. I don't really think about it except when I'm cleaning the window sills. It's a great shelf for knicknacks."

"Good insulation?"

"I don't know. It's what I'm used to."

There was a big brick garage next to the house that was obviously built at a later date. "You have other cars?"

She laughed. "Dad was a packrat. Lots of junk and half-built projects."

"Ouch."

They laughed. She poked his ribs. "You at least finish your tasks. Dad had a lot of junk that I really ought to get rid of. But I haven't. Not in all these years."

She pulled back onto the street. "Come on, I've got something else I want to show you."

...

They stopped at a convenience store for gas and drinks and then got on the interstate.

"Elephant Butte Reservoir isn't all that far away, and we've got time to kill."

Luke asked her about getting into nursing. When her father died suddenly, Anna's mother wasn't in the best of health. It was before the local hospital had been built and she tagged along on several visits to the hospitals many miles down the interstate. The nurses impressed her, both with their expert knowledge and their one-on-one personal care with the patients. When high school started putting pressure on the students to plan for their future, Anna researched nursing.

"I guess part of my plan was to take care of Mom when she got older, but when that fell through, I chose to stick with it and finished the program."

He nodded. "And Sailor Moon?"

She blushed. "You know there's a Las Cruces Comic Con, right? Well it was a welcome change when I needed it, and I added a collection of manga to my medical books."

She took the marked exit, and shortly, the lake appeared on the horizon.

Anna pulled into the marina parking lot, at least the current one. The lake level was down considerably. "When I review my budget, the slip rental fee just kills me. I'd have cancelled it a couple of years ago, except I don't really want to face the task of pulling the boat out of the water."

"So, you have a boat?"

She nodded. "Dad's last project, and his biggest. Come look."

They hiked down the narrow path to marina's walkway. Anna had a key to the slips. Luke was impressed when she stepped aboard her cruiser.

"Wow. That's quite a powerboat."

He followed her aboard and Anna opened up the hatches. "Let it air out a bit. I only take the boat out two or three times a year. It's a bit much for handling solo, so I generally make a party of it. Here's hoping I didn't leave anything last time to grow mold."

Luke glanced at the neighboring pontoon boats. "This is pretty big cruiser for a lake this size."

She nodded. "Dad's big plan was to finish outfitting the boat here, and then trailer it to the west coast. From there, we'd cruise all the way up to Alaska."

"So it was designed for sea travel."

"Yes, it's got big diesel tanks. Dad claimed three hundred mile range. I haven't topped it up in two years. Luckily diesel doesn't go bad."

When they went into the cabin, Luke nodded. "You could live in this place."

"That was the idea. Dad's big dream was to travel the world."

"Three hundred miles at a time."

She nodded, "But that's enough. You hop from port to port, restocking as you go. All of North and South America would be easy. Using Greenland and Iceland as waypoints, you could reach Europe, Africa and Asia, and even Australia. Only the Pacific Islands would be out of reach."

"Antarctica?"

She sniffed. "It would be too cold, and the boat wouldn't handle the weather down there."

Luke nodded. "Sounds like a plan. When do you leave?"

She smiled. "When I win the lottery. More likely, I'll be looking for a buyer when my money runs out. Until then, let's go for a little cruise."

Luke handled the mooring ropes while she started the engine and checked out the controls. Soon, they eased out of the slip and stayed centered in the channel. As soon as they were past what looked like floating breakwater made out of big truck tires, they sped up.

Anna pointed to the depth finder. "There are a lot of shallows on this lake, and the *Enchantress* has a deep hull."

"That's the name?"

"New Mexico is the 'Land of Enchantment'. Dad thought it was a good name. Look at the decoration on the bow."

He grasped the railing and leaned over. There was a sketch of a sorceress near the name.

"So he had a flair for the fantastic as well."

She chuckled. "Maybe. He didn't often show it."

They toured the lake. Luke declined the offer to wet a hook. "I wouldn't know what to do with a fish if I caught it."

"I'll teach you sometime."

There was enough cell signal that Luke could keep a running check on the printing back at the warehouse. Eventually, they docked back at the slip and filled up on burgers and fries in nearby Truth or Consequences.

By the time they reached the warehouse, the sun was going down and Sailor Moon was getting the top of her head printed.

Anna changed back into her costume and they recorded the moment when the print job finished.

She set up her camera where Luke worked to carve away the scaffolding and buff away any irregularities.

"Watch where you're putting your hands," she said.

He chuckled, "Hey, you're the one who ordered a figurine with long legs and a short skirt."

Soon, he presented the finished statue to her. "Here, these are the paints you should use."

He packaged it carefully in one of his Maker Products boxes with plenty of padding and she declined his offer of supper. She was excited to get started on the painting phase back at her home.

He waved as she left. It had been a fun day.

· · ·

Luke waved at Anna the next day at work, but they both looked worn out. He hoped she didn't try to do all the detailed painting when she was exhausted, but that was her call.

He had intended to get to sleep early, but when he tested the vacuum chamber and found no leaks, he re-ran the last ion tube's test and noted right away that the exit stream of ions was much more pronounced than any of the others that he'd seen. The flow-through reading had been real.

Was he getting close to the ideal deposition settings?

Quickly, he set up abbreviated tests on the next set of tubes. Instead of measuring the gas pressure, he took cell phone snapshots of the glowing exit plume. It was much faster to tell the relative difference that way.

By three in the morning, he had a rough plot of deposition time vs. ion plume length. It was plain that he'd passed the optimum. There was a critical point where the whole tube interior was coated with the tin alloy one atom thick, and that was where the 2D effect was strongest. More tin just cancelled the effect.

He started another batch of tubes on the printer, crashed for the night, and slept through his wake-up alarms. He was late getting to the hospital, but luckily no one was waiting for him. It didn't help him lose the guilt for missing his self-imposed deadline, however.

He was still at work, doing a little unpaid overtime as penance, when a link showed up on his text.

Anna had posted his Maker Products promo. He was fascinated by what she'd done, editing together clips from the convention, some words from him that he really didn't remember her recording, and bits and pieces from the Sailor Moon project.

It reminded him that the Lubbock convention was coming up soon, so he went home and edited his web site to include the promo.

Luke: **Hey, Anna, I've incorporated your video into my site. Thanks a lot. It'll help.**

Anna: **Great. Still working on SM. I'll have that stream out before too long.**

Luke took a look at his inventory for the next con and sighed. He really needed to start up some items. He took a good look at the spreadsheet he kept that told him which items sold best at which conventions. Lubbock was a college town, and that made a difference in which items were popular.

Soon enough the warehouse was abuzz with active printers making colorful trinkets for sale.

Buick by the Road

The crowd at the Lubbock Memorial Civic Center was happy and energetic. Luke caught a glimpse of Sailor Moon in the crowd on Saturday, but she had made connections with a whole crew of like-costumed females, and one butch-looking guy with a beard also in a Sailor Moon costume. Apparently, one or more of the voice actors for the anime were guest celebrities at the event and people were lined up to get signatures.

Luke realized that if he'd just printed a half-dozen smaller statues like Anna's, that they would have sold well. He really needed to pay more attention to the guest lists at these events.

Still, he "made his table" soon enough. With that expense covered and his motel expense likely to be paid off as well, he'd be looking at actual profit before too long.

Sunday, he had the idea of playing Anna's promo video on his iPad, propped up in the middle of his display. He didn't want to have the sound blasting loud, but the moving lights did attract a few people walking the aisles. He even discussed a couple of custom jobs, but by the time he mentioned the all the costs involved, nothing came of it.

About three in the afternoon, when the after-church crowd began to fade, Anna came by smiling at her video, still playing on the table.

"I looked for you yesterday," she said. "A bunch of us were going out to eat after the show, but you'd already spread your sheet over the table and I didn't see you."

"Sorry about that. A drive-thru salad at Whataburger was my speed. I scout for the cheapest motel in town."

She nodded. "Well, I'm heading home. I met all my friends and got some pictures signed. I guess I'll see you back at work."

He nodded. "Yeah, it'll take me an hour or so after the close to pack up my stuff and load it into the van. I hardly ever stay another day after a convention. An extra motel day could turn a profit into a loss."

"I guess I'm lucky. I've never tried to make money at an event. For me it's always been about networking and growing my audience." She handed him a splashy laminated business card with her links.

He waved it off. "Save it. I've already got your links bookmarked."

The convention announcer came on to give the warning. "Make your last-minute purchases. The vendor floor will close in fifteen minutes."

She shrugged, waved and wandered off.

It was always a gamble during closing. He wanted to pack up and get on the road as soon as possible. It was six-and-a-half hours to drive home— getting him there after midnight even if he was extremely lucky.

Still, it was common enough that there was a last minute buyer who'd been putting it off and was in a rush to get that final item. Often people like that weren't in the mood to haggle over price.

He started putting away his displays; turning off the iPad and boxing up things that needed padding.

When the final announcement came, that last minute buyer never showed and his packing sped up.

He was sweating heavily by the time he wheeled out his boxes and packed them in the van where they wouldn't shift around while driving. He topped up the gas tank, bought drinks and ice for the trip.

He chose the Brownfield/Roswell route because it looked like fewer miles and hit the road.

He was still in Texas, heading west through endless irrigated fields, when he saw an old Buick off on the shoulder. The color was right. He had a bad feeling and slowed down.

It was Anna's car.

She looked startled when he walked up and knocked on the window. "Oh! Luke! I'm so glad it's you!"

"What's the problem?" Although, he'd seen the oil streak on the pavement, so he had an idea.

"I don't know. The car lost power and all I could do was pull over to the side. The engine runs, but it makes noises and I'm afraid to try anything."

He could see she was still partly in her costume, covered with a sweater and looking almost normal.

Luke nodded. "You've left a streak of transmission fluid on the road. I doubt you can do anything here. It'll have to be towed."

"Oh, no. Um. You're not a car guy?"

He chuckled. "Hardly. I could change a fuse and take my van to get an oil change, but beyond that, it's out of my skill range."

She sighed. "It'll be a fortune to call a tow truck out here."

"You don't have triple-A or one of those services?"

She shook her head. "Never thought about it. This was Mom's car and I just took it over when she passed. Like you, I know where to take it for an oil change but it's been so reliable, that I never worried about it."

"We're in cell phone range. We could look up a local car service place, but I'm sure it'll take days."

She nodded sadly. "If we were home, I have a guy who has always handled Mom's car troubles. It'd take it there, but it's still hundreds of miles away. Towing it that far would cost a fortune."

Luke looked at the big truck passing by on the highway. "You know, I saw a U-haul place back aways. They have trailers for hauling cars. We could go back, rent a trailer and I could pull your Buick behind the van."

"Would that work? Are they open Sunday afternoon?"

He shrugged. "It's worth a phone call, at least."

It was a small place, and the owner felt like answering the phone call. And yes, he did have the right kind of trailer.

Anna locked the Buick and got in the van.

"Be careful with your costume. The van hasn't been cleaned in some time."

She nodded. "At least it's not oily. It'll be fine. It's my fault for not changing when I had the opportunity."

It took over an hour and a half while they went back, rented the trailer, and returned to the abandoned Buick. Anna took the opportunity to change into jeans and a blouse while Luke winched the Buick up onto the trailer.

Two hours delayed, they got back on the road. Luke decided to drive slowly and carefully with the extra load, taking advantage of every passing lane to let the other vehicles get ahead of him.

Anna held out her hand. "I'm still a little jittery. I've never really been stranded on the road before."

He shrugged. "I have, but then I'm not a girl. I can imagine it's a little more stressful for you."

"Yeah. If I was in town, there were people I could call. I was in a panic."

"You had my number. You knew I had to be close."

"Yeah, but I was a little distracted. It's just lucky we chose the same route."

"It's the fewest miles."

She shrugged. "I chose it because of Roswell. I like the lampposts with the alien eyes. I was going to eat at the spaceship McDonalds there."

"We still can, but parking will be more difficult with the car in tow."

"Don't bother. It's not important."

But, when they got to Roswell, Anna went in to get them burgers while Luke circled the block a couple of times. He wondered what it had been like for some fast-food executives to decide to make a UFO-themed MacDonalds. Luke had driven by it several times before, but he'd never been inside.

The burgers were standard. She got a Big Mac and he got a plain cheeseburger. He liked McDonalds for the fries anyway.

"Tío Gonzales will be asking about you, once I get home."

"Oh," Luke frowned. "Should I be worried?"

"No, not really. Mom and I just had these neighbors that stepped up and made sure we were okay when Dad died. They helped out and then when Mom died, they let me know I was family. They haven't really been nosy about who I date, but when I tell them about this rescue, they'll have questions."

"What do they think about you dressing up as Sailor Moon and attending conventions?"

She wrinkled her nose. "It's a mix. Abuela Donna doesn't understand or approve, but her daughter Maria came along with me the last time we went to Las Cruces. She didn't go in costume, but she bought trinkets and posters for the family."

Luke laughed. "Was she spying on you?"

"Maybe. But I must have passed, because she wants to go along again sometime."

When they finally arrived home in the small hours, they took the time to unload the Buick in the parking lot at Anna's preferred auto repair place. She turned the steering wheel while Luke pushed.

He nodded. "I'll return the trailer to the local U-haul place in the morning."

"Keep the receipt. I'm paying for it. I really owe you for this."

"Will you have a way to get to work?"

She nodded. "I've ridden my motorcycle to work before."

"Oh!" He smiled. "What kind?"

"Oh, a 300 Sport. I could never handle one of the big ones. But I can get anywhere on mine."

"I've always wanted a motorcycle, but never made the jump."

He dropped her off at her house. When the lights came on and she waved from the doorway, he drove off. He really needed to catch some sleep. It had been a very long day.

The Accident

The first day back at work was a struggle, since he woke up at dawn like usual, giving him less than three hours of sleep. But he managed to run the last tests on his ion tubes. He was confident he had the right settings. Now what?

He'd told Anna about his plan to make a honeycomb block, but would that really work? It was a good next step anyway.

He toyed with the plans in his head on the way to work. He spotted Anna's motorcycle in the lot when he arrived. It looked like she beat him to work.

By noon, he knew he could get away with leaving early. He waved at Anna in the hallway.

"Surviving?" he asked.

She shrugged. "Odd hours are part of the game. I know a few tricks."

"Did you call your repair guy?"

"Yeah, but it'll be a couple of days before he can even take a look at it. I'll be dealing with helmet hair for a while."

"If you need a ride somewhere, let me know."

"Thanks, but I'm covered."

He nodded. "I'm taking off early. I've got to drive down to Las Cruces."

"Oh?"

"Yeah. The perils of keeping my old California bank account. There's no local branch here, and half my sales are in cash, so I'm driving around with a fat bundle and it makes me nervous. Too many ways to get that lifted."

"So I've heard. Well, be safe."

Luke had a burger for lunch and dozed about an hour before he took off south to find his bank. All he really needed was an ATM that accepted cash deposits, but he hadn't found one any closer than Las Cruces. He just needed to keep enough to make change if a buyer at his next convention brought nothing but $100 bills. It had happened a few times.

Normally, he took this bank run as an opportunity to visit the stores not available closer to home, but he was still mulling over his next ion tube project. The whole thing was likely to be a dead end, but the experimental process was exciting on its own. He had all this cool equipment, but if he only used it to make toys for other geeks, then it was something of a waste.

When he returned home with a fatter bank balance and a lighter money bag, he had the design in his head. He went to his modeling software and took the core ion tube design and built a triple-row of tubes, thirty units long. He packed them as close together as he thought safe. All he really needed was enough plastic between each tube so that it would be structurally sound and have no possibility of leaking between the tubes. He staggered the center row so they would pack efficiently, just like the cells in a honeycomb.

The end result was a thin slab about half an inch wide and less than three inches long. But, if he had ninety times the ion flow, then he could start on the next step, building the magnetic focuser that could separate the carbon ions from the other elements.

He processed his model through the slicer software to make the G-code for the 3D printer and started it going. While the printer worked, Luke went to the laser to program it, allowing it to carefully bore out the smooth interior of each tube in the array. It was all standard computer numeric control features built into the machine. All it needed was the right numbers, then magic of CNC would get the job done efficiently.

Step by step, he worked to finish the test array. Once it was polished by the laser, he added a surface coating of aluminum that only went a quarter of an inch into the tube, then the tin deposition, which he hoped would work the same on the whole array as it had on a single tube. Then finally he grew the silver igniter crystal needles on the mouth surface.

When it was all done, he extracted the honeycomb array from the silver solution and set it out on the work surface to let it dry.

He closed his eyes. He'd lost track of the hours, and he'd started with a sleep deficit to start with. He dozed.

...

I should have gotten more sleep. I'm stupid!

Luke winced in pain as he held his hand tightly on his left arm.

"Hey, Siri!" He couldn't reach his cell phone, but it was in voice range.

"Call Anna Bushnell."

There was noise as the call started.

"Hello, Luke?"

He clamped his teeth. "Are you off work?"

"Yes, you sound funny."

"I've had a little accident at the warehouse. Could I get you to come over and treat a burn?"

She was all business. "How bad is it? Should we get you to the hospital?"

"Not life threatening. My arm. But I can't have any questions right now. Trade secret stuff. You're the only one I trust." He looked over at the floor where it was still spinning.

"Okay, I'll grab my kit. How big is the burn?"

"Maybe three inches long. I've got my hand clamped over it. It hurts."

"Ten minutes. I'll be right there."

"Thanks."

He could hear her packing something. About when her door slammed shut, the phone connection stopped.

Luke just stared at the floor, trying to make sense of what he was looking at.

He hadn't locked the front door, so when he heard her knock, he yelled. "Come on in!"

She stepped inside. "What in the world?" Her eyes were drawn to the plastic device spinning on the concrete floor.

"That's my gadget. It burned me. Be careful."

She stepped closer to him. "Can I video that?"

"Yes, but not for the public. Not yet."

She nodded. Recording the spectacle of the broken plastic slab spinning on its own on the floor, giving out sparks and glowing—she gave it a few seconds and then turned her whole attention to his arm.

She pulled up a chair next to his. "Lift your hand." She winced. "It's mostly second-degree. I don't think you'll need a skin graft.

"Come with me." She led him to the bathroom and although it was difficult, they managed to get the burn under running water.

"We'll keep it like this for a few minutes and then I'll put an antiseptic on it and bandage it up."

He nodded. "Sorry I panicked. It hurts quite a bit and I'm not thinking straight."

She shrugged. "All normal. Now, tell me about that thing on the floor."

Through the open bathroom door, they could still see it spinning and sparking.

Luke sighed. "It's impossible. That's what it is."

"What do you mean? You made it, right?"

"Yes. I built it with my printer and added all the details. I know exactly what it's supposed to be."

He closed his eyes as the pain spiked again. He tried to concentrate.

"It's a block of plastic—ninety tubes stacked together like a honeycomb. With pressure from an air tank and voltage to ionize the gas, the plasma would stream through. I was going to measure the flow.

"That's what it's *supposed* to be."

She checked that the water was still flowing over his burn. "But there's no tank of air."

"Right. I walked over to where I'd left it sitting on the table. I reached for it and—I guess I sparked it with some static electricity or something. Anyway, within a second or so, it started glowing and sucking in air all on its own.

"Have you ever seen a bottle rocket take off without its stick? That's what happened. It was like a rocket engine with no stability. It flew around the warehouse, randomly bumping into things. I tried to grab it—that's when it burned me.

"Then it slammed up against one of the ceiling supports hard enough to break it. One piece fell down inert. The other started spinning. Its thrust was now lopsided. It fell to the floor where it's still spinning."

She sighed. "You set off a rocket indoors."

"Not really a rocket. It's an air-breather. A jet."

"Still."

He shrugged. "You can call me stupid. I just never expected it. I never measured the thrust of the ion stream when I was dealing with single tubes. It's surprising to me that it has the thrust to lift off and fly around.

"But that's not the worst part."

"Oh?"

He nodded, then winced when his burn shifted. "It's still going."

She looked out at the spinning gadget. "Yes, it is."

He sighed. "I've got a device sitting on the floor of my warehouse that is endlessly spinning, making noise, glowing and giving off sparks. There's no fuel in the air to supply the energy for this. If the metal plating or the plastic body were burning to supply the thrust, then it should have burned itself out in seconds. Instead it's been going for... nearly thirty minutes now."

Anna moved his arm to check the burn again, then put it back under the water. "You sound so sad about that. It sounds like an amazing discovery to me."

He shook his head. "You've heard the term 'Perpetual Motion Machine'?"

"Hmm. Maybe. Yes."

"Well people who invent PPMs are either con men or deluded. If anyone announces the existence of a machine that produces work with no fuel, nobody even bothers to look at the evidence. It violates the laws of physics to get something from nothing."

She chuckled, "So I shouldn't try to sneak that video out on my stream to get more viewers?"

He shook his head. "Well maybe. Your stream is named *Anna and the Fantastic* so it's right up your alley. You'd maybe get some fringe followers that way. It's just that I'm not ready yet."

"What are you waiting for?"

"I need to understand it!" She winced at the force of his statement.

He sighed. "Just discovery isn't enough. I need to have a reasonable, testable scientific explanation of why this works. If I don't then 'Luke Moore' will be just another name on the list of deluded tinkerers who didn't know what they were doing."

She turned off the water and dabbed the skin dry. She applied antibiotic ointment and bandaged it.

"You could invite people over to see the gadget on your floor."

He shook his head. "I'd get some locals. There would also be a few mythbuster types who would want to take a jackhammer to the floor to look for a hidden magnetic coil or something. I wouldn't get any serious scientist out here."

She sniffed, "Well, I want to document it. Can I take more pictures?"

"Be my guest, only be very careful. That thing is still spewing out high velocity ions. I really don't know the minimum safe distance. I know I got too close!" He cradled the burned arm with the other.

Recovery

Anna stayed at her recording a while, getting down on her hands and knees with her camera as close as she dared and taking high frame-rate video. Luke put up the slowed-down sequence on his biggest monitor.

"Every time the casing gets close to this blemish in the concrete, an electric arc flashes. I'd bet there's a piece of rebar close to the surface and the device is grounding itself out."

Anna frowned. "So it's continually making more electricity?"

Luke nodded. "I guess that makes sense. The igniter is electrically charged and splits the air molecules into positive ions and free electrons. The tin plating channels the ions down the center of the tube, but the electrons scatter. Probably half of them strike the inner surface of the tube and just raise the voltage. It would have to spark to get rid of the excess eventually."

Anna shrugged. "Physics isn't my thing, but positives and negatives attract. If the tube wall is negatively charged, then ions should be attracted to the wall of the tube as well."

Luke nodded vigorously. "That's the magic that makes this whole ion tube business work. A layer of this tin alloy, one atom thick, on the inner surface of the tube causes positive ions to bend their path, according to this scientific paper I read. They tested it on a flat surface, so I thought having it on the inner surface of a tube would cause the ions to concentrate along the centerline, never touching the tube wall and flowing like a superconductor for ions. I think that works."

"So that's your discovery?"

"Yes. Although it's so obvious someone else will discover it sooner or later."

"You need to patent it."

He chuckled. "I'm a garage tinkerer, not a corporate scientist. I don't even know how to patent something."

She shook her head. "We'll take a look at that. For now, document everything. If you write it down, make sure you add the date and time. I'll take time-stamped videos."

He smiled. "You're going to be my public relations expert?"

She thought a moment, then nodded. "I think so. Give me the exclusive rights to all the PR stuff and we'll work together to get this puzzle solved."

He nodded. "That's a deal I can't turn down. You'll do the stuff I'm no good at anyway."

They took more videos, and then when Luke felt up to it, they decided to stop the spinning dervish.

"I'd just let it spin, but it's too dangerous." He kicked the dirt loose from a metal grid that he'd used by the front door. He stepped close to danger zone and then carefully dropped the grid on the spinning device. A couple of big sparks told that he'd shorted it out and the glowing stopped. For the first time he realized how noisy it had been as the room went silent.

Anna kept recording as Luke picked it up in his gloved hands and put a strip of tape across the air intake side.

"That ought to do it. With no more air to suck in, it can't charge back up." He took it over to the work bench and gently clamped it into a vice. Speaking for the camera, he said, "I'll do more experiments with it later, but I need a little time to sleep and to heal."

She nodded. "Call in sick tomorrow and catch up on your sleep. I may do the same, if I can get away with it."

. . .

Luke opened his eyes at dawn, but then buried his head under the pillow and went back to sleep. It was afternoon before he woke. He called in and explained his absence. There were a few repairs to take care of, but they weren't urgent, so he promised to be in the next day and decided to rest.

Of course, rest included a few experiments with the broken gadget in the vice. Removing the tape and connecting some electricity immediately caused the ion streams to start back up. He hesitated, then shut it back down.

Pulling out his camera, he did the same thing as before, narrating each step.

"If I want to be able to use this jet thrust for something useful, I'll need an easy way to turn it on and off. I'll need to try a few things. Controlling the electric igniter would be easiest, if possible. Adding a valve to turn off the air flow is more mechanical and subject to failure."

Once he shut it back down and turned off the camera, he went to the internet and looked up proper record keeping for patents. His existing notes weren't up to recognized standards, so he took the time to make a video, time-stamped of him slowly turning the pages, recording his notes. He had kept the video running as he showed off his spreadsheets as well.

It wasn't bulletproof, but at least he was making the effort to document everything. He also got on Amazon and ordered some bound notebooks like those recommended for scientific note keeping. It was extra work, but if he ever had to prove he was first to discover this, then it would be helpful to have documentation.

If I really do have a perpetual motion machine, it can't help but make money.

But he still couldn't quite make himself believe it. Seeing is not believing, when it goes against everything you've ever believed before.

They're going to call me a cheat and a con man.

The urge to just drop it and hide the discovery nagged at the back of his mind. He'd struggled so hard to be respectable. Being a teenage boy without a mother made people look at him with suspicious eyes. Especially those parents of potential girlfriends. And then when his brother Ted moved halfway across the continent to get away from home, it didn't help.

It was just too much for Dad, and he'd jumped at the chance to be on the road all the time.

Luke had a couple of credit cards and a phone number if there was trouble, but there he was at eighteen, living alone and definitely without the extended family Anna enjoyed. Dad's death hadn't made much of a change, other than a month or so of nightmare paperwork.

But through it all, Luke followed the rules. He met every deadline, paid every late penalty, and followed the advice of the court-appointed lawyer who handled the settlements. Through it all, he was on his own. His brother Ted replied to the lawyer's letters asking where to send his portion of the settlement, but there was never a word for Luke.

Luke knew in his heart that all he had going for him was a solid reputation. He could live on his own and make his own way in life, as long as people trusted him.

Declaring himself insane on the internet didn't sound like a good move.

...

Anna caught up with him at work the next day.

"How is your arm?"

He shrugged. "I bought another bottle of Tylenol, but it's not too bad."

She looked at his arm. "We should probably change the dressing while we're at it."

He shook his head. "I can't use the hospital's supplies."

She gripped his arm tighter. "Yes, you can." She pulled him over to the nurse's work station.

"Mary, tell Dr. Pereli that I'm going to change Luke's bandages. He picked up a burn a day or so ago."

They went into one of the rooms and Luke sat on the bench. "I want to pay for everything I use."

Anna cut the old bandage away with scissors and cleaned the area. "Everything is under my signature. You're an employee and I don't think it'll be an issue, but I'll let you know if there are any charges."

He sighed. They were in her area of expertise. He'd have to go with it.

"How's your car?"

She sighed. "It was the transmission. I've got to decide whether to spring for a junkyard replacement, let him attempt to take it apart and find replacement parts, or just sell the Buick as junk and get a newer car."

Luke nodded. "Do you want a newer car?"

She shrugged. "Some days, but I'm used to the old clunker."

She smiled at him. "Want to 3D-print me a new one?"

He shook his head. "No. Cars aren't my thing. About the best I could do would be an electric golf-cart, and it wouldn't be street legal."

"Aw, I thought you could build anything."

"Maybe I could, but you can't imagine the paperwork involved in making a new car for the American market. I read an article once. It's a nightmare.

"Even just a one-off custom that you could drive on the highway would be beyond me."

She nodded. "And you're busy."

He nodded. "Yeah. I've got a URL for you."

"Oh?"

He flexed his new bandage and then pulled out his phone and sent her the links to his research for patent applications.

She tapped and looked. "I'll read this on break."

He nodded. "And get the junkyard replacement transmission. It won't be cheap, but it should keep the Buick running another year or so while you make your long range plans for its replacement."

She nodded. "I was considering that."

"Until then, if you need any highway trips, I'll take you in my van."

She smiled. "Thanks."

. . .

Dr. Easton walked into his workroom. Luke looked up from the circuitboard he had clamped under a magnifying glass.

"Hello, Luke."

"Dr. Easton."

"I've heard you had a burn."

Luke held up his arm. "Yeah, a couple of days ago. No big deal."

"Was it a workplace injury?"

Luke shook his head. "No. Just a mistake at home. It's healing up okay."

Easton nodded his head. "That's good. Less paperwork for me to deal with."

Luke nodded. "I wanted to say that Nurse Bushnell changed my bandage here, so if there's a charge for the supplies or anything, I'll certainly pay for it."

The doctor shook his head. "If it comes across my desk, I'll approve the use. We certainly have to keep our people healthy.

"But I was wondering if you'd considered our last talk."

Luke sighed. "I have. I'm afraid I'll have to decline full-time status for now. Another project has come up that will take a lot of my time—unrelated to the hospital. I just can't in good conscience sign up for a full-time schedule."

Dr. Easton nodded. "Sad to hear that, but it's your call. What's your new project?" He was plainly trying to be upbeat about it.

Luke shrugged. "It's hard to explain at this early stage. It's an industrial thing that I can't talk about yet."

Birthday Party

Anna knocked on the warehouse door, but didn't really wait for his response.

"Hey, Luke! Coming in."

"Over by the vacuum chamber!"

She came and sat down, just out of the camera's field of vision. "What are you doing?"

He flicked his fingers at his camera and she nodded.

He spoke to the camera. "I'm trying to nail down more details about what's happening. This is the original broken honeycomb unit and I've visually determined that forty-one of the original ninety ion tubes are still working."

Anna asked, "You have everything clamped down?"

Luke chuckled. "Yes, I'm not making that mistake again. But in any case, for this experiment, I'm going to be sending the output of the ion tubes into a five-liter glass bottle with a gas pressure gauge attached. I'll run the ion tubes for one minute. After it cools down, I'll measure the new pressure. By finding the pressure change, I can calculate the mass of the air that has been pumped through the honeycomb. I've already measured the force of the thrust that has been produced.

"Using the standard formula; force equals mass times acceleration, I'll be able to calculate the acceleration the gas ions undergo while inside the ion tube."

Anna frowned and nodded. Her job for these videos was supposed to be the ordinary person, not trained in the physics of it all.

"I think I remember F=ma in school, not that I ever used it."

Luke nodded. "It's useful. Starting now." He flipped the switch and tapped the timer.

They went through the exercise as he'd described it and he worked the math on a whiteboard with the camera watching.

He shook his head at the numbers. "Some very strange physics is happening in the tube to get this kind of acceleration. My tubes are all fifty centimeters in length, but I'm not at all confident that the acceleration is uniform, since the diameter shrinks from the mouth opening down to the smaller exit port. I'll need to make some adjustments to test that out."

Anna asked, "Does that mean you'd get more force with a longer tube?"

Luke nodded. "That's a good bet. The problem is that my machines can only make the honeycomb tube array in certain sizes. To make bigger ones would take larger printers, and bigger deposition chambers. That's a good experiment for when we want to go commercial, but I just don't have the money to buy more equipment right now."

He turned off the camera and copied the details into his new log book.

Anna watched. "You're getting in the habit with these notes."

"I was already taking notes, this is just following more rules."

Anna said, "Dr. Easton asked me if you were planning to quit."

"Oh?"

"Yes, he's worried some other company is about ready to hire you away from him."

"What did you say?"

She shrugged. "I claimed ignorance. I just thought it was amusing that he asked me about it."

He gave her a look. "We talk a lot at work. People know about the Buick rescue business."

Anna looked to the side. "And that brings up another point."

"And that is ...?"

She gave him a side look. "I've been asked to invite you to Tía Margarette's birthday party."

"I don't have to speak Spanish, do I?"

She grinned. "You'll get by."

...

Three days later, Luke found himself leaning up against the rear fence with Race Gonzales, Anna's voluntary uncle. They were both holding plates, eating one-handed. Luke made a half-hearted effort to wipe the edge of his mouth with the back of his hand.

"What's in this? The fast food taco place I visit would beg to have this on their menu."

Race chuckled. "Donna wouldn't share her recipes with the likes of me, and certainly not with some chain place."

The picnic tables and the folding table were covered with other dishes and the yard was full of people. All the neighbors were in attendance and there wasn't a seat to be had—which was why they were leaning against the fence, juggling their plates.

Anna was there at the table, helping fix plates for the guests, dressed in something that looked traditional, although Luke hardly knew what that style was called. It was colorful, at least. And she fit right in with the others.

"Are you and Anna a thing?" asked Race.

Luke blinked and realized he had gotten distracted. They had been talking about cars and how the Rio Grande was lower this year than before.

Luke chuckled. "Oh, I wouldn't be opposed to the idea, but really Anna and I are just working together. We both work at the hospital and we share some other interests as well. I made a statue for her with my 3D printer."

The man grunted. "I saw that. She was painting it, just like I did with my model cars when I was a kid."

Luke nodded. "That's the thing. None of my printers can print more than one color at a time, so you have to add the details afterward."

"Anna said you were some kind of tech guy? I'd expect a guy like you with skills to be working over at the Spaceport or something."

Luke laughed. "That would be fun, wouldn't it? Seeing those space planes take off and such. But no, I'm just working on my own projects for now. Working at the hospital to pay the bills."

Race nodded. "I've seen that big-wing thing fly. I took a trip out to the Spaceport last month. They've got the site blocked off to casual tourists, but I was lucky enough to see it in the air from the road. They've got the original Virgin Galactic spaceplane parked by the entrance gate so people like me can take pictures of it."

"I've never been. How far is it?"

"Not bad, if you don't mind a few unpaved roads. An hour maybe. They've got a dozen space-oriented companies out there, although I've only heard about a couple of them on the news."

Luke nodded. "I've heard the news as well. I guess I never realized the place was so close."

Race pointed. "Just over that way. Beyond it is White Sands where they test military missiles." He chuckled. "Commercial airlines keep their planes far away from that part of the desert. It's a good place to launch rockets and such."

Anna came over and pestered Luke to wander around and meet more people. He gave his birthday greetings to Margarette. The lady, who wasn't very fluent in English, seemed happy to meet him. Everyone knew he worked at the hospital with Anna, but some thought he was a doctor. He had to drop their expectations.

Eventually, Anna walked him over to his van.

"Thanks for coming."

"Oh, it was fun, and the food was good. I'm stuffed."

"Did Race Gonzales question you? He was worried about you before."

"No. Seems like a nice guy. If anything, he acted like he was trying to get me to go to work out at the Spaceport. Where does he work? I never asked."

She shook her head. "Oh, he works at the market. He's a buyer for local produce in the area and trucks stuff around."

Luke nodded. All along the Rio Grande River, there were seemingly endless fields of chili plants and pecan orchards being watered by the canals that branched off the river. He suddenly realized some of what Race had been saying about the water level in the river.

"Anna, are you up for a little excursion in about a week?"

"Hmm. What kind of excursion?"

He made sure there were was no one in listening range.

"Well, there's an experiment I'd like to try—one that has to take place outdoors. I want to make a honeycomb ion system purposely designed to be a jet engine. My idea is to launch it like a model rocket, and then track how high it goes."

She chuckled. "I can see why you want this outdoors. Can I record it?"

"Sure, but it has to stay out of the public eye. You read that stuff about patents, right? We can lose our patent rights by an early public disclosure."

"You take all the fun out of it. I just know I could make a viral video out of it! Have you seen all the weather balloon YouTubes where some school teacher and the class sends their balloon up to the edge of space?"

Luke shook his head. "I doubt we could get that high. It's an air-breather, so when the air gets thin, the thrust drops off. I'll make an instrument package and a parachute to recover it when the engine shuts down."

Anna was thinking about it. "Can you make it so it'll send video back down to us? A launch would be cool, but a video from on-board would be great."

"I'll take a look. I haven't even designed it yet. Something Race said about rocket launches at the Spaceport got me thinking in that direction. I'll have to design and build everything from scratch."

She nodded seriously. "Take good notes and I'll come by to get some pictures of your construction in progress. I like this! When it comes time to reveal it all, having step-by-step development would make a nice presentation."

As Luke drove home, he shook his head. *Now I've done it! Once I tell Anna, I'm committed. What kind of a craft is this going to be?*

The Launch

Luke was in show-and-tell mode. It was a lot easier now that Anna was there behind the camera.

"My first thought was to just take a standard model rocket and fit the ion jet into it, but that was all wrong. The traditional rockets have a long and skinny rocket engine. They are long to hold enough of the solid rocket propellant to get an extended flight.

"But the ion tubes, arranged in a honeycomb are only fifty centimeters long because of my current manufacturing abilities. To get more thrust, I need more tubes in the honeycomb array. A more powerful engine needs to be wider.

"Since I knew I'd have to design a new craft, I built the engine first and did a test firing to find out how much thrust it could produce."

Anna said, "You did this without me?"

Luke shrugged. "Well, it was late at night and I knew you had a long day at the hospital. I did set up my camera to record everything. It was pretty boring, just running the engine and measuring the tension on the chains I used to secure it."

She sniffed. "I'll look at it, but you really need to let me film these things. I'd have made it less boring."

"Sorry."

She waved him on. "So tell me about the design."

Luke nodded. "So ... to even take off, the weight of the craft has to be less than the thrust."

"You're going straight up? Jets can take off from a landing strip."

He smiled. "That's right, but since the ion tube produces so much thrust, we can take off straight up, like a rocket. If I were making a remote controlled airplane, then I'd have to design the remote control system that would work when it got out of line of sight, and that's not what I'm trying to test. I want to see how the thrust weakens at higher altitudes. That's why I'm making this like a rocket launch, straight up, with passive control fins to keep it oriented properly.

"All I need to be able to do is to shut down the thrust when it weakens and pop the parachute so we can recover the craft on the way down. I can easily make a simple circuit to handle that."

He went on to detail the craft, with an air scoop at the top, feeding directly into the engine, with a housing space for a gutted cell phone to send the video and GPS readings to the ground. The rest of the craft included the thin, spindly fins that extended well below the engine to give aerodynamic stability to the craft.

"It's simple. When the center of mass of the craft is in front of the center of pressure, the drag, then it'll fly straight. Think of an arrowhead and the feathers at the rear. As long as there's no significant winds, the craft should go straight up until it runs out of thrust."

"No wind? We need to check on that."

Luke nodded. He'd launched model rockets in the past. If there was a gust, the rocket tilted into the wind and never gained its full altitude.

It took a few days to build the craft, but most of the work was disassembling the cheap cell phone he'd bought in Las Cruces. He needed it fully functional, but he didn't need the weight of the case. A little glue allowed him to aim the camera down the length of the craft so they could see the land below. A custom app program was in charge, sending video and GPS data. He programmed it so that if the elevation peaked and then started to drop, then it would trigger its ringer. A little extra wiring went to the igniter circuit to shut it down and then trigger the little explosive charge that would deploy the parachute.

...

In all, it took ten days to prepare.

Luke shook his head. "If I'd known it would take this long, I'd have tried a different experiment."

Anna sat beside him in the van as they bounced over the unpaved road. Luke had pored over the local maps, trying to find a piece of Bureau of Land Management acreage that was out of sight of any settlement and far enough from the major cities and airports so that no radar would likely detect the flight.

Anna hadn't seen the need. "It's plastic. Radar won't pick that up."

"Maybe. The ion plume might be visible, I don't really know."

Anna checked her phone again. "The signal is weak. I really don't want to get stranded out here in the middle of nowhere."

"Don't worry. Just over that ridge, we'll start picking up the Interstate-10 cell towers. They're tall and far apart. I checked this out before I chose the spot. We need cell coverage to get our video as well."

Anna didn't look confident.

On his map, the marker was visible. "We're here."

The land was dry and vegetation was just occasional sage and cactus.

They got out. Luke pointed. "That's a good spot. Nothing to burn if there's an accident."

Anna swept her phone around. "Two bars of signal. I'd prefer more."

"It's okay. The rocket will be at a better altitude. The video is being captured by my computer at home as well. Even if we get drop outs here, everything will be safe."

She nodded. She tapped a button and began recording, explaining for her eventual audience what they were trying to accomplish here.

He let her talk while he pulled out the pieces and began to assemble the three white fins that would keep the craft stable. It formed a tripod, so they could launch straight up without a platform or launching rail. On two of the fins, there was a 30-gauge wire. The two wires led up to the igniter circuit. He attached a tiny little alligator clip to each, giving him a few yards of wire leading to the starter switch. Everything, including the igniter, was powered off the cell phone's battery, but nothing would start without him sending that first signal.

Anna said, "I can see the gravel. It's a little out of focus."

"Let me get it on my phone. You can get the takeoff sequence on your phone."

"Okay. Can I push the launch button?"

He laughed. "Sure. Just wait until I'm ready."

He connected to the stream the jet/rocket was sending. "Got it." It was a little out of focus. He'd set it for long distance images, so that wasn't surprising.

Anna said, "It's now 2:34 PM and we're ready to launch the first craft powered by the ion tubes. Five, four, three, two, one. Lift-off!"

She stabbed at the button and there was an immediate cloud of dust as the ion jets fired. It was less than a heartbeat before the odd-shaped craft lifted off. *The alligator clips came free okay.*

On the screen of his phone, he could see the widening view of the ground. In the center was the exhaust plume.

Anna was narrating as she tracked the plastic test vehicle higher and higher.

Luke said, "It's got a slight spin. I can see the van in the view, rotating around."

"Let me see!" He swapped phones with her as he tried to track the receding plume. It was getting hard to see. The ion stream wasn't very visible against the blue sky.

"I've lost it," he said eventually. "What's the altitude?"

She handed him his phone and she switched hers over to the aerial view as well, but they were getting dropped frames. They were losing signal.

He switched over to text messaging, where the phone was sending simple GPS data.

"Wow, it's up to five miles," he said. "I never got that altitude on any of my model rockets. Nowhere near."

Anna asked, "What do you expect to achieve?"

"Well, I'm actually happy it got off the ground. But, air pressure should already be down to a third normal. If the thrust is down to a third, then it should start to slow down."

Anna shook her head. "Video is gone. Did we lose signal?"

"It went too high. I'm still getting texts, but I don't know how long that will last."

He kept his eye on the GPS altitude reading. It was slowing down, but it hadn't stalled out yet. He kept calling out the readings.

Anna said, "Eight miles high? I'm getting a song in my head."

Luke said, "I'm worried about the instability. Did you see that fin shaking earlier?"

"Yes, maybe. Is that a problem?"

"Maybe. I didn't build it very strong. I didn't think it was an issue."

Anna shook her head. "But it's slowing down. When will the engine shut off?"

"When the altitude stops climbing. I thought for sure it would have happened sooner. If it's still going, we're above ten miles."

She laughed. "We're going to space!"

"We can't—" But even the texts had vanished. He waited, going through all the possibilities in his head.

He sighed, eventually. "We've lost it."

"Oh?" She sounded disappointed. "What happened?"

"There's no more signal. But it has to have started coming down by now. We should have gotten more texts, if it was still intact."

"You think it exploded?"

"No, but if it was going too fast when the parachute deployed, the shock could have ripped it apart, enough so that the cell phone circuit was damaged."

"Is that likely?"

Luke laughed, and then laughed again.

"What's so funny?"

He shook his head and reached for a bottled water. He took a big sip.

"I forgot something. The government was worried about terrorists using GPS for rockets or something. They engineered a hard limit into commercial GPS chips, like those in cell phones. If the GPS gets above 18,000 meters, it starts resetting itself.

"That's what happened to us. We reached the limit, somewhere over eleven miles high, and the GPS went crazy. My app reacted and fired the parachute too early."

She frowned. "What do we do now?"

"There's nothing we can do. I was counting on the GPS signal to guide us in recovering the craft. It'll just tumble down and crash on its own. I just hope it crashes hard enough to shatter the engine."

"Why?"

"Because someone else could find it first. If they were really smart, they might puzzle out how it works before we can get the patents filed."

She frowned. "We can't have that."

"I know. But I really don't know what we can do about it. If I'm right, then it was over eleven miles high when it came apart. I have no idea which way to go looking for it."

They were in sparsely populated lands. All they could do was stare at the sky and hope for a miracle.

Talking Strategy

Anna gestured at her house. "Come on in. I can fix dinner easily enough."

Luke looked at the surrounding houses. "I don't want to cause trouble."

"Oh, no trouble. Besides, we need to talk some more. You've been a grumpy bear all the way back. We need to talk strategy."

Maybe she didn't care about what her neighbors would say about his visit, but he really didn't want to be the object of speculation. Still, he was upset about the flight and talking about it might be a good thing.

"Okay, but nothing fancy."

"Frozen pizza?"

He nodded.

Anna went on in and started the process. Luke eyed the living room and opened the front draperies a little more and sat down on the couch in plain sight.

Anna brought out a Diet Coke. "Fifteen minutes until it's done." She settled down on the couch beside him.

"So give," she said. "What's the problem?"

He sighed. "It's just... every time I think I've got a handle on the ion tube issue, I realize that I'm just fooling myself. I don't understand it. I'm not sure I'll ever understand what's going on.

"I was thinking of making a first stab at writing the patent claims, but now I don't know."

"What's changed?"

He shrugged. "It's the thrust. I designed the craft to be lighter than the thrust supplied by the test engine. I thought it would fly up maybe a mile or two at best, and then when the atmospheric pressure dropped off, the thrust would fade and that would give me the data on how the thrust acted with reduced air pressure.

"But, it didn't drop off like that. There was still plenty of thrust even as it got ten miles high! The air pressure there is just a fraction of what it is on the surface. I really don't understand what's going on at all."

He shook his head. "Maybe I ought to just pack it all away and forget it. I only came to New Mexico to sell all this equipment in the first place. I ought to focus on finding a buyer and forget about this crazy ion tube stuff."

She frowned. "You can't do that. You *do* have a discovery. You have to make the most of it. It's ridiculous to pack it in just because your experiment didn't go precisely like you expected it to do. You haven't even analyzed the data yet."

Luke nodded. "Yeah. I guess you're right. I'm just so far out of my depth here, what with all the patent application stuff and all. If I try writing it now, it'll be plain as day that I don't really know what's going on."

"So wait a little longer. Analyze your data. Make your spreadsheets. You'll figure it out."

"I just hope no one discovers the engine."

She took his hand. "So what if they do. If you're willing to give it all up now because it's too hard, then what's the loss? Besides I doubt anyone will make sense of the honeycomb engine even if they do find it sitting smashed in the dirt."

She sighed. "It's frustrating to me, too. I'm ready to start putting together a set of videos promoting the magic ion tubes and I can't do that until we've got the patent ready."

Luke nodded. "And we can't reveal the patent until we have some kind of definitive proof that the effect exists."

Anna nodded. "Yeah. We need some kind of big PR splash, something that nobody can ignore."

He said, "I'm glad we didn't try it with today's launch. Losing the craft isn't exactly the kind of proof that we're looking for."

"No, that wouldn't look suspicious at all." She chuckled.

There was a buzz from the kitchen. She hopped up. "I'll be right back."

. . .

With Luke's suggestion, they ate their pizza slices on the front porch, waving at neighbors that happened to walk past.

Anna said, "I'm going to go ahead and edit the video, up through the launch and the loss of the craft. You go do your spreadsheets and we'll add a summary interview after you do that."

He agreed and went back to the warehouse. He cued up the saved flight video on his computer and watched it through to the end.

It definitely has a different curve than I expected. I need to work the numbers.

With the video set to pause once a second, playing on one monitor, he typed in the GPS readings into a spreadsheet on another. He added the data from the text messages. It was a long, laborious process, but he didn't know anyway to automate it, now that the flight had ended.

If I do this again, I won't use a cell phone. They make light-weight GPS trackers specifically for model rockets. I should have used one of those.

But after a couple of hours, he had a spreadsheet he could visualize with charts.

He picked up his phone. *Too late to call her.* He texted instead.

Luke: **Hey Anna, I've got a chart. It seems that I misunderstood the whole air pressure thing completely. I've got a much better understanding of it now. I'll tell you tomorrow.**

But the phone rang a couple of minutes later.

"Hey, Luke. I'm still up. Tell me. What did you find?"

"You should be getting your beauty sleep for work tomorrow. But the chart is pretty clear.

"I thought that the thrust would scale with the air pressure, with one atmosphere being the most thrust. That's not how it works at all. Probably it's all controlled by the geometry of the ion tube. There's a maximum flow of ions that the tube can process and the tube can suck in that volume of air from a much weaker pressure than one atmosphere.

"The thrust actually climbed until the craft got up to about four miles high, and only then did it start dropping off. Even when we lost cell signal completely, there was still enough air to produce thrust."

"So you've got the real numbers now?"

"No, I doubt it. I had an air scoop on that engine. I can't calculate the air pressure from the GPS altitude, not with the craft ramming more air into the honeycomb due to its velocity. I'll have to run some static tests here at the warehouse.

"But the thing has got me wondering how much I can alter the thrust by changing the internal dimensions of the ion tube. I've got so many more experiments to run."

Anna sighed. "So we can't plan our big demonstration any time soon?"

"Probably not. But do be thinking of what that demonstration should be. You're the one who knows what goes viral. I'm only good at table-top tinkering."

"Then I'll probably just take your advice and get some sleep. Maybe you should get some rest as well."

"Sleep sounds good. Maybe it'll all come to me in a dream."

"Stick to your spreadsheets. We can't patent dreams."

...

Luke closed his spreadsheet and considered going to bed, but he really wasn't quite sleepy enough. Idly, he tapped his web browser and clicked on bookmarks.

Netflix came up and he realized he hadn't watched anything in a while. Scrolling down through all the lists, his eye caught on a Sailor Moon series. He remembered watching one of the episodes, but couldn't remember anything about it. He went back to the first episode of the first season and started it up.

Right off the bat he started wondering about this tuxedo guy. Sailor Moon was only fourteen. How old was this strange guy she was crushing on?

The episodes were short, so he watched the Sailor Mercury and Sailor Mars episodes before he closed it down and went to bed. He hoped the plot would develop enough to keep his attention. This was Anna's show, so he ought to watch it through to the end so he'd understand it better.

When he woke at dawn, he had a vague memory of a dream where there was a magic crystal inside his ion tubes that made them generate energy, but he shook it off. He definitely couldn't believe in magic crystals.

But something is harvesting energy inside the tube. It has to be because of the geometry and the metamaterial channeling the ions—somehow.

Over breakfast, he reviewed more science abstracts. It was interesting stuff, but not as interesting as his ion tubes. If someone else had made the discovery as well, then they were keeping it quiet for now.

He went to his design software and designed a sequence of tubes, ranging from one with a wider interior down through one with nearly microscopic dimensions the whole length. He started the printing process and went to work.

On the way, he turned on his van's radio and scanned the channels. He was surprised the radio still worked. He hadn't tried it in years. It didn't sound like anything had changed in all that time—just music he wasn't interested in and angry people who liked to gripe about their pet peeves.

There was certainly no local news item about a strange engine falling out of the sky.

Anna is right. I can't worry about that. I'll either get my patent application done in time, or someone who is smarter than me will figure it out first.

Zero

They sat together for lunch.

Luke said, "I've started work on the patent claims, but I stalled out."

Anna brushed her hair back and adjusted the stethoscope she was still wearing around her neck. "What's the problem?"

"Oh, I put a diagram of the ion tube into the document, but when I tried to annotate and describe the features, I realized that I still needed more experiments to clear some things up. It's one thing to have a vague idea of what's going on, and quite another to explain in detail how it works."

She sniffed. "Just how detailed do you have to be?"

"I don't know. What I've done is download a lot of the Apple and Intel patents off a website and see how they phrase their claims. They always seem to claim the world. They explain in detail one variation but also claim other ways the same device could be built.

"The critical item is a good description of the special feature that makes this a patentable invention. Unfortunately, that's where I'm weak."

"You can't fake it? I hear all the time about bogus inventions that were granted a patent."

Luke nodded. "And those end up in court. If I can barely afford to apply for a patent, then I certainly can't afford the lawyers to defend it.

"You see, the thing about a patent is that it's supposed to be detailed enough so that some other engineer could make a working version of it from your description. That's the deal. You make public how it works in exchange for a monopoly license for several years."

She waved her hand. "But you *can* make an ion tube from your description, so what's the issue?"

Luke shook his head. "The patent examiners might just decide that the ion tube claim is just fluff and nonsense and deny the patent. I have to convince them that it's real. I don't think many perpetual motion machines get a patent."

Anna nodded. "So we need that demo."

He smiled. "Any ideas on that?"

"Not yet. By the way, were you planning to go to Albuquerque?"

He frowned. "A comic con?"

"Yes, I saw advertising for it, a couple of weeks from now. I'm not really sure if my Buick will be back in service by then. I thought maybe we could go together."

Luke sighed. "I'd certainly take you, but I never signed up for a table there. You see, this isn't the big Albuquerque Comic Con. It's a smaller event and I didn't think it was a good gamble."

He told her about his experiences with several smaller events.

"There are big companies running conventions as well as some great ones run by well-established science fiction clubs. But anyone can decide to run a convention and not all of them know what they're doing. Since I'm trying to make money at this, I've had to pay attention to the organizations behind the conventions. Some know how to promote their event and others don't. I've paid for a table where I only sold one or two trinkets. I have to be cautious."

Anna nodded. "So, you're not going?"

"If you're enthusiastic about doing your cosplay stuff, even at a smaller event, I'll be your chauffeur, but I'm not paying for a table."

Anna shook her head. "It was just a thought. I haven't bought a ticket. And I wouldn't drag you all the way there just to be my driver."

"Sorry. My next convention is in Midland, Texas. I have to sign up for a table months in advance, especially when they are popular and sell out early."

She nodded. "I'll put that on my list."

...

Days later, Luke printed out side-view diagrams of all of his ion tube variations. He had thrust test data now for a dozen variations. It was time to compare them all and make sense of the numbers.

The fat tube, with bigger core dimensions had zero thrust. The tin plated interior did help the ion flow, but there was definitely no thrust.

The thrust effect only works when the interior is nearly microscopic.

The ultra-thin tube that narrowed quickly from the entrance throat and then stayed at the tiny dimensions for nearly the whole length of the tube had just a trace of the thrust.

The thrust isn't just because it's microscopic.

The hybrid cone, which narrowed quickly at the throat and then gradually narrowed for the remaining length, with the majority of the length in the tiny dimensions had the best thrust of all, even better than the original cone shape.

The thrust is best at microscopic dimensions, but only when the tube's geometry is still a narrowing cone.

All the rest of the test versions tended to back up that analysis. He could get the best thrust by extending the narrowest portions of the cone shape, but the cone geometry was critical to the function.

He just didn't understand *why*. Was a detailed explanation of *how* it worked good enough for the patent claim?

He made a stab at it, reworking his patent claim to describe the dependency on the tube's geometry and the microscopic scale. He wasn't happy with it.

. . .

The phone rang. Luke broke himself away from the screen and grabbed his phone after the third ring.

"Hello?"

Anna said, "Luke, are you okay?"

"Um. Yeah. Fine. I'm just distracted a little. What's up?"

"Luke, you never showed up at work today. Dr. Easton asked about you."

He flinched. "What day is it?"

"Tuesday."

"Oh! I totally lost track of time." He glanced at the clock. It was late in the afternoon.

Anna chuckled. "But you're okay? No accidents?"

"No. I've just been deep in the research."

"Any luck?"

He hesitated. "Um. Yes."

She spoke lower. "Good stuff?"

"It could be."

"Okay, I'm going to tell the doctor that you've had some insomnia and overslept. Have you eaten?"

"Not really."

"Okay, I'll be at the warehouse in thirty minutes. I'll be bringing something. Okay?"

"That'll be great."

"Okay then. Later." The connection dropped.

Luke looked at the clutter that covered his work table. He'd been printing out paper copies of certain websites to help him work through the math. The place looked like a tornado had ripped through.

He started picking up things and making piles.

. . .

Luke carved into his enchilada. "I've been starving. I just didn't realize it."

Anna was still in her scrubs, but with a leather jacket for protection while riding on her bike. "I thought you might like it. They don't usually do call-in orders, but they knew me."

"Thanks." He took another bite.

She was working on her dish as well. "So, don't keep me waiting. What have you discovered?"

He paused. "Don't think I'm crazy."

"You have to tell me first, then I'll make my decision."

He nodded. "Well, have you ever heard of zero-point energy?"

She frowned. "Um. Yes. In the Stargate series. They had super-powerful energy gadgets they called zero-point modules."

He chuckled. "Yes, I guess I first heard about it in science fiction as well. But … it's a real thing. It's a quantum mechanical thing.

"I was reading my science abstracts and came across a report talking about nano-robots and the problems they were having with Van der Waals forces mucking up the action. I wondered if there was any link to my ion tubes, so I started tracking things down. Van der Waals forces led to the Casimir Effect."

Anna frowned, "Kashmir? Like in India?"

"No, Casimir. Named for a Dutch physicist. Seventy or eighty years ago he was trying to work out why the Van der Waals forces worked at microscopic dimensions, and talked with Neils Bohr. He then worked out the math that described it."

Luke waved at the stack of papers. "Honestly, the math is beyond me. But I think I've got the gist of it."

Anna chuckled. "I thought zero-point energy was just the usual sci-fi technobabble."

"Maybe in Stargate it was. Here's the idea.

"Space is filled with infinite energy, but it all cancels out, so in a vacuum, it looks like zero energy. In the description of the Casimir effect, you have two plates very close to each other and it masks some of that infinite quantum fluctuation. The end result is that the two plates feel an attractive force."

Luke was waving his hands. "Now in my ion tubes, the 2D plating causes the ion stream to be focused into the center of the tube, but there's still the Casimir effect at play as well. Because of the synergy between the ion focusing and the attractive force at microscopic dimensions, this zero-point force ends up accelerating the ions.

"It's a delicate balance caused by the geometry of the tube, the 2D plating, and the Casimir effect. If any of the components are off, it never happens. But in my original ion tubes, enough of the cone-shaped tube was just in the right zone to get some thrust.

"I've tinkered with the shape and can make ion tubes with even more thrust."

Anna looked stunned. "You made your own zero-point modules?"

He laughed. "In any one ion tube, the amount of thrust is small. I can hardly lift cities into space like they did in Stargate, but with the right geometry tube, amplified by the honeycomb array, I can make a thruster that needs no fuel."

She nodded. "We knew that already."

"Yes, but I didn't know *why* it happened! Now I do. That makes all the difference!"

She frowned. "But you still need a big splashy demo, right?"

He smiled and dug into his food. "Oh, certainly. Maybe even more so now that we're going to be using sci-fi technobabble terminology to describe it."

Checking the Cruiser

Luke shook his head. "Absolutely not."

He put his hand on the motorcycle's rear fender. "I'm not going to put an ion booster on your ride. Nor on the Buick when it gets out of the shop."

Anna grinned. "It'd be so cool, though! I can just imagine hitting the interstate with an ion jet! I bet I could outrun any of the cop cars."

Luke tried not to smile. "We don't know that. And even if you could, I don't think peeling the paint off the car behind you is really a good idea. We don't have any rocket cars on the highway for a good reason.

"Besides, I'm not confident you could control it. Even if I can reliably dampen the igniter on the jet on demand, your brakes were never designed for really high speed. No road vehicles! I just won't do it."

She shrugged. "It was just a suggestion. We've got to come up with some kind of splashy demo."

"I agree with that, but it's just too risky."

Anna nodded. "Okay, but what can you do with a zero-point thruster that will make a big splash?"

He shrugged. "We could put it on your boat. You say the boat has a three hundred mile range with full diesel tanks. We could take it to the coast and sail a thousand miles."

She hesitated, thinking about it. "I've taken the boat up pretty fast once, racing home when a storm was coming in over the lake. The waves got rough. I don't think we could risk a fast trip. Thirty miles per hour feels uncomfortable, and I don't think using the thrusters would change that."

Luke nodded and pulled out his cell phone. "San Diego to Hawaii is 2600 miles or so. So... you could do it in four days, but that's going fast all the way. And that's assuming I could make thrusters that would push your boat that fast."

Anna giggled. "I've dreamed of doing something like that, but I knew the diesels could never make it that far. Would the thrusters last that long? They're made of plastic. Would they melt?"

He sighed. "I really don't know. My lab tests were rarely more than a minute or two, and we lost the one we sent up into the atmosphere. The one that burned my arm didn't melt."

She said, "How do we test it?"

Luke thought a moment. "I could make some thrusters that I could bolt onto the back of the boat. We could circle the lake for a while and see how they hold up."

She said, "Just circle the lake? For how long?"

"I don't know. A couple of days? It might get boring."

She giggled. "A two-day vacation on the water actually sounds pretty good right now. I could stock the pantry and fill the water tanks. That is, if you're willing to come along as tech support."

"Of course I'd be coming along."

She shook her head. "I didn't know. You turned me down when I suggested a trip to Albuquerque. People might talk about us being together."

He sighed. "Yeah. I do worry about that. I really don't want to push it."

"How could you be pushing when it's my invitation? I'm not trying to cause a scandal, but we've been working together with no problems for some time now. I was just wanting to be clear."

He smiled. "I've been asked by people several times what our relationship is without a good answer. What should I say?"

She frowned. "It's really none of their business, but I know my neighbors have been asking me the same thing."

"What do you tell them?"

"Co-workers. It's true, but I'm not sure they buy it."

He looked her way. "We could claim to be dating. It's what they believe anyway."

She frowned. "Hazardous. If we open that gate, then the questions will get much more personal. I've seen it happen with others."

He nodded. "I really don't have close gossipy friends, but I could imagine there would be questions I might not want to answer."

She nodded. "For now, let's just be co-workers. Good friends with common interests. Not dating but we do spend time together."

"That's fine," he said. "And if there are any questions, you can just say I'm naturally timid."

She laughed. "I knew that already. I'm really surprised we've even been able to talk about this."

He shrugged. "I've gotten used to it. It's comfortable to be with you."

...

They made an evening run to Elephant Butte Reservoir.

"If I'm going to make a thruster mount to fit your boat, I need to take measurements first."

They walked out onto the marina. Anna sighed. "The water level has been down lately. The smaller the lake, the more the times we'd have to turn around."

"Is there a bigger lake we could use?"

"I don't think so. Besides, I'm not confident the trailer is safe to use. It's been sitting behind the garage for years now."

"I'll check it out. But for now, I just need to look at your cruiser."

The boat was sitting under a big canopy that protected the more expensive slips.

"I need to go check the pantry."

He nodded. "I'll get started here."

The cruiser had pod props under the hull rather than the common outboard motors, so the transom was bare. There was even a fold-down platform for swimmers to use. Luke began photographing and measuring everything. He had experience in making 3D models from real life objects, but this was a little larger than what he was used to. Luckily, his phone had all the measuring tools for the job.

Soon, he had everything he needed, with measurements down to the fraction of a millimeter.

"Anna?"

"Yes, I'm down below."

He followed her down. She was pulling moldy hamburger buns from the pantry.

Luke said, "I need to know everything about the electrical system."

She frowned. "Okay. Give me a few minutes and I'll walk you through it."

Putting aside the trashbags she was filling, they walked through the cruiser. It had two levels, an enclosed living area below that could be sealed off in bad weather, and the piloting deck where the wheel and the throttle sat beside the captain's chair. Both were large enough to hold several people.

She pointed. "The refrigerator is handy on weekends, but for the most part I keep it turned off and aired out so no mold grows inside when I'm away."

"What's its power source?"

"Three-way. There's battery power, propane, and even 110 volt AC for when we're plugged in at the dock."

"No 110 away from the dock?"

"Well there's a generator, but it hasn't worked in some time. I never got around to getting it fixed. It requires its own gasoline tank and I never bothered."

"Not diesel?"

"No. That would have been handy. But the only thing that runs off the generator is the room air conditioning down here and the refrigerator. I normally just open the windows and use the battery or propane for the fridge. The cooking stove uses the propane as well—just those standard bottles you can get everywhere."

Luke nodded. "I can make sure the thruster's igniters can be controlled off the batteries, but if you really wanted to do a trip to Hawaii then I can imagine having a working generator would be great to make the living conditions tolerable."

He wondered if there was a handy diesel replacement for her generator. If they didn't need the big diesel tanks for running the engine, then it just might keep electrical power running for a long time. It would be more efficient than charging the batteries from the main engine.

The level above was more open, although the windows could be closed. That was where the navigation controls, the depth finder and GPS system were housed. The captain's chair felt comfortable as he sat down and explored the system.

"Can I start the engine?" he asked.

"Yes, but make sure the gear is in neutral."

The diesel rumbled to life on demand. All the indicators and instruments lit up and he found the circuit breakers and took a look at the wiring.

Anna stretched out on a couch across from him, watching as he worked.

He found the controls for the generator and heard its starter whine on command, but nothing happened.

"Where is it located?"

She crooked her finger and led him to the cabinet on the main deck. He poked around, but it was like any other gasoline engine that wouldn't start for him. This wasn't his skill set.

She asked, "Do you want to take us out for a sunset cruise?" The sun was very low on the horizon.

Luke shook his head. "No. If we're doing this, I'll be getting plenty of cruising time. It'd just get us home pretty late."

She nodded. "Okay, but come up on the bow and we can watch the sunset from there."

He followed her through the upper deck and out the hatchway to the bow. There were seats there. He sat beside her. The smaller boat in the slip facing them didn't reach as high and they had a good view of the cliff on the horizon.

She handed him a box of cookies. "A little old, but they're still good."

He chuckled as he bit into the shortbread cookie stamped with the Girl Scout emblem. "I've had these many times."

She nodded. "I used to sell them, ages ago. When they're in season, there's usually someone selling them in the Dollar General parking lot."

"Let me know when that is. I only discover them at the wrong moment, when I'm rushing somewhere else or don't have any money handy."

"Girl Scouts take credit cards these days."

"Oh? That's good." He watched as the sun began to dip below the cliff to the west.

She leaned up against him. "Would you really fix Dad's boat up to make it all the way to Hawaii?"

He shrugged. "That's the plan. But we've definitely got to make this weekend trial run first. I think it will work, but we won't know without a real test."

She sighed. "Dr. Easton won't like an extended trip. Especially, if we both take a long vacation at the same time."

He nodded. It was just starting to feel real. What would it really be like, spending days on end together with her like this?

"Do you think the girl scout cookies will be on sale before we leave? This box isn't going to last long, at the rate we're eating them."

She giggled. "I'll ask around."

Looking for an Assistant

Dr. Easton said, "Luke, I'd like you to help find an assistant."

Luke frowned. "An assistant?"

Easton shrugged. "I've got to face facts. You may not stay here for very much longer, and Carlos can't handle everything on his own. I'd hate to be caught with no one around to keep the electronic stuff running. When it comes to machines and electronics, you've got a better idea of what skills are needed than I do."

Luke said, "I haven't really been planning to leave."

"Yes, but it's obvious you're spending long hours on other projects unrelated to the hospital. And it's not just that you're spending more time with Anna Bushnell." The doctor shrugged. "If it was just romance in the air I'd be pleased with the chance that you'd have a stronger motive for staying on here, but I can recognize a different kind of distraction with you." He smiled. "You've got a techie itch you have to scratch, I bet."

"Probably true," Luke nodded. "I'm sorry it's taking so much of my time."

"No help for it, I'm sure. But just to be on the safe side, having an assistant would make both of us more comfortable. Are you up to posting some kind of advertisement for someone?"

"I'll ask around. I've never tried this before."

"Well if you can't do it, I can try other methods, but I'd prefer you find someone local rather than advertise more widely."

Luke promised to give it a shot. It wasn't a good start for the day. He'd been up long hours working on his boat thrusters. Making them was a sequential process, even with the design finalized, he could only bulk print one at a time, out of the ten he thought he'd need. As the next one printed, the first went into the laser for fine shaping, and in sequence, the next steps, deposition of aluminum and the tin alloy came next. He was always taking one thruster out of one machine and putting it into the next, and everything was slowed to the pace of the 3D printing step.

Adding his regular hospital duties, and now this hunt for some technical assistant was going to be a load on his waking hours.

And I haven't even finished the design for the igniter screen.

Controlling the thrusters was a critical design change. He couldn't rely on his earlier embedded silver crystals to spark the ions into being like he did on the earlier test tubes. This was a thruster that had to be controlled reliably from the captain's chair. He couldn't risk a runaway voltage buildup like he'd seen before.

He was building a separate, detached igniter that could never be swamped by the electron buildup in the throat of the tubes. But, he still had some features to work out.

He texted Anna.

Luke: **Hey, you're local. I need to pick your brains about the teachers at the local high school.**

Anna: **Sure. Busy til six.**

Luke: **Later then.**

...

The high school building looked strangely familiar, as if high schools all over the country had been built to the same blueprints. Maybe there was some architectural firm that specialized in schools. Certainly poor school districts might be happy to reuse a tried and true design that was in use elsewhere, if it was cheaper.

He went straight to the office and got his visitor pass, then on to the counselor.

"You're Luke Moore?" She shook his hand. "I was surprised to get the call from Anna yesterday. How is she doing?"

Luke had a seat and chatted. He told her about Anna's work at the hospital and told the lady with gray streaks in her black hair about Anna's cosplay as well. She smiled and told him about Anna's time in school.

"But what I came for was to let you know that the hospital is looking for a tech worker, a trainee. Basically, I'll be training an assistant to do the job I'm already doing. So, when I thought about the kind of person I wanted, I thought about who I was back in high school—a computer and software nerd who was comfortable taking things apart and putting them back together again."

He shrugged. "I'm new here. I don't know all the local people. But I suspect you know someone who might fit the description. I don't want to tempt anyone to drop out of school over this, so maybe the ideal person would be someone who has already graduated, but hasn't gone on to college or found a great local job. I've really never hunted for anyone before, so I'm just looking for advice, really."

She nodded. "I'm always happy to find out when there are more job opportunities locally, and I have some ideas. But your best bet is to talk with the guys in the Technology Department that keep all our computers running. I'm sure they know the right people. Let me call them."

Not too much later Luke was talking to his counterpart and explained the situation at the hospital.

Carl Andrew nodded. "We regularly have bright students that ask if they can get a job in our department, but really there are already three of us and we aren't hiring. I can make you a contact list. You say you'd rather have graduates?"

"Yes. I don't really want to cause anyone's grades to drop."

Sooner than he'd really expected, he had a list of people to call. He stared at the list, feeling greatly out of his depth. Of the eight people, three were girls, and two didn't really speak any English.

I can just imagine hiring the Spanish-speaking girl. I'm supposed to train her, but I wouldn't even be able to talk to her. Anna is the only girl I can really talk to. And I don't know enough Spanish to train anyone.

Yet, he couldn't count her out, not in this community where anglos like him were the oddballs. He was tempted to sort the list with the comfortable candidates at the top, but he couldn't do that with a clear conscience.

Should I kick this back up to Dr. Easton? But that was just bailing out on the task that was assigned to him.

...

Anna shook her head, "I can see your problem, but I can't tell you what to do."

Luke sighed and took another bite of his burger. "Dr. Easton declined to make a decision for me either. I bet he hopes I'll give up and just become a full-timer."

"Oh, he's not that devious. He just doesn't want to get into that diversity conflict. It'd probably look good on his state statistics if you *did* hire the latina. But he can't make the decision based on that either. And besides, he handed that job over to you in the first place, right?"

Luke sighed. "I guess I could train someone with textbooks, or maybe with a translator. Do you think that you—"

"No. No way. I've got a job that's consuming too many of my waking hours as it is. I'm not going to be your translator. Besides, I probably wouldn't know all the technical jargon in the first place."

She poked at her salad. "I should have gotten a burger as well. That looks too tasty for my health."

He smiled. "I've got a pocketknife. I can split it for you."

She chuckled. "Afraid of an indirect kiss?"

He shook his head. "Isn't that just a Korean anime thing?"

"I always thought it was Japanese, but I could be wrong."

He handed his burger over, and she bit a chunk out of it. She chewed with obvious pleasure, but handed the rest back to him.

Luke said, "If I send out email invitations to all eight at once, then there'd be no favoritism. I can request they send me a resumé or something like it. I can then choose the best two or three that reply. That'll give me time to come up with a translator if necessary."

She nodded. "You'll have to make that clear up front. And maybe get some help making your choice."

He nodded. "Of course, I really ought to make the invitation bilingual. Do you think you could translate it for me?"

She sighed. "Only if it's simple enough."

...

Luke gave the candidates a week to reply, and that gave him time to concentrate on making the boat thruster.

The honeycomb blocks were finished, as well as the frame he'd use to mount them on the transom of the boat. It was the igniter and the control circuitry that was taking the time.

For now, he used the mounting bolts to hold a thin sheet of aluminum up against the air intake side of the blocks. These were so much larger and potentially much more powerful than the original unit that burned his arm. He wanted there to be no chance one or more of them would self-ignite and run wild inside the warehouse. But with the sheet blocking the air intakes and also being connected with a grounding wire to the frame of the building, he was confident they would stay inactive.

He formed the igniter out of four-inch strips of window screening, each with the silver crystals grown on the metal surface. The whole thruster, when mounted, would be six feet wide with eighteen of the strips arranged side by side the whole length of the bar. Each strip was electrically isolated from the others and connected via an electrical switch to the igniter high voltage system. The controller could apply voltage to the strips in any combination, and instantly switch them back to ground state.

Luke was annoyed at how expensive the high voltage switching transistors were, and his design needed thirty-six of them. His first vision for the igniter would have been an array of one-inch panels, so that he could light up the thrusters with fat pixels like a billboard display, but that would have taken hundreds of those expensive transistors and a much more complex controller board.

Maybe in version two.

The whole idea of carving the igniter into segments was to carefully control the thrust. His static tests hadn't given him a real gut feel for how powerful the thrusters were, and he was taking extra care to keep everything under control.

Burn me once, shame on you, burn me twice, shame on me.

. . .

Three days later, he was out at the boat dock, hauling the components of the thruster out to the boat. The dirt walkway was some distance from the parking lot with a sixty-foot climb to get back to the van. Carrying everything in several trips was laborious.

But as soon as he got all the frame pieces to the boat, he fitted it carefully over the transom and secured it with C-clamps. He just wasn't ready to start drilling holes in Anna's cruiser.

"Hey, what're you doing to Jase Bushnell's boat?" The man's voice came from the slip to the left.

Luke set down his wrench and met the man's eyes. His boat was a sixteen-footer with a Johnson outboard engine and a little electric trolling motor. "Oh, hello. I didn't see you there. This is Anna Bushnell's boat. She inherited it from her father. I gather he died a few years ago."

The man's wrinkled face frowned. "I didn't know. I guess it has been a while since I saw him around."

Luke shrugged. "I never met him. And as to your question…" He stamped his foot on the swimming platform folded down from the transom. "I'm installing party lights. I gather Anna likes to take the boat out for party cruises."

The man sniffed. "Just so long as she doesn't play loud music when I'm out fishing."

Luke chuckled. "I'll let her know."

The man frowned and waved his hand. "No, I'm not wanting to cause trouble."

The Plotter

Luke took José Garcia and Julia Flores to the cafeteria and said, "Go ahead and have lunch. I'll be back in about thirty minutes. This afternoon, we'll try working on one of the monitors."

José turned to Julia and gave her the translation. Luke hurried over to Dr. Easton's office.

"Can I have two assistant trainees for at least a month?"

The doctor put down his pen. "Explain."

Luke shrugged. "I got five responses to my invitation, and chose three to show up for interviews. Only two showed, but they both look capable, from what I can tell this morning. However, one of them, Julia Flores, doesn't speak much English. José Garcia, the other candidate, knows her and just started translating for her on his own.

"If I had the two of them for a month, then it'll be obvious which one is the better candidate. That'll also give me a chance to learn a little more Spanish and Julia a little more English. I'm pretty sure she can read a lot better than she can speak it."

Luke had to promise a few more things, like limiting his overtime to reduce the budget, but he was happy to agree.

Back at the lunch table, he sat with his candidates.

"I've gotten permission to hire you both on a one-month trial." He explained the situation.

"At the end of the month, we'll see how it goes, but at the minimum, you'll have work experience for your resumés and a month's pay."

He smiled, "And to be honest, if you do great work, Dr. Easton may just fire me and keep you both on."

...

At home, after work, Luke's good spirits crashed. He was glad to be training the two, but it would also mean his own paycheck would be thin.

Money was becoming a problem. The rapid pace of the thruster construction had required quite a few purchases, from the bulk plastic used to build the honeycomb blocks to the silver plating solution he used to grow the needles on his igniters—none of it was cheap. His neighbors were eyeing all the Amazon trucks that rumbled up to his warehouse.

And in the back of his mind, he just knew that whatever big demo they came up with wasn't going to be cheap either.

Just the trip to Hawaii is going to take a lot of money, and my bank balance is getting dangerously low.

The convention sales were too low and erratic to count on. He had three conventions scheduled, but just wasn't in a mood to schedule more of them. Toy sales weren't going to dig him out of his hole.

He looked around the warehouse. He came here to make a bundle by selling this equipment. *Where is that list?*

He got on the computer and re-examined his salvage inventory.

...

Anna took them to her favorite restaurant. He was glad to get some decent food.

She giggled. "Julia Flores talked to me."

Luke didn't pause with his fork. "Oh, what did she have to say?"

Anna shook her head. "I think she must have heard some gossip."

"About us?"

She nodded. "I think she was just a little intimidated by you."

Luke frowned. "Why?"

"Well... I think she was worried about going to work for a young good-looking anglo."

Luke sniffed. "She's working for the hospital, not me. Did you relieve her mind?"

"Well, I said that you were timid around girls and that we were spending a lot of time together."

He frowned. "That'll get back to the gossips."

"Like that's not already common knowledge."

He shrugged.

Anna asked, "How are the boat modifications coming?"

"It's done. At least all that can be done while it's sitting in the slip. People were already curious about what I was doing on Jase Bushnell's boat."

She looked curious. "Who said that?"

He told her the story.

She sighed. "I guess there were people we never were able to contact when he died."

"That always happens." He had his own family memories.

"But you say the boat is ready?"

"Yes. Almost. Once we leave the slip and move away from the marina, I'll have to remove a protective metal sheet and tighten a few thumbscrews. Five minutes work."

She nodded. "Then I guess I'd better finish the grocery shopping. Can we do it this weekend?"

"Probably. All I have to do is walk on board. I guess I'd better tell my assistants that they'll be on call."

She smiled. "Let them know how horrible hospital hours are right from the beginning. And you! Bring a bathing suit and comfortable clothes. I have towels."

...

When Luke's phone vibrated in his pocket, he wondered what Anna had forgotten to tell him.

But the number was unknown. *A spam call?* But the caller id said "Palmer Industrials" so he answered.

"Hello?"

"Yes, this is Palmer in Albuquerque. I saw your posting on the equipment exchange. I was intrigued by your flatbed plotter. The price looked much better than what I've been seeing."

Luke nodded to himself. "Yes, I acquired a variety of equipment during a bankruptcy proceeding. It was all crated up before I took possession.

However, I have uncrated three of the items for my own use and they've all been in good working shape."

"Bankruptcy? What company?"

"Sorry, but that's all under non-disclosure. All I can tell you is that it was a small semiconductor house."

"Hmm. Given your location, I can probably guess which one. But that's beside the point. Can I send someone down to take a look at the plotter?"

Luke thought a moment. "The earliest I could walk you through it is Monday afternoon or Tuesday. But I can show it to you now via Zoom or FaceTime."

The Palmer buyer agreed and they switched apps. Luke walked over to the crates and showed the bundle of documents that came with it and pried open the lid. After some haggling, Palmer agreed to handle the shipping and Luke agreed to wait for payment until after they uncrated it and checked for damage.

Palmer Industrials was getting a high quality large format plotter for less than half price and Luke could really use the $35,000 to boost his sagging bank balance.

...

"Can I come over and see?"

Luke chuckled. "Not much to see, but yes, the truck has just shown up and if you hurry, you might be able to watch."

"I'll be right there." Anna's call ended.

He yawned. Palmer Industrials had been in a hurry to acquire the plotter so Luke had to clean up the warehouse, again. This time to make sure that none of his ion tube experiments were visible to the outsiders. It took hours to make sure that everything was put away and all his log entries were up to date and secured.

He really had no fear that there were spies out trying to look at his discovery, but he just wanted to avoid the casual question that might catch him off guard.

One of these days I might need to get better locks on the doors and install a good security system. Better put that on the agenda before I file the patent application.

Once he started the paperwork, all that would be out in the public eye and he knew there were companies that regularly trolled the filings looking for something newsworthy.

Right now he was blessed by security-through-obscurity, a notoriously weak defense.

Anna parked her motorcycle at the far edge of the parking lot and hurried in. The truckers were hoisting the large crate on the forklift and inching it out from the other containers.

She asked, "That's a plotter? It's huge."

"Yeah. It makes very large plots. It's bigger than a pool table."

She shook her head. "What would anyone need that for?"

Luke shrugged. "The company I got it from made integrated circuits. I suspect they printed out a blow-up of the design so they could eyeball it, but I'm just guessing. I don't really care why the buyer wants it, as long as they pay me for it."

She looked at him. "I haven't asked, but are you short on money?"

He kept his eye on the work, just hoping that everything would go smoothly.

"Who isn't a little short of cash? But this sale should help me get through the next few months."

He nodded toward the other crates gathering dust. "I need to sell all of these, eventually."

She looked at them. "Better you than me. I've been letting my garage sit idle for years. It's packed to the gills with Dad's stuff. Mom didn't have the will to get rid of it, and I just turn a blind eye."

"What did he collect?"

She shrugged. "Stuff. His projects. I can't really complain. I just bought a new toy this week myself."

"Oh, what is it?"

She grinned. "I bought a drone. One of those hovering copter things with a good camera. I thought I'd use it to take pictures of us in the boat."

"You'd trust it over water? I bought one a couple of years ago and promptly crashed it into the trees."

"Oh, I got one that advertises all the bells and whistles. It can steer itself and follow you around. Auto-landing. All that kind of thing."

He nodded. "It'll be great, if it works. I've been wanting to get a good video of the thruster at work from behind—without walking into the danger zone."

She chuckled. "Yes, I'd want to stay well above the flames."

They watched as the forklift eased the crate into the truck. Luke signed the papers and they watched it drive off. He sighed.

Anna elbowed him. "So you're rich now. You can pay for dinner."

He sighed again.

Lake Cruise

Luke grabbed two of Anna's bags. "We have to hurry if you're going to get your drone footage."

She nodded, still dressed in her scrubs and carrying two bags herself. They hurried out the wooden walkway dodging around a fisherman with his own ice chest. They loaded everything into the boat.

Anna unhooked the ropes. "You take the boat out, stay under five miles per hour until you get past the no wake zone. I've got to change clothes."

He nodded. He'd never driven anything as large as the *Enchantress* before, but he had some experience with fishing boats.

Anna had been delayed getting off work when a farmer came into the ER with a big cut from a slipped machete. They had raced to her house to unload all the groceries and her bags and get to the lake before sunset.

They had two days off work, and they were going to make the most of the time.

Luke turned the key and the diesel rumbled to life. He glanced at the inactive thruster panel he'd installed, but that had to wait until they were well clear of the marina.

He tapped the throttle down to minimum and shifted into reverse.

The water sloshed below and they eased out of the slip. It took a few false moves before he got the handle of steering the boat out backwards. Luckily, they were only moving at a crawl.

Clear of the slip, he turned the wheel and shifted into forward. Only when they were clear of the other slips did he nudge the throttle higher. The speedometer was a simple needle gauge, probably connected to a pressure hose. It barely bounced off the zero pin. He didn't trust it to tell him when they reached five miles per hour, but he experimented.

The no-wake zone was marked. He could see the reason for caution. A big wake would cause all the boats in their slips to slosh around, possibly causing damage.

Anna stepped up beside him.

Luke's mind went blank. She was dressed in a bright blue bikini with a yellow scarf around her neck. A part of his mind noted she was even wearing makeup.

She smiled. "I'll take over here. You go set up the thrusters."

"Um. Right." He pulled his eyes away from her and hurried back to the transom.

He loosened the bolts, removed the aluminum safety plate, and then tightened the igniter into place. Cautiously, he plugged the control cable into its socket.

Anna yelled, "Your circuit board lit up!"

"Don't touch it yet."

"Got it."

He leaned over the transom and gave the row of honeycomb blocks, all fitted tightly together side by side, a quick look. Everything seemed in place.

He went back to the captain's chair. Anna looked like a picture out of a sporting magazine.

"You're distracting."

She giggled. "I have to look good for the video. You take over here." She pointed at the floating breakwater. "That's where the no-wake zone ends."

He sat in the chair, thinking more about how Anna looked than about his thrusters. He forced himself to concentrate on the task at hand.

The big technical problem was that he didn't have a throttle for the ion thrusters. It was either on or off.

He had two possible solutions; either pulse the thrusters on and off rapidly to simulate partial thrust, or to only turn on some of the thrusters at any one time.

His control rig was set up to do both. It was just a Raspberry Pi, a tiny computer, connected to a tiny display and a keyboard. He typed the setup command and the display lit up with a grid showing all eighteen zones, outlined but unlit. He typed another command and it shifted to nine zones. This was his simple mode. He'd start there.

The boat rumbled out past the breakwater and Luke steered off to the side, just in case there might be other traffic coming in or out of the marina at sunset.

He made sure the steering wheel was in the neutral position and turned off the diesel.

Anna was over by the couch, digging out her drone. She looked up. "Give me a minute. I want to launch this before you start."

"Okay, we've got maybe twenty minutes until sunset."

"I'm hurrying."

Luke pulled out his cell phone and tapped an app he'd written. His screen turned into a duplicate of the controller's screen. He'd never really tested it, other than with dummy indicator lights instead of the real thrusters, but it ought to work.

The buzz of the drone's spinning blades caught his attention. Anna was out on the rear deck and tossed the drone up into the air. It stabilized and began slowly circling the boat.

Anna switched to her phone.

"Greetings! This is a special episode of *Anna and the Fantastic*. This evening we're going into uncharted waters. Take a look at this odd contraption strapped to the transom of this cruiser. This is a totally new kind of engine. It's a Luke Moore-designed ion thruster, like a solid-state jet engine. You've never seen anything like it before.

"If you've been following my recent episodes, you'll certainly remember us launching an ion jet, like a rocket, into the upper atmosphere. Well this time, the same technology is strapped to a big cruiser. Let's see if we can get some real work out of this thing!"

She turned her head. "Luke, are you ready?"

"In just five seconds." He had been watching the drone circle the boat. Just as it got behind the boat, still twenty feet up or so, Like tapped the center square and it lit up.

The center two panels on the transom hissed to life. He could see a little of the glare reflected from the waves.

The boat began to move.

Anna steadied herself. "It's working!"

Luke called out, "I'm adding more thrust. Hang on."

He tapped the two outer squares, as closely together as he could manage. The boat surged faster.

No one was at the steering wheel. Luke hurried back to the captain's chair. The speedometer climbed to near fifteen miles per hour.

That's with three of the nine zones. Full thrust might be too fast for this hull.

Anna yelled, "Hey, we're leaving the drone behind."

"Okay, dropping back to one zone." He tapped the keyboard: 1,↓,9,↓

The outer two zones turned off, leaving just the center thruster on.

He glanced back. Anna was watching her drone catch up and she tapped something on the controller and it curved down to land on the deck beside her.

She picked up her little drone. "I'm good. You can speed back up."

"Come on up here," he said. "I want to show you how to work this thing."

She came up and he let her have the chair.

"Maybe the drone could have caught up on its own, I just wasn't sure."

He nodded. "Better to play it safe with new equipment."

He picked up his logbook and made a couple of entries. "I really want to keep that central thruster on for twenty-four hours. I want to give it a chance of melting from its own heat."

"You want it to melt?"

"No, but it would be better to find out now, when we have the other thrusters and the diesel engine to back us up. It's a trial by fire."

She nodded.

He showed her how to work the controls with the keyboard.

"One through nine selects the thruster zone. Type the number and then the up or down arrow to turn it on or off. I've been trying to keep things balanced."

He tapped: 1,↑,9,↑

The boat sped up.

She nodded. "Could you steer the boat with just the thrusters?"

"I don't know." He tapped. 1,↓,6,↑,7,↑,8,↑,9↑. On the little screen, all the lights on the right hand side were lit.

The hissing from the jets was louder, although not as noticeable as the diesel engine. The cruiser began turning toward the left.

He shrugged. "It's probably easier just to use the wheel, but it works."

She grinned. "Make me an autopilot. Sometimes having to sit at the wheel for long periods of time gets old."

He chuckled. "I could probably do it, if I had time. I'm running short of sleep hours these days."

She nodded toward his phone app controller, "It'd be really handy on the trip to Hawaii."

"Wouldn't work. No cell phone internet out there in the middle of the ocean."

"Oh." She sniffed. "That's right. I forgot about that. How in the world am I going to post my streams during the trip?"

He shrugged. "One other thing. Hit the zero key and everything shuts off instantly. It's the safety switch. Don't do that until my twenty-four hour test is done."

She nodded. Glancing off to the west, she said, "Sunset."

"You get us back on course," he said. "I'm going to go inspect the thrusters."

"Carefully."

While she played with the thrusters and steered them back north, he pulled out a hand mirror and looked over the lip of the transom at the jets coming out of the thrusters. The ion tubes in the honeycomb were so closely packed that it was hard to make them out individually. It was just a blue-white, unwavering flame. Holding his hand cautiously over the edge, he could feel the radiated heat.

They just might melt, after all.

Peering out along the path of the thrust jet, he could see heat waves shimmering in the reddish light of the sunset.

The thrusters changed. Anna had shifted to a 1,3,5,7,9 pattern. They were moving pretty fast.

. . .

"We're at the northern limit of the lake, for the cruiser." Anna pointed at the depth gauge. "One time we got too shallow and ran aground. We had to get another boat to drag us free. I never want to go through that again.

"You can see on the map how it's deepest here in the center. This is the original Rio Grande River path. In heavy rain years, the lake can be forty miles long extending up the river, but it's much less than that now."

She smiled. "You take over now and drive us back to the marina. I'll fix us something to eat."

"Okay, don't be surprised if I play with the thrusters. I've got some experiments to run."

"Of course you do." She smiled and turned to leave.

Luke had a sudden, most overwhelming urge to give her a playful swat on her rear. He resisted, but when she was out of sight, he took a deep breath.

That bikini was going to do him in, if he didn't watch it.

The Pact

Luke was using his phone for everything, from running a flickering pattern on the thruster array to checking the boat's response on a GPS-based speedometer app.

And then the phone rang, from Anna.

"Hey, there," he said.

"I'm about ready to bring up the food. Could you keep the boat steady while I'm carrying things?"

He chuckled. "Yes, I can do that. By the way, it got a little chilly up here once the sun went down."

"Yes, it does that. I'll be up in a minute."

He shut down the rapidly changing patterns on the thruster, leaving only that center section running. The boat settled down to the slow speed. Luke peered off into the darkness, making sure there were no running lights visible in their path.

Anna appeared like a dark shape in the doorway. She was draped in a blanket and carrying a shopping bag in each hand.

Luke grabbed a bag. "Let me help with that."

She shrugged the blanket off onto the couch and sat down beside it. She was wearing a light sweater over her swimsuit.

"I've got drinks in your bag, and food in mine."

Luke took another glance ahead of them and sat down beside her. "I'm starving. What do you have?"

"I guess the closest thing to call them are breakfast tacos, but it's my own filling." She handed him one.

He nodded. "Bacon, eggs, and corn? I like the texture. It's a little spicy."

She shrugged. "Close enough. You have to learn what you can cook on board. And that's green chili."

He couldn't stay more that a minute away from the captain's chair. They were only going at a slow pace, but there were still other boats out on the water and he didn't want to cause any issues.

"How many of those did you make?"

She grinned. "I made you two. But I have dessert."

He told her about his experiment, trying to make the thrusters smoothly change power by turning individual units on and off rapidly.

"It fails if I flip them faster than about quarter-second intervals. I guess there's a lag time for the ions to form and then clear out of the tube. I've tried to play games by alternating one section with another to get a finer-grained adjustment, but I'm not sure how much that'll be worth in real life use."

"If you do it too fast, you might get a buzzing noise," she said.

He nodded. "I think I'll quit the experiments for now, and just keep the center thrust running through the night. It'll be hard enough staying awake and making sure I don't run into anything in the dark."

"Oh, I'll take a shift. I was planning that from the start. But before that, I've got watermelon."

They ate and chatted about his new helpers at the hospital, and kept a watch out for changes in the depth gauge and any obstacles. Off in the distance, they'd occasionally hear an outboard motor, but other than that, there was just the white-noise hiss of the thruster and the occasional splash of water against the hull.

He'd exaggerated how chilly the night air was at first, just in hopes she'd cover up all that bare skin—and it had worked. He'd half hoped it wouldn't.

But now, the air truly was getting cooler. When he looked over at Anna, she had draped the blanket over her shoulders again and in the dim light, he wasn't really sure if she was still awake.

It was going to be hard to stay alert. He often stayed up late, but that was working on computers with the warehouse lights on bright. The boat was barely lit, with just a single 12-volt light overhead and the display lights from the GPS and depth gauge. Probably the only other lights on the boat were the red and green navigation lights up front and the white light on a pole at the rear. The central thruster probably was visible from a distance as well, but it didn't help him stay awake.

He glanced over at Anna and saw that she was stretched out on the bench, probably asleep. It didn't look comfortable.

A glance at the GPS showed them far from shore. He nodded and stepped over to the bench and tried to lift the bundled girl.

Her arms reached out around his neck and she clung to him. He pulled her up. She wasn't as heavy as he'd feared, especially with her help. Her breath on his neck was warm.

He carried her a few steps to the rear doorway.

"No," she mumbled. "I can walk. You have to stay on the lookout."

They locked eyes, barely visible under the starlight. Reluctantly, he released his grip and she stood on her own. She looked down. "I'll set an alarm. Come get me if you're dozing off."

"Okay." He watched her go down the steps into the lower level.

He sighed. *Yes, I'd better not get distracted putting her to bed.*

He forced himself to go back to the captain's chair and look hard at the GPS map and watch the depth finder occasionally show passing fish.

The quickest way to sabotage this whole project is to make a mistake with Anna.

It had been great having a partner in this. She'd gotten him back on track when he'd gotten discouraged and there was no one better to talk with when he needed ideas.

But, she was cute and ready to jump right into this…. This weekend alone on a boat with him, dressed in a sexy bikini and with not a word of warning to set a boundary line.

He shook his head in internal argument. She wasn't ready to tell people they were dating. She'd said as much.

I have to make sure I don't step over this invisible line.

...

Anna showed up a little after three in the morning.

"We're turning?"

Luke nodded, barely able to keep his eyes open. "We're in the middle of the lake. I've got the rudder tilted, running us in small circles. There's a little wind from the east, so there's some drift, but I was worried I'd fall asleep."

"I'll take over. You go below and get some sleep. I'm good to go."

He nodded and stumbled off. He was asleep the instant he stretched out on the bed, still warm from her presence.

...

The sun was up and the closed cabin was getting a little warm. He went up.

Anna smiled. "All the fisherman are already out with their lines wet. I was about ready to go shake you awake."

The cruiser was near the canyon walls. Luke could see other boaters taking advantage of the weekend. Some were fishermen. Others were water skiers, cutting pathways around the clear water.

Luke pointed. "Did you ever do that?"

She nodded. "Back when I was younger, Dad would have parties with other boating families and we all skied. It's fun. But the cruiser is a little too big for it. Not enough maneuverability."

"And I'd hate to ski behind an ion thruster-powered boat."

She laughed, then pointed at his jeans. "Why aren't you in your bathing suit? This isn't your warehouse."

He nodded. "Yes, I guess we need to look the part. What exactly is our role, anyway?"

It threw her off. "Um. I guess ...." She looked off in the distance and adjusted the wheel. She said, "I guess we're a couple having a weekend alone on the water."

He nodded. "I thought that might be it. But you'd said before that we shouldn't tell people we were dating. I just didn't know what you had in mind."

She sighed. "I know what people think. But you see, we're telling a story as well. I've got to make my videos, and those have to tell a coherent tale."

"Storytelling." He nodded. "We've got the gossips. You've got your tale for *Anna and the Fantastic*. I've got my patent claims. It's just ... I really don't know what the real story is—the Luke and Anna story."

She smiled. "Yeah, I've been struggling with that one myself."

He breathed out, confessing, "I don't want to mess anything up."

Anna nodded. "It'd be stupid to get tangled up in ... personal stuff when we're on the verge of this big reveal. Your discovery can change everything and we have to walk a fine line here."

"I was thinking the same thing last night."

She nodded. "Luke, you've got to file your patent. We've got to make our big viral demo that will get your name on everyone's lips. And then ... then we can see where the Luke and Anna story really goes."

"Okay then," he said. "We make a pact. I'll get the patent ready. No waffling this time. You get the video stuff ready. Then the big demo. But before that—"

"Right. Before that, what we present to the world can't sabotage the story we're telling. And we can't sabotage ourselves."

He nodded. "Pact."

She bumped fists with him.

"Okay, but all that said," she frowned, "our next video shoot with the drone needs to show the two of us in bathing suits on the deck of the boat."

He winced. "Really?"

"Yes, really. I'm going to be promoting you as a sexy young inventor who's changing the world. And I really need some shots of your bare chest."

The Crack

Luke winced when the park ranger boat pulled up beside them and waved, ordering them to cut their engine.

It was short of his twenty-four hour goal, but he stabbed the zero button on the keyboard and they drifted to a halt.

Anna was already at the gunwale. "Hello, is there a problem?" she asked in her pleasant voice.

The ranger tilted back his cap, and then nodded as Luke came to stand beside Anna.

"That's what I'm asking you. I've heard some reports about this cruiser driving around all night with search lights. I was afraid you'd lost something."

Luke shook his head and laughed. "No, I'm sorry. That was just the party lights I installed. We were testing them out."

"Party lights?"

Luke waved his hand. "Yeah, light panels. I can control them with a phone app. Make them flicker and scroll and such. Just an experiment for now."

"Well, if there's no problem, then okay. I would have been around earlier if it weren't for some idiots waterskiing near the marina."

Anna shook her head. "No, we're fine. Just taking the weekend off to relax for a change." Luke edged closer to her, showing them as just a couple of twenty-something's out on the lake together.

The cop headed away. Luke asked, "Did we look sufficiently like a couple?"

She chuckled. "Yeah. No doubt in his mind. As long as we fit in a standard category, he'll never give us another thought. But are you ready for me to bring the hibachi out onto the rear deck. I've got steaks or hotdogs."

He laughed. "Not ready to hold the hotdogs out into the ion jets?"

She grimaced. "The way your arm looked—no way I'd try to cook over those things. They'd turn to charcoal immediately. How hot are those flames?"

Luke shrugged. "Too hot for my IR temperature sensor and way, way too hot for a physical thermometer bulb. It's plasma hot, and out of the range of something I can measure."

He looked over at the portable hibachi and said, "Steaks are always nice. I'll hold off shaking the boat until after we eat."

There was an anchor they could toss over the side, but they were far enough from shore that they didn't bother. Steaks with corn on the cob cooked in foil made a pleasant meal as they watched the other boaters.

Luke noticed that they were getting closer to the western shore. "I think the wind may have picked up. Did you check the weather?"

Anna looked off at the clouds to the east. "Sorry, I'd checked earlier in the week, but not recently. Yesterday was busy."

"I didn't check either. But, I guess I'd better get back to running the experiments—just in case."

Luke helped stow the hibachi and get the meal tidied up and then went to the captain's chair to check their position. Soon, the "party lights" were flickering and he was reading their gradually increasing speed on his GPS.

Anna pulled out her drone and captured video from various angles. She called Luke out onto the deck a couple of times to get some pictures of the two of them having fun on the boat as the thrusters pushed them along. A few other boats passed by close enough to get a look at the lights and Luke and Anna waved.

But that didn't last too long. Late afternoon, Anna came to where Luke was working and handed him a jacket. She was wearing her sweater.

"It's my dad's. He left it here. The breeze has turned chilly and I'm worried about rain."

Luke slipped it on. "Thanks. I've been noticing that the lake is clearing out. People are heading back. I wonder if we should as well."

"How much more experimenting do you want to do?"

He shrugged. "A little more. Part of this is to examine the wear and tear on the thrusters. The more hours they're in service the better."

Anna nodded. "The cruiser was designed for ocean travel. It'll stand up to a lake squall with no trouble. The waves might get bouncy, but we should be in no trouble."

"Okay. Mmm. You're more experienced. I'd like to try a short run at full power. Is that okay?"

She sat in the chair and steered them north. "Okay, let'er rip."

Luke tapped all the thrusters on, and the cruiser lunged forward like a ski boat. The hull was planing quickly, and they started bouncing on the waves.

All too quickly, Anna called out, "Enough! Too fast."

He dropped them to half power and the boat settled back to normal. Anna chuckled nervously. "I've never been that fast before. I was afraid I'd lose control."

"If it was faster than the diesel could manage, probably the hull was never designed to go that fast." But that was just a guess.

He'd read that the diesel was rated at 450 hp. If that was true, then he needed to revise the power of his thrusters upward.

Not twenty minutes later, they heard a thud.

"What was that?" he asked.

Anna looked over the side. "We hit a piece of driftwood. We're getting into the shallows." She looked up at the dark clouds. "I wonder if there's been a rain nearby. The water looks muddy."

She turned the wheel, putting them back on a course to the deeper end of the lake.

Luke stared at the sky. He could see the streaks of rain. "It's coming. Do we make a run for the marina?"

Anna tapped the keyboard and they edged a little faster.

The rain, when it hit, instantly drenched the deck and there was no visibility. When the wind whipped spray into the cabin, Anna said, "Close the front hatch!"

He latched it, and although there was still water everywhere, it wasn't coming in anymore.

Anna shook her head and dropped the speed. "I can't see well enough. And what's that noise?"

Luke could hear it too—a popping noise. He tugged the coat's collar up and dashed out to look at the thrusters.

The thrusters were still working in the downpour, but instead of an even hiss of the flame, there were loud popping noises mixed in. The hand mirror was nearly useless, but he could see it, too. The flames were exploding in places.

He rushed back up to the controls.

"Something wrong with the thrusters. Shut them down."

She stabbed the zero button. Almost immediately there was a loud crack, like a baby thunder strike.

"What's wrong?" she asked.

He wiped his face and dashed into the rain to see.

The mirror wasn't necessary. Part of one of the thrusters had its top edge chipped off, with a three-inch chunk missing. Wiping the mirror free of droplets with his hand, he looked over the edge.

He checked the whole length and dashed back.

Anna looked at his face. "What is it?"

"One of the thrusters cracked. Don't use the seven or eight button. I don't know how bad the damage is. Maybe we should just use the diesel to get back."

She shook her head. "Visibility is too bad. Just toss the anchor over the side and wait it out in the cabin below. You're soaked to the skin. You need to dry out and warm up."

He nodded. "I'll do it. Where's the anchor?"

She gave him directions and raced to get below herself.

Anna had a towel for him when he sought shelter.

"Now aren't you glad I had you wear your swim suit? You can change to your dry clothes in the bathroom. I'll fix us something warm."

When he came back out in his shirt and jeans, he saw that Anna had changed to her scrubs as well. She was stirring something over the stove, holding the pot steady as the wind gusts rocked the boat.

She poured them large mugs of hot chocolate. "Sorry. no marshmallows. I forgot."

"No problem. This is great."

She sat down beside him. "What happened? Was the engine too hot and the rain cooled it too quickly?"

He stared at the steam coming off the mug. "Maybe some of that, but there was more. That popping noise was the first symptom."

He described what he'd seen.

"What I think happened is that there was so much moisture in the air that the igniter was able to split the water vapor into hydrogen and oxygen. When it came out the exhaust as plasma, there was enough hydrogen in the mix that as it cooled, it recombined explosively and made that popping sound."

He sighed. "When I told you to shut down the thruster, there was enough of that explosive mix inside the tubes that it exploded and shattered the block. I think only one of them cracked, but I can't be sure without testing."

Out the window, the rain was still pouring down.

Anna said, "I looked on my phone. This is the remnants of a tropical storm that came out of the Gulf of Mexico over Texas and drifted this way. Everyone else had plenty of warning. I just didn't pay attention."

He shrugged. "It's warm enough in here now. We can wait it out."

She sighed, "Well don't mope about your cracked engine the whole time. Figure it out. The diesel probably would have had trouble if the air intake sucked up a bunch of water as well."

"Yeah." He hadn't really looked at the diesel engine, but he suspected there was an air intake somewhere. There should be a filter to protect the engine from dust and other things. How would he do that for the thrusters?

If he had his computer handy, he'd start designing it.

But that had to wait. He needed to take everything apart and determine the exact cause of the crack.

He sighed. "You say you have a trailer for the boat?"

Just then, the window lit up and there was an immediate crack of thunder. Even inside, it was deafening.

Anna gripped his arm. "Did that hit us?"

"It was close. It probably did hit us. I'm glad we're down here."

She was shivering. "I've never been this close."

He put his arm around her. "We're probably protected. The lightning grounded out." But he was worried as well. What would a lightning strike do to his thrusters or the electrical wiring that ran down from the controls?

Checking Things Out

When they arrived back at the marina in the morning, under diesel power, the place looked a little different.

Anna nodded. "It was a big rain. All the tributaries are full, and the lake level is creeping up. I can see the difference on the shoreline—it's up maybe a foot."

"The area needs it." But Luke would have preferred that the rain happened before their trip. Cautious testing showed that many of his igniters had been damaged in the lightning strike. He could get a little thruster power, but it wasn't balanced and he really didn't trust it in the occasional drizzle.

They had decided to go home early, after he dismounted the central thruster and the cracked one for analysis.

Anna looked at the broken block. "Better it happen here on the lake than on the way to Hawaii, I guess."

He carefully wrapped the thrusters and put them in a cardboard box to carry to the van. He frowned. "I'm wondering if we really need an entirely different demo. The Hawaii trip would only intrigue people familiar with cruisers and their fuel capacity. There's so many ways someone could fake a long range boat trip, whether from hidden extra tanks or a midway refueling rendezvous."

Anna nodded. "I've had the same doubts. Plus, it's not really exciting. It's more than four days to make the trip. You can't make a video that'll keep people engaged for nearly that long."

On the trip back, they brainstormed demo ideas. They needed something short, but long enough for the word to spread. The more people they could get to watch it all live, the better.

Anna said, "I haven't released any of the ion tube videos yet. I could use them as teasers for the big event, or even as fillers if the big demo has slow periods. But I have to get a big crowd of people emotionally engaged in the demo."

Luke frowned. "Probably there needs to be an element of danger. There has to be a risk of failure. I remember when SpaceX was launching all those rockets and filming the crashes. It made the eventual success something to cheer about."

Anna nodded. "I should have had the camera recording when the engine exploded. I just never thought it would happen."

He grinned tightly, "Now you know. I can't think of everything, and when I miss something as simple as rain, bad things can happen."

When they arrived at Anna's house, he helped her bring the remaining food inside.

"Do you think I could look at your boat trailer? You say it hasn't been used in years."

She nodded. "Are we still planning the Hawaii trip? I thought we decided that wouldn't work as the demo."

He shrugged. "That doesn't mean we can't do it. I pretty much promised to make it happen. Besides, if I'm going to redesign the thrusters for the boat, it'd be a lot easier if the cruiser was on its trailer at the warehouse."

Anna thought about it. "And I could stop paying the slip expense. Sure. That would work. Come with me."

She led the way into the backyard. It was overcast, with some occasional drizzle, but it wasn't enough to bother him.

Sitting next to some rusting car parts, the boat trailer was up on concrete blocks, its tires removed, and protected by a tarp that had begun to fall apart from sun damage.

Luke inspected it. "Where are the tires?"

"In the garage. They're probably buried under boxes, but I remember them."

"We can look for them later." He checked the fittings, the trailer hitch attachment and the wheels.

"I'll need to lube the axles, but the trailer looks functional. If the tires are good, then it'll work. I was afraid it had been all rusted out. Your father took good precautions."

When Luke returned to the warehouse and unpacked the broken thruster, he separated the pieces and turned on a magnifying work light.

And then the phone rang.

He recognized the voice. It was Julia Flores, but her rapid-fire Spanish zipped by too fast for him to make out anything, other than a name "Carlos Smeeth".

"Julia, wait. What about Carlos?"

She was having trouble understanding him as well. Her reply wasn't any better.

Hurriedly. Luke fished out his phone and pulled out the translation app he was experimenting with.

"Okay, repeat what you said."

She said it again, slowly.

The app twirled a half second and said, "He fell off the ladder and hurt his ankle."

"Okay, I'll be right there. Diez minutos."

Luke turned off the lamp and hurried out.

If you're going to fall and hurt yourself, the hospital was a good place for it. Carlos winced as the nurse was wrapping his ankle.

"Sorry," he said as Luke walked in. "I didn't get the girl to hold the ladder steady. It wasn't her fault."

Luke asked, "How's your ankle?"

"Just a sprain, but I'll be hobbling for a few days. You'll need to cover for me."

Luke nodded. "No help for it. What were you doing on the ladder?"

"Overhead light in Exam Room Two."

Not ten minutes later, José Garcia hurried in. He saw Luke and frowned. José spoke to Julia and then he turned to Luke. "I told her to call me first. I knew you were on the lake."

Luke shrugged. "We got rained out. It's okay. But now that the both of you are here, let's go look at the light."

Luke held the ladder while José climbed and replaced the fluorescent tube.

"You have to be careful about the lighting. We're using 277 volts for the high efficiency lighting in the building, and that's more than double the 110 volts on the wall sockets. You have to make sure the right circuit breaker is thrown for the right electrical line."

José was translating for Julia as he worked. Julia asked why the 277 volts and Luke actually understood enough of the question.

"The hospital uses an industrial grade electrical system. We're powered by a 3-phase/4-wire 480 volt system and phase to neutral is 277 volts on that setup. Running the lights that way means we don't need a transformer." He explained more, telling them about the big air conditioner and other systems that ran more efficiently on the 3-phase power.

José stumbled his way through the translation, but Luke could see that she was understanding it all. After they fixed the lights, he gave them a tour of the circuit breakers and the big emergency generator that was primed to come on immediately if there was a power outage.

Luke offered to take Carlos home in his car and walk back, since his place wasn't that far from the hospital.

Carlos commented, "That kid is sweet on the girl. He's always in a panic that she'll get in trouble because she can't speak English."

Luke shrugged. "I'm just glad he is. I'm feeling very much the outsider here because I can't speak Spanish."

Carlos chuckled. "Then learn."

Luke nodded. "I've got the app, and I'm practicing, but it feels like it'll be forever before I can get up to speed."

"Luego pasa más tiempo hablando español."

Luke frowned. "Time, speak, Spanish. Spend more time speaking Spanish?"

"Sí, gringo."

Luke sighed. "I'll try. I can understand more than I can speak."

...

Anna's bike was at the warehouse.

"Where have you been?" she asked when he entered.

He was tempted to answer her in Spanish, but he lacked the vocabulary to even start. He explained the minor problem at the hospital. "I'll be handling an extra shift for a few days."

She frowned. "Did you make any progress understanding the crack?"

He shook his head. "You can help."

They peered at the cracked block under the magnifying glass, and then set up a camera to get a much more microscopic look, projected on the computer display.

"There!" She pointed. "It's got micro fractures."

There were three neighboring tubes that had the tiny cracks all at the same point. Luke nodded. "You're right. That's where the explosions happened, and the shock wave from one triggered the others."

She frowned. "I'm frustrated. Is this a deal-killer for the Hawaiian trip?"

"No, but I've got to engineer a way around it. I need to block rain from getting into the igniter, and maybe even set up some kind of software to make sure the tube is clear of hydrogen before shutting it down.

"It's a fixable problem, but it adds complexity."

She gripped his wrist. "That's all I want to hear, for now. But I have too much food at home. It's not too late, come over and eat."

He hesitated, but she shook her head. "If I leave you alone, you'll stay up all night fretting over some new design problem."

He felt the rumbles as she mentioned food. "Okay, you go ahead. I'll be right there."

She waved her finger. "No more than ten minutes. I'll start cooking."

As her cycle rumbled away, he glanced at the other thruster block he needed to look at, the center one which had the longest continuous run time, but if he opened it up, then he'd be late for dinner and Anna would be upset.

He turned off the lights and camera and settled for that.

At her house, food was still cooking. "Is your garage unlocked?"

She reached for a pegboard and pulled a keyring for him. "Don't get dirty. I haven't cleaned in there, ever."

He turned the key in the side door, and fumbled for a light switch. Old fluorescent tubes blinked to life. It was packed with boxes. At least they were in rows. He navigated around to the bay door side and peered down the rows, hoping to see the trailer tires packed somewhere.

Against the far wall, he saw something black. He eased into the tight passageway, knowing he was going to be nagged at for getting dirty.

There were eight black tires, the right size for the trailer, stacked together. Likely they were still usable.

But then, he saw two more tires, smaller, just beyond them. He edged closer.

There were several large pieces, wings and a fuselage. He reached into a cardboard box and pulled out a thick logbook. Hand written notes on the first page explained it all.

He took it back into the house.

Anna frowned. "Did you roll in the dirt? Go clean up."

"There was a kit-plane in the garage." He held the logbook. "It looks nearly complete."

Anna nodded. "Daddy's airplane. I sometimes crawled into the cockpit when I was little. Momma said it was just another of his projects that he never finished."

Luke wondered about that. He needed to read that logbook.

Under the Dust

Anna was a little frustrated that he ate with the logbook in one hand. "Don't you like the food?"

"No, it's great." But he turned another page.

She sniffed.

Luke asked, "Anna, how old are you exactly? When's your birthdate?"

"You're not suppose to ask a lady that."

"Seriously. I need to know."

She told him. Luke nodded.

"Listen to this, from the last page: 'I just cancelled the engine order. Called the company and made my pitch that I needed the money for medical expenses with the new baby. They were sympathetic and had a backlog of orders, so they gave me a full refund. Maybe some day I'll finish this.'"

Anna frowned. "Mom told me that they had to take me back to the hospital when I was just a few days old. I don't know the problem."

She sighed. "So Dad had to give up his airplane because of me. I never knew that. He never said anything."

Luke shrugged. "Could have been any reason. I've heard that the majority of accidents with homebuilt airplanes happen during the first flights. Maybe he just didn't want to risk leaving his family alone. From the log book, he spent nearly two years making the plane—well before you came into the picture. It was just bad timing."

She put her hand to her forehead. "I don't know how many times I've just repeated what Mom said, about Dad never finishing his projects. It was really unfair of me."

He shook his head. "So you've learned a little more about your father, and gained a little more respect for him. How is that a bad thing?"

She nodded.

Luke paid a little more attention to dessert. But he was still fascinated by the plane. "It was a Long-EZ. Mainly built out of blocks of foam that were cut to shape and then covered with fiberglass. It's nearly complete, from what the logbook says. Everything but the engine."

She chuckled. "Put thrusters on it and fly around the world."

He nodded. "I had that thought as well. It might make a good demo." He shrugged. "You don't happen to have a pilot's license, do you?"

She shook her head. "Nope. Never thought about it."

"Me, neither. I wonder how long it takes to get one."

Anna asked, "Are you seriously thinking of getting Dad's plane to fly?"

He hesitated before saying. "It's worth thinking about. A plane would give us a more spectacular platform for the demo than the boat. Faster things would catch the eyes of more people."

"How long will all this take?"

Luke shrugged. "Right now I've got extra shifts at the hospital, more analysis of the boat thrusters, designing a rain baffle for the boat thruster—and the same kind of thing for a plane thruster.

"I need to finalize the patent application, and add whatever words that will include it being used as a flight thruster.

"I'd have to familiarize myself with the Long-EZ and get a pilot's license."

He sighed. "It looks like months of work. Maybe I should get that provisional patent."

"The patent-pending thing?"

"Yes. I've dug into the patent website and I'm just still not certain I can pull it off myself."

He looked like he'd tasted something sour. "It can be done by a do-it-yourselfer, but so much of the advice says that you need a patent attorney to make sure everything is done properly."

Anna asked, "Are you worried about the money, or about the secrecy?"

"It's several thousand, no matter how I look at it. And I suspect that any reputable patent attorney has iron-clad privacy rules."

Anna frowned, "They wouldn't want a cut of the deal, would they?"

He shook his head. "That's not what I'm seeing on the sites I've visited. They just charge a disgustingly high price for their hours of work. The thing is, it might be worth it. Lots of patents are rejected, sometimes multiple times, before they're accepted. If I do it myself, I'm sure to be rejected at first because of some stupid error."

She thought about it for a moment. "I'd say, go ahead and put together a provisional patent application, and then that gives you a year to get all the details together. And, do you have enough money for this?"

He said, "In an ideal world, it'll probably take five to ten thousand dollars. Some sites say you should budget twenty thousand. I really need to sell something else in the warehouse to get my bank balance pushed up higher."

"I have some money. Abuelo Pérez was a big farmer and Mom was well off. I haven't been hurting."

Luke shook his head. "I'd rather not take your money."

"Why not? Aren't we in this together?"

He hesitated. "We can't do this without a company. You know how I got that signed document from Dr. Easton about the scrap? I'm going to need us to form a partnership or something—on paper. Our verbal agreement isn't enough. Not now when it's getting so real."

"What," she asked cautiously, "are you thinking about?"

He smiled. "A *business* document. Let's form a legal New Mexico business with the both of us as owners. Then we can track the money stuff and even file for the patent in the company name."

She frowned, "How do you do that?"

"I haven't a clue. There's probably something on the state website. Why don't you put that on your to-do list? I'm buried in stuff right now. You're probably better at it than I would be anyhow."

"Thanks a lot." She sighed. "Where do I start?"

"Look up what it takes to form a partnership or a corporation according to New Mexico laws. After that, we just follow the checklist."

Still, she hesitated. "Wouldn't it be easier for you to just hire me as an employee of Maker Products? Don't you already have that business set up?"

Luke shook his head. "Wasn't our verbal agreement more of a partnership? I'm not going to back out of what I agreed to earlier."

"That was before we realized how important your discovery was. You could make millions with this. I can't take half just for some videos."

He smiled. "You're helping me a lot more than just that. If we really do pull this off, your contribution will certainly be worth a fair share."

...

It was a hectic week. With the extra shifts at the hospital, Luke was there early each day. He had to have a talk with José.

"Now, I appreciate the translations, but you're not helping Julia by showing up every time she does. You're not the only bilingual person around here—not by a long shot. Julia has to be able to handle any plant operations task thrown her way when she's the only one of us here. And that means she needs to rely on any of the other nurses or secretaries or whoever is available if there is a language issue."

José frowned. "She almost didn't apply for the job, afraid she'd not fit in at the hospital. I promised her I'd be there to help her if there was an issue."

Luke nodded. "I'm glad you convinced her, but she's not the problem. There are plenty of people she can talk with. I may need your help in translating certain training sessions, but in day-to-day work, she needs to stand on her own. If she can't, then she's the wrong fit for the job. She needs to either rely on a wider pool of people to translate for her, or to enhance her English skills."

He pulled out his phone. "And I'm hardly a model of bilingualism either. I'm struggling to get through these language lessons on my app. I should have started this when I first moved here. It's not fair to make everyone speak English just to communicate with me."

José nodded. "I'll have a talk with her."

Luke smiled, "Well, make sure she knows that I've been impressed with her work. I'm really pushing the idea that the hospital should hire the both of you. I just don't want the language issue to sabotage that. Dr. Easton will be concerned if you're always at her elbow. He won't hire you to be around as a translator."

...

Nearly every day after work, Luke was in Anna's garage, carefully moving boxes around. The trailer tires came out first and he got his hands horribly dirty lubricating the axles and making sure the brake lights were still working properly.

He bolted the tires back into place and jacked the trailer up to remove the supporting blocks.

"Anna, I'm ready to pull the trailer out. I want to take it to my place first and make sure everything will fit in the warehouse."

"Okay, but we take the boat out of the water on Monday, like we planned, right?"

"Sounds good. But for now, I'd like your help as I back my van into your back yard. Extra eyes would be useful."

"Got it."

Zerpo

Anna bumped Luke's shoulder. "How's it feel to be officially partners now?"

He stepped out of the Doña Ana Courthouse in Las Cruces. "Not partners. We're a limited liability corporation. Although I'm not sure how well I like Zerpo LLC as the name. It reminds me of Zeppo Marx. I'm sure people are going to mispronounce it all the time."

She smiled. "Yes, but once my videos come out and people start talking about zero-point energy, then it'll make sense. Besides, so many of the good names were already taken."

She pointed. "Do you want me to show you where I went to school?"

He glanced at his watch. "Yes, if it doesn't take too long. I've got to be back at the hospital by four."

...

Scheduling became increasingly important. After a long day working in Anna's garage, Luke carefully unpacked the pieces of the homebuilt plane and transferred them to his van. Luckily it looked like the wings were designed to be dismounted from the fuselage for transport. It was surprising how lightweight the plane was. With Anna's help, they had no problem moving everything.

Reserving space to work on the boat, when they brought it from the lake, Luke poured over the diagrams and made sure that all the pieces of the plane were present and accounted for.

Anna came over for supper after her shift at the hospital a few days later and marveled at it. "I never saw it all put together like this. It's a strange-looking plane."

"Yes, with the main wings in the back and the canard wing up front, it certainly looks strange enough."

"So, do you think it would work if you put some ion thrusters in the back?"

"Probably. I've done a little research. The Long-EZ has been modified quite a number of times with experimental engines. There's been a rocket version, one with an automobile engine, another with twin engines on the wings, and there was even a NASA version where they were testing pulse-detonation engines—whatever that is. Whenever we announce a Long-EZ with ion thrusters, there will be a number of people who won't bat an eye."

Anna giggled. "Let's get in. I'm the pilot!"

She opened the canopy onto its starboard-side hinge and climbed into the pilot seat. She looked tiny in the space.

"Get in," she urged. "The seats are designed for big people."

Luke put his leg in then climbed into the passenger seat behind her. He settled back. "These seats are going to need cushions."

She nodded. "The last time I played in here, I was about twelve. I didn't remember the hard seats."

She closed the canopy and latched it down. She put her hand on the stick at her side. "Where are we off to?"

He smiled. "Hmm. Let's go buzz the Statue of Liberty."

She giggled again, made motor noises with her mouth and said, "Taking off."

Luke watched the elevators on the canard at front wiggle as she worked the stick.

She looked off to the side. "Oh! The things on the wings work, too."

"Ailerons."

Playtime lasted a few seconds longer, but adult Anna couldn't keep it up. She sighed. "I could play at this for hours back then. When I was a teen, I even watched videos about flying."

"And you never thought about getting a pilot's license?"

She shook her head. "Not seriously. Those pilots-eye-view videos were great while up in the air, but I got nervous during the landings. And then there was that Rocky Mountain singer guy who died during a plane crash."

Luke nodded. "John Denver." He tapped the plane body. "I think it was in one of these planes, as a matter of fact."

"Oh, no! Wasn't it safe?"

Luke shrugged. "I just ran across a mention of it when I was researching the plane. He'd just bought the plane and it was his first flight in it. One of those simple errors that got out of hand, I think."

She shook her head. "I'm not a pilot. I don't think I have the right skills for it."

"We'll see. I'm definitely looking at pilot training for me, and the sooner the better. We can't get the plane certified to fly without some test flying, no matter what kind of engine it has."

They opened the canopy and he climbed out. He helped her up and out. With her head close enough to whisper, she said, "You will be safe, right? This whole project isn't worth you dying in a crash."

He gave her a squeeze. "I'll be careful. I'm not interested in becoming a statistic either."

. . .

It was afternoon a few days later when Luke was moving some of his machines around—making room for the boat when they pulled it out of the lake the next day—when he saw a small head peering around through the opened bay doors.

Luke smiled. "Hello?"

The boy winced, but only had eyes for the Long-EZ. "¿Es una nave espacial?"

"What?"

The boy ducked away and dashed out the gate, racing home.

Luke frowned and pulled out his translation app. He chuckled. *So the neighbor kid thinks I have a spaceship in my warehouse.*

He looked at the plane again and grinned. It did have that look to it.

. . .

Luke waded into the lake water, listening to Anna over the phone in his bluetooth earbuds.

"I'm lined up," she said. "Let me know when to approach."

The cruiser was drifting slowly toward the boat ramp.

Luke said, "Okay, looks good. Give me five seconds and then make your approach." He climbed up onto the boat trailer. There was a submerged platform just by the bow support and he spooled the hook and cable out a few feet.

There was the rumble of the diesel and the boat approached. Anna was spinning the wheel back and forth to keep it lined up.

The hull slid onto the rollers, the engine died, and Luke scrambled to the ring with the hook. "Snagged it! Let me crank it up."

"Not much I can do here. Let me know."

"Hang tight."

Luke worked the hand crank as fast as he could, worried the boat was drifting a little to the left.

A stranger waded into the water and shoved at the side of the boat to hold it steady. "Got it!" he yelled.

"Gracias!" Luke called out, hauling the boat up into the V-shaped cavity lined with rollers. The more the boat was wedged into the slot, the less it had a chance to drift. When the bow squeezed tight against the front support, Luke called out, "It's secure."

The stranger waved and waded back to his own boat on the trailer beside him on the loading ramp.

"Anna," Luke spoke into the phone. "Stay put. I'll be hauling the boat up to the parking lot."

"Okay."

The van's tires slipped a couple of time before they got traction on the wet concrete. Luke eased the heavy load up to the parking lot and got out.

Anna went to work, running the bilge pump and removing the transom plugs at the rear of the boat. They needed to drain every bit of lake water out of the boat before they hit the road. There was always the chance that an invasive life form was riding along in the bilge and they didn't need to spread it.

Luke was adding the clamps that secured the boat even more firmly into the trailer's rollers. He fully intended to drive slowly and carefully, but he remembered that bus that was run off the highway. Accidents could happen.

When Anna shut down the boat's electrical system, Luke was there to help ease her to the ground.

She patted his chest. "You're soaked. Did you bring a change of clothes?"

He shrugged. "Didn't think of it."

She put her hands on her hips. "Well, I always do." She showed off her shorts. "You should get in the habit."

They drove back to the warehouse. He eased up his gravel road at less than five miles per hour. At this time of day, there were always children out playing with their friends.

He saw a familiar face. He told Anna about the boy.

She giggled. "I thought it was a spaceship myself a couple of times."

Backing the cruiser, high on its trailer, into the warehouse took a while, with Anna watching for clearances as he eased it back, inch by inch.

When they cranked the trailer free of the hitch and Luke parked the van outside, he came back in and shook his head. "It's going to be cramped in here for a while."

She said, "You could park the *Enchantress* outside."

"I still have a lot of work installing the redesigned thruster system and it'll be easier to do that indoors."

"How urgent is that? Isn't the plane a higher priority?"

"Yes, but the more people see the thrusters out in the open, the more chance there will be of early discovery. I'm just glad we've got the boat with the 'party lights' back out of sight. Leaving it there in the slips was a risk."

Anna giggled. "Well, we'll always have some eyes on us." She pointed at the open bay door, where two boys and a girl were peering in at the spectacle.

When they realized they were seen, they scattered at a run.

Juan

Dr. Easton sighed. "I've been expecting this."

Luke shrugged. "I intended to stay on the job for another few months, but it turns out that I'll be needing to leave earlier."

"May I ask, is it a tech job?"

Luke shook his head. "I really can't explain too much at this time. There are corporate secrets involved. But as soon as I can, I need to leave for a training school in Las Cruces, and I'll be there full time for nearly a month. I just can't keep this job at the same time. It won't work."

"Well, I appreciate the two-week's notice. Carlos is back on schedule and I suppose the trainees will need any last minute advice you can give them."

"I'll let them know. I just needed to notify you first."

"I appreciate it." Easton frowned. "Is there anyone else involved?"

Luke was puzzled for an instant. Then he smiled. "As far as I'm aware, Anna has no intention of leaving her nursing job, although she will be needing to take her vacation time."

"That's a relief. Staffing is always a nightmare. You assemble the perfect team and then talented people find even better jobs and it's time to start looking for new people all over again."

Luke smiled. "You could always hire an assistant to help with that."

Easton shook his head. "And when I get a much bigger budget, I'll consider that."

...

Anna asked, "How did he take it?"

Luke shrugged. "He was almost relieved. He'd been expecting something. I think he was more worried about losing you."

She smiled. "I'm never leaving nursing. I've spent too much of my life getting here."

"That's basically what I told him."

She nodded thoughtfully. "But you'll be living in Las Cruces for a month?"

He sighed. "I think I have to. Getting a private pilot's license the normal way might take half a year, but going the intensive route, I can get it in a month, maybe. But that's all I'll be doing. What with the pilot training and cramming in as much aeronautical design as I can, I won't have time to do much more than eat and study."

"You're worried about the plane, aren't you?"

"Yes. There's more than just slapping some thrusters onto the back of the plane and crossing my fingers that it'll fly. There was a passage in the design documents that talked about how adding an electric starter and the heavy wiring that took would affect the way the plane flew.

"A plane has to be balanced, and I just know that replacing a two-hundred-plus-pound engine and a prop with a block of lightweight, honeycombed plastic *has* to throw the plane out of balance. I can't even start to make those modifications until I understand how it all works."

She sniffed. "Classes, study time, sleeping and eating. No time for a visit from your friend?"

He smiled. "Not much of one. I figured we'd be texting a lot."

"I have no objection to driving down in the Buick from time to time. Just so you know."

...

"What's your name?" The figure in the warehouse doorway was just a silhouette.

The boy, maybe ten years old, said, "Me llamo ... my name is Juan."

"Good to meet you Juan. You live across the street."

He nodded.

Luke gestured. "Do you want to look at the machines?"

Juan nodded vigorously.

"Go ahead. Just don't do more than touch them."

Juan went straight to the Long-EZ and ran his hand along the smooth white surface.

"¿Qué es?"

Luke came up and tapped the wing. "It's an airplane. It's a special kind, but it's not finished yet. I'll be making changes to it over the next couple of months."

"¿Puedo ayudar?"

Luke pulled out his translation app. "Sorry, my Spanish isn't good."

The app came up with the answer as Juan said, "Can I help?"

Luke considered it. He remembered how he was at that age.

"I could use some help, maybe for an hour or so after you get out of school. I would need to have written permission from your parents. And sometimes I'll be gone for a long time."

Juan nodded and ran out of the building, hurrying across to his house.

Luke sighed. He didn't know whether to hope that the boy's parents would approve or not.

. . .

Luke was connecting the vacuum pump to a tank of water when they arrived.

"Hello, there." Luke got up from his work. "You are Juan's mother?"

The short woman nodded. "Delores Rivera. You want Juan to work here?"

Luke shrugged. "Juan seems interested in the machines and comes by to look. And, as you can see, the place gets pretty dirty. I could use an extra set of hands to sweep the floor and do a few simple tasks.

"I just thought that, after school, he might come by for a little while to help and I could pay a little for that."

Delores looked at the boat, the plane, and all the strange machines. "Is it dangerous here?"

"Some of the machines can be dangerous, but I won't be using them when Juan is here."

The mother was a little suspicious of the anglo, but he was a neighbor and nobody had said anything bad about him since he'd come to live on their street.

"Is the nurse your girlfriend?"

Luke smiled. "You know her?"

"I've seen her at the hospital."

Luke nodded. "I've been working at the hospital as well, but I'm starting a new job soon."

They discussed Juan's working hours and how much he'd be paid. It was understood that Delores could show up at any time to see what was going on, and at least until the weather turned colder, he'd be leaving the big bay doors open while Juan worked.

Soon, she gave her approval and went back home.

Luke looked at Juan. "Let's get started then." He walked over to one of the workbenches and picked up a remote. He handed it to the boy.

"This controls the robot sweeper. Keep steering it over the floor to get the worst of the dust up. In places where the robot can't go, you'll need to use a broom."

The boy had never used a robot sweeper before, but he quickly mastered the remote control and had a blast running the robot all over the place.

Luke went back to his work with the vacuum pump, only glancing at the boy and the robot from time to time.

"What are you doing?" Juan asked, watching the water bubble in the jar.

Luke said, "I'm making cold steam."

The boy looked puzzled.

Luke put his fingers in the output flow from the pump. "Feel it."

Hesitantly, Juan put his fingers in the stream of fog where Luke's had been.

"It's wet."

"Yes, it is."

"Why?"

Luke smiled. "It's a secret project. I can't tell you."

After about an hour, Luke handed Juan his cash and sent him home. Once the door closed, Luke connected a test ion tube to the vacuum output and fed the pure water vapor into the igniter. At first, he didn't think it worked, but it was just because the hydrogen-oxygen flame as it recombined was nearly invisible.

It didn't explode. It didn't crack the tube. It didn't even produce the popping noise they'd heard on the boat in the rain.

He connected a small honeycomb thruster to the water vapor and confirmed that it was indeed producing thrust very much like the normal oxygen/nitrogen mix from the air. The only real difference was the voltage necessary to split the water molecules versus what it took to split oxygen and nitrogen molecules.

Two hours later, he found the right combination to trigger the explosive pops. Rapidly shifting between pure water vapor and the air mixture caused the imbalance necessary to trigger a detonation. Even then, he never duplicated the thruster-cracking explosion they'd seen on the boat.

The dangerous point is when raindrops fell onto the thruster intake holes. That's what I have to avoid.

He started working on designing the boat's new thruster bar, complete with the rain shield.

Smash Them

Anna pulled up into the warehouse parking lot. She frowned at the sight of the boy energetically hammering away.

"What are you doing?"

Juan smiled up at the nurse. "Lo que dijo el jefe."

Luke called out. "Hey, Anna. I didn't know you were coming."

The hammer went down on the white plastic honeycomb block and it shattered into pieces. Juan eagerly turned his attention onto the largest of the fragments and smashed it into even smaller pieces.

Anna hurried inside. "What's he doing?"

Luke nodded, whispering. "I'm having him destroy and trash all the excess and experimental thruster blocks. I'm going to be gone starting next week so I don't need to leave any unsecured evidence lying around while I'm away."

"Don't you need them?"

He shook his head. "All the designs are in my notebooks and computer files. Besides, the next generation thrusters will be a slightly different design anyway."

She wasn't happy. "Those might be valuable someday."

"We have pictures and videos. Keeping all those prototypes around just increases the risk that the secret will get out. Losing our patent rights is too big a risk to worry about the future museum value of the old junk."

Anna looked over at the boy sweeping up the white powder into a trash sack. There was a stack of blocks yet to be destroyed. He'd be at it for a while.

"So when do you leave?"

"Sunday. I've signed up for the accelerated private pilot's training and I've got a cheap motel with a decent weekly rate. I get started in classes Monday morning."

Anna chuckled. "Better you than me. It was quite a celebration when I finally left school."

"Yeah, not looking forward to going back either. But this should be different."

"Are you going back to the hospital?"

"No, I've logged my last hours and filled out the HR paperwork. I no longer work there."

She frowned. "Oh! We should have had a going-away party or something."

"I didn't want that. There would be too many questions."

Anna sighed. "There will still be questions, and everybody will ask me what's the deal."

"Tell them the truth. I went to Las Cruces to get a pilot's license."

"Really? You want that out there?"

"Why not? You're going to have to start building anticipation for the big reveal eventually. A few puzzling hints in advance might not hurt."

"I'll think about it. Do we even have a schedule for the demo?"

He sighed. "I'll know more once I learn a bit more about airplanes. If I have to take apart the Long-EZ and rebuild it, then it will take a lot longer than if I just have to design and install the new thrusters."

"Is that why you're holding off on filing the patent?"

"Yes, once I get the provisional patent, then there's a hard one-year deadline to finish the main utility patent. I've actually gotten the thing written, I just need to know how much time it'll take before I really pull the trigger."

Anna nodded. "Okay, then let's go out to eat this evening. You didn't get a proper going-away party at work, so let me treat you."

Luke smiled. "Sounds good. Let's go let Juan know his work time is over."

Anna introduced herself to the boy and he was happy enough to quit work on the demolition. He complained his arm was getting sore.

. . .

"Juan, baja eso." Luke realized he'd gotten sloppy when he saw the thruster block in the boy's hand the next day.

Juan frowned but set it down like he was told. Luke slipped some gloves on. He typed into his translation app, "Juan, if it's this color, then don't touch it. It's dangerous."

As the app spoke the Spanish, Luke sorted out all the blocks that had the built-in igniters. He carried those over to a plastic washtub and soaked them all in water, then added acid to the mix to dissolve the silver needles. *It was stupid of me to leave those around.*

He still had vivid memories of the block that self-ignited and flew around the warehouse and burned his arm. It was criminal that he'd let the boy collect those. It was just luck that none of them had gone off.

"¿Que?" Juan asked.

"The blocks with that color on one end are like matches. They can catch on fire if you're not careful."

The boy nodded. "Incendio."

Juan worked over three hours before heading home. He was disappointed that the warehouse would be locked up for a month, but Luke promised to have him back when his "escuela de vuelo" was over. Juan was intrigued that there was a special school to learn how to fly an airplane.

Luke spent the whole weekend securing the warehouse for his absence. The leftover thrusters that Juan hadn't managed to destroy were packed in a crate and labeled as plastic building material. His computer records were all backed up and encrypted on the cloud after he changed all his passwords. His logbooks were wrapped in weatherproof plastic and stored in his van. He was taking those with him.

Anna came over several times, when her hospital shifts allowed.

"People miss you already."

He shook his head. "Carlos and the new kids can handle everything."

Anna bumped him. "*Some* people just like having a cute guy around, walking the hallways."

He shrugged. "It was a nice job. I just don't have time for it anymore."

Flight School

Luke: **Hey, Anna. Guess where I am? I'm in an examination room, getting a physical.**

Anna: **If you wanted a physical, I could have done that.** ☺

Luke: **Hey none of that. I don't need an elevated heart rate right now.**

Luke: **It seems the first thing you have to do at flight school is get a physical. They don't want pilots ready to have a heart attack or something.**

Anna: **I can see that.**

As soon as he'd typed it, he wondered if he'd made a mistake reminding Anna about her mother's heart attack.

Anna: **Let me know if you pass the test.**

Luke: **No worries. This is just something I have to take care of. I've already started cracking the books.**

...

Anna: **Hey Luke, it's been a week. I need more updates.**

Luke: **Sorry, it's been pretty intense here. Most of the other students are getting commercial pilot's licenses and they're pretty focused.**

Anna: **How many in your class?**

Luke: **It's not really like that. More like college, with different people studying different things.**

Anna: **Have you flown yet?**

Luke: **Yes, actually. Not ready to handle the takeoffs and landings yet, but I can fly straight and turn. Lots of practice ahead.**

Anna: **Be careful.**

Luke: **The instructors really don't want any crashes on their record. They're taking care.**

· · ·

Luke: **I got your voicemail. Sorry, it's been an intense day and I didn't have time to deal with the phone until now. What do you mean you got in trouble with Juan?**

Anna: **Ah! Finally. You know I do get worried when you go silent on me. I can imagine the worst.**

Luke: **Nothing worse than a long day. Juan?**

Anna: **Oh, I went by the warehouse and tested the doors, just to make sure everything was all locked up tight. It was. But Juan challenged me like I was a burglar.**

Luke: ☺ **Did he call the cops?**

Anna: **No, but he called his mom. We had a nice long chat. She was puzzled about you going off to flight school.**

Luke: **What did you say?**

Anna: **Oh, stuff. I told her about Dad's plane and how you bought it from me.**

Luke: **So you made stuff up.**

Anna: **Well, we DID transfer it to the LLC. That's the same thing.**

Luke: **More or less.**

Anna: **FYI, Mrs. Rivera knew me from the hospital. I had treated her when she had a fall last year. She also basically said that she only let Juan work for you because she knew I was your girlfriend. Did you say that?**

Luke: **No, she said it. I just never denied it. I just changed the subject.**

Anna: **Skirting the terms of our pact** ☺

Anna: **Not that I mind. I know how it can be. Mary at work pesters me constantly.**

Luke: **Either be proactive talking about our work partnership, or change the subject. Protesting too much is a meme.**

Anna: **Harder to talk about our partnership when you no longer work at the hospital. But I understand. "The lady doth protest too much, methinks" — Hamlet.**

Luke: That old. I was never into the classics.

Anna: Hmm. That gives me an idea. I think I'm going to protest too much.

Luke: What do you mean?

Anna: Well, you've got your flight school, but I'm going to head out next week to the Santa Fe Comic Con and do my streaming gig.

Luke: I canceled. I just don't have the time for comic con events right now.

Anna: And I'll mention that in my stream. I'll protest that we're not 'involved' but that I miss your presence.

Luke: And your motive?

Anna: When the demo happens, I'll need the biggest possible viewer number to make it go viral. Why not tease a few romance addicts into watching my streams more closely?

Luke: Okay, that's your area of expertise. Just send me the link.

...

Luke: Anna, what's the make and model of your drone. I never looked that closely.

Anna: Why? You can't take my drone apart! It works too well as it is. I got some great shots flying through the convention room before they made me stop.

Luke: Yes, I saw that. Did you get into trouble?

Anna: Not really. I was so apologetic and nearly made some fake tears when they came to me with their complaints. I looked so pathetic, they just made me promise not to do it again.

Luke: I would have liked to see that. I can't imagine you looking pathetic.

Anna: I can act. But why do you want to know the model of my drone?

Luke: I just talked with some of the other students here. Some are getting helicopter ratings and there was lunchroom talk about VTOLs and such.

Anna: VTOL is...?

Luke: Vertical TakeOff and Landing. Like helicopters and harrier jets.

Anna: **Harrier? Give me a movie reference.**

Luke: **Okay. True Lies with Arnold Schwarzenegger. The harrier was the jet plane that he flew around that skyscraper.**

Anna: **Okay, I remember that one. So… what's your plan?**

Luke: **No plan yet. I was just toying with making my own drone with thrusters instead of propellers.**

Anna: **That's a great way to start a grass fire when it lands.**

Luke: **Well… no idea is perfect.**

...

Anna: **Whatcha doing?**

Luke: **Touch and go's.**

Anna: **What's that?**

Luke: **You fly around in circles and practice landings. Only instead of stopping, you speed back up and take off again for another loop. Over and over again.**

Luke: **The idea is to make takeoffs and landings so automatic that it's smooth and comfortable.**

Anna: **So you're texting and flying? Isn't that dangerous?**

Luke: **At times. I've got my earbuds under my headpiece and most of this is dictation. I have to make corrections because of the noise.**

Anna: **I'll leave you to it then. Don't make a mistake because of me.**

Luke: **Okay, later.**

...

Luke: **Can I track you?**

Anna: **My, how forward of you! But yes. I was tempted to ask the same. What prompted this?**

Luke: **One of the other students. He checks up on his wife and she's always calling him when he's back at the hangar after a flight.**

Anna: **Are they jealous, or lovey-dovey?**

Luke: **Sounds like the latter. Newlyweds.**

Anna: **Okay, how do I do this?**

Luke: **Expect a popup any second now.**

Anna: **I see it. There.**

Luke: **And… you have permission to track me.**

Anna: **I can see your icon. You're at an airport.**

Luke: **Nearly all the time. And you're at the hospital.**

Anna: **Yes, until eight.**

Luke: **I just want you to know that I'm close to getting my certification.**

Anna: **That's good. Is there a graduation ceremony?**

Luke: **Hardly. But if you're willing, there might be a way we could celebrate.**

Anna: **Tell me.**

. . .

Luke: **I've just taken off.**

Anna: **I've been watching your dot on my phone. Are you coming here?**

Luke: **That's the plan. I should be at Hatch airport shortly.**

Anna: **I'll probably beat you there.**

Luke: **Later.**

Luke slipped his phone into the jacket pocket and concentrated on his compass heading. It wasn't far—just fifty miles or so. He kept the river and Highway 185 in sight over to the right.

Soon enough he saw the single runway. There was no tower, and the place was deserted with no other planes in sight. Just one car parked near the 29 marker at the south end.

Luke went into automatic, honed from all those hours of practice, and lined up for the approach, easing down onto the pavement in a smooth landing. He pulled to a stop and killed the engine near where Anna was waiting, standing beside her Buick.

She hurried over.

"Is this the plane you've been flying?" She put her hand up to the Cessna's overhead wing.

"Mostly, although some of the other students get to play with multi-engine planes. I don't need that, so I didn't pay for it. So … get in."

Once she was buckled up and put on the headset, he started the engine and they turned back to go the other way.

"Normally, I'm supposed to take off into the wind if I have a choice, but there's hardly a breeze stirring today so it doesn't matter."

They took off and Anna giggled. "I haven't ever been in a real-life small plane before. I took a commercial flight once."

He nodded. "You can put your hands on the yoke, if you want to."

"I'll pass. I'm just the passenger today."

They circled around and cruised over the low desert mountains south of Hatch. Luke pointed out the road they had traveled in the van the day they had launched and lost the model.

"I suppose we could hunt for it."

"Not today," he said. "We're just doing a little tour."

Anna nodded. "The atmosphere is hazy, isn't it?"

"Yes. It's hazy above us as well, but it's really obvious when looking down at the ground. If I fly too high, it'll be harder to see details."

Anna pointed out some landmarks, especially when they flew over the river.

Luke pointed off to the east. "I can't go there—restricted air space."

"Is there a map?"

"Yes. I have to check it all out before I take off. I really don't want to get in trouble."

He flipped the switch on the radio and got a weather report.

Luke smiled, "That's from Spaceport America's tower."

He sighed. "This is so much easier getting into and out of an uncontrolled field. The hardest part was learning how to talk to air traffic control."

"But you're done? You've got your license?"

"Yes, but of course, it's never done. I've got to log my flight stuff. It's a lot of work for one demo."

"You're not going to keep flying?"

He grinned at her. "Of course I'll keep flying. It's addicting."

He took her back to Hatch field, and after promising to call her once he was back home, he took off for the flight back to Las Cruces.

Y the Drone

Anna walked in. "Ah! That smell. I remember that."

Luke got up from his workbench. "Yes, I've been running the 3D printers pretty heavily since I got back. How was work?"

She shook her head. "We had three separate grandmothers come in with breathing problems. There was a little concern that we might have a new disease, but it's starting to look like food poisoning. They all shopped at the same roadside market."

Luke frowned. "Still, that's concerning."

She nodded. "Dr. Easton called someone at the state level and they're sending investigators."

"Are the ladies okay?"

"Pretty much. Antihistamines and oxygen are keeping them stable. One of them is ready to go home. She's insistent that she has to fix supper."

Luke chuckled. "Sounds like someone's abuela."

Anna looked at the workbench. She pointed, "What's that?"

Luke picked up a foot-long Y-shaped plastic fixture that was laced with wires. "I'm making a drone. It seems there's open source software for controlling drones. I'm hoping I can make a thruster drone."

He snapped some additional pieces in place and plugged in the connectors.

Then he stepped back with a video game remote in his hand.

Anna said, "You're not going to try to fly that in here are you?"

"I think it's okay."

She took a step back. "I've got my first aid kit in the car."

Luke tapped the button and there was a hissing noise. It was a little unsteady, but the triangular craft lifted a foot into the air. He giggled. "It works."

He tried more buttons and managed to steer the skeleton of the drone around the warehouse and back, before he landed it on the concrete.

Anna laughed, a little unsteadily. "So ... why three thrusters instead of four like my drone?"

Luke picked it up off the floor and set it back on the workbench. "Give me a minute and I'll show you."

He walked over to his regular paper printer and pulled off a sheet he'd printed earlier. With scissors, he cut out the template and folded the tips up. With tape he put it over the Y-shaped drone and it was suddenly very clear.

Anna said, "It's a model of the Long-EZ."

"Yes, a crude one, but it helps you visualize the idea."

Anna pulled out her phone and started taking a video. "Explain it to me, Luke."

He cleared his throat, speaking for the camera.

"The idea is to prototype a possible alteration in the plane." He tapped the remote and the drone with its paper cut-out making it look a little like the Long-EZ. As she recorded, it drifted over to where the real plane sat on its landing gear.

Luke continued. "If I can add thrusters at the nose and the wing tips that can support the plane and lift it vertically into the air, then our plane can become a VTOL, a vertical takeoff and landing plane. This would allow me to land and take off from anywhere, including my own parking lot, and avoid the airports altogether.

"Adding this capability to our demo plane would greatly increase our flexibility."

He made the cut gesture with his finger and she stopped recording.

"What do you think?" he said as he steered the cobbled-together drone back to the workbench and turned it off.

She said, "You could still make it a four-spoked drone if you put thrusters on that short front wing."

Luke shook his head. "I really don't want to make much change to the shape of the plane, especially the wing surfaces. When I realized the open source controller software was flexible enough to handle three engines, as well as any number up to eight, I just had to try it out."

He frowned at the controller in his hand. "The only failure is that I can't rotate the drone. The software uses the changing torque of the propellers' motors to cause the rotation. I'll have to come up with an extra side thruster to give me that capability."

Anna nodded. "I think I like it. I can just imagine the shock people will have when the plane takes off straight up, or comes to a hover overhead."

"Not directly overhead. We still have to worry about the heat of the plasma."

She giggled. "Yes, don't start any grass fires when you take off!"

Luke scrubbed at a scorch mark on his workbench. "Or melt the asphalt landing on pavement."

. . .

It was a week later that Juan was sent to warn all the homes on the street that there would be another big truck coming through to pick up more equipment that Luke had managed to sell.

"Tell all the mommas that I've warned the trucker that there are kids playing in the street, but maybe it would be safer if the kids were warned to stay behind their fence."

Juan raced off to handle the job. Luke was grateful to have a helper. Anna really had a full time job of her own and her focus was still putting together a media blitz when the time came, not helping him with the mechanical stuff.

Juan was at a nice age—too young to really understand what Luke was building, but still capable and able to stay on task rather than get too distracted by his friends. Plus the cash money at the end of the day was something he could brag about to anyone who asked. Luke was forced to turn down several other kids who had offered to help as well.

. . .

Based on the original diagrams Mr. Bushnell had used when building his plane, Luke worked out the alterations he needed to make. He had Anna over for a design review. Even though they'd both agreed to turn the ownership of the plane over to their company, Luke really wanted Anna fully on board before he started cutting holes in the plane her father had built.

"Water?" she asked.

Luke nodded. "Yes, to keep the plane balanced, I need the new thrusters to weigh roughly what the original engine and propeller would have. The only way to do that is to build a ballast tank around the thrusters and fill it with water. I'll also be filling the two gas tanks in the wings with water as well.

"The alterations will make a cosmetic change to the plane as well, but it can't be helped. Putting the ballast tank around the thrusters will make a bulb-shape back there, and replacing the nose with the hovering thruster and the pitch-and-yaw steering thrusters in the front will force me to make the nose a little bulb-y.

"Here is what it'll look like." He put the rendering of the plane up onto the big screen.

Anna tried to focus on the design, rather than on the esthetics. "So the wing thrusters won't change the shape?"

"It shouldn't. I'll be piping the air to all the thrusters through an internal channel I'll have to cut. It'll be difficult, but it won't change the external shape much."

Anna pointed to the air scoop on the belly of the plane near the rear. "This is new."

"Right, and it'll make people think this is just a simple jet engine, at least until we reveal the truth during the demo. I've used this scoop design so that it can be unbolted and I can replace the internal filter. I don't need a high volume air scoop, but I do want to keep out dust and rain as much as possible."

Anna nodded. "What will you name her?"

"What?"

She shrugged. "Just like the boat is the *Enchantress*, the plane needs a name."

Luke frowned. "Well, once I get the FAA airworthiness certification, I'll have the tail numbers."

"Yes, but you need a name! I'll need a name when I'm making all that breathless commentary as you fly up into the sky. 'Luke's plane' or 'Number 020' just won't do."

He shook his head. "I just don't know. I've never thought about it."

Anna nodded, "And we'll need an artistic image on the side as well. Have you seen the Virgin Galactic plane with the pin-up girl floating weightlessly on the side of the cabin?"

Luke sighed. "Probably, but it didn't stick. And I'm not the one to design an image like that. I can do technical drawings, but not artwork."

"Well, think about it. I've interviewed a few artists for my stream. Once we settle on a name and a theme, I can find someone who can draw the image for us."

...

"¡Eh, jefe! ¿Qué estás haciendo?"

Luke looked up from under the wing where he was measuring the location where he needed to make a cut.

"Hola, Juan. I need to make many changes to the plane before it can fly."

"Changes?"

"Sí." He gestured. "There is no engine."

Juan's eyes went wide, as if he'd never noticed that before.

"Will you take me on a ride when you're done?"

Luke laughed. "I think tu madre might object."

Juan pouted. Then he asked, "But if she agreed?"

"We'll have to see about that. I have to get the plane fixed before anyone gets to fly."

Luke climbed out from under the plane and showed Juan the new thruster modules he'd been making, sitting under plastic wrap on the shelf.

"You broke up the old ones, but these ones are new and have to be kept very clean. No dust. No fingerprints. Do you understand?"

"Sí, jefe. No touch." He looked puzzled. "What are they?"

Luke grinned and put his finger to his lips. "Shhh. It's a secret. Tell no one. They make the plane fly."

Finishing the Plane

"Are you crazy!" Anna yelled at him. She dug into her first aid kit and produced an antihistamine inhaler.

Luke coughed and tried the inhaler.

"Sorry, I just got caught up in the work."

She pulled out a washrag and began wiping the white dust off his face.

"If you're going to be cutting into plastic and fiberglass then please, please be wearing a face mask and goggles when you're doing it! This can get serious. I mean it. Your lungs aren't designed to handle breathing in all that gunk."

Luke gave another hacking cough. "Believe me, I know."

Anna looked at the door. "And I don't think Juan should be working in here when the air is filled with that stuff either."

Like nodded and got up to reposition the box fans. There was still a bit of dust in the air.

She picked up her bag. "Let's get out of here until the air clears out. We're eating at my place."

He nodded and made sure the windows were open all the way and they locked the place up.

...

It was nearly a week later, well after dark, when Luke slid the first of the vertically oriented wing thrusters into place and made sure that the wiring harness was connected to the igniter. Practically all of the thrusters he'd made for the plane were oddly shaped, no longer simple white bricks. The sides had grooves that allowed the thrusters to interlock with each other for physical support. There was also a long locking pin that held all the thrusters in place, even when the plane was maneuvering in the air.

Luke had designed the system so that everything could be disassembled and pieces replaced if necessary. Thus, no glue to hold everything together.

But for right now, there was only the single thruster in place at the tip of the left wing. A wide yellow towing strap was looped over the top of the wing and held down with a pile of cinder blocks. Luke hoped it would be enough.

He secured the locking pin and then climbed into the cockpit. He picked up the game controller and pressed the start button. On the cockpit dashboard, the little display he'd built lit up and showed zero thrust on all three positions, not that the nose or the right wing even had any thrusters installed yet. This was mainly a test to see if the control system even worked.

With the game controller, Luke raised the thrust level. He could hear the hissing noise start, faintly. With his eyes on the strap, he raised the power. The wide yellow strap showed some tension, but the cinder blocks were weighing the wing down properly.

Luke raised the power, and then played with the controls, experimenting with the thumb-stick and the other ways he could individually control the thrust.

He nodded. Everything was working as predicted.

But he sniffed a little dust in the air. The ion thrust directed downward was kicking up residual dust off the concrete floor.

...

Two days later, the left wing vertical thruster system was installed. By the end of the week, the right wing system was complete and balanced against the left one. The nose system took ten days to complete, considering it had a vertical thrust component and three other smaller thrusters, one to push the nose of the plane to the right, one to push it left, and one to push the nose down. This made up the yaw and pitch thrusters Luke was sure he would need if he ever took the plane up into the very thin regions of the atmosphere where the elevators, rudder and ailerons could no longer do their job.

The final part of the rebuild of the nose was the smoothing and polishing the skin of the plane so that no irregularities would cause trouble during normal flight. He had to look at many examples from other planes to make sure he had it right. He didn't want the plane to constantly require trim adjustment just because of the shape of the nose.

Anna said, "It looks really good."

Luke was collapsed in his chair. "Maybe. But I guess now it's time to shift to work on the main engine."

"Have you tried to lift the plane with the drone controls?"

"It's not balanced yet. Without the weight of the engine and the ballast tanks, the drone software can't be adjusted properly. I don't want to do it twice."

Anna walked closer and put her hands on his shoulders and massaged. He sighed.

She said, "I think you should take a break. Maybe a day or more. Just to relax. The last time I was here, even Juan was worried about you."

Luke grunted.

"Have you eaten?" she asked.

"A little."

She walked over to the plane and looked at the newly polished nose bulb. "We could paint our logo here. Have you decided on a name?"

"Sailor Moon?" he suggested.

She shook her head. "I appreciate the offer, but we'd better steer clear of trademark issues."

"Sailor something else?"

"Most of the planets are taken."

"Sailor Sky? Or maybe Sky Sailor."

She chuckled, thinking about it.

Luke mumbled. "*Celeste.*"

Anna blinked. "I like it. And we could make a logo that is loosely reminiscent of the Sailor Moon style, but something all our own. What do you think?"

There was no response for a moment, and she thought he was deep in thought.

When she turned, she could see he was asleep, stretched out in his chair.

She smiled. Quietly, she went over to his portable space heater and adjusted the temperature a couple of degrees warmer, then turned off most of the lights and locked the door behind her. He needed the sleep.

. . .

Juan looked at the main thruster. "Eso no parece un motor a reacción."

Luke hesitated, translating it in his head. "No, it's not a normal jet engine. It's an ion thruster."

Juan frowned.

Luke said, "It's like no other engine in the world."

Juan nodded, not really satisfied. Luke understood. Only at a distance did it look like the exhaust port of a jet engine. Up close, it was just a dense array of ports too small to really see. There was a large metal hoop circling the exhaust that was supposed to help with the buildup of positive electrical charge as the ions streamed away. The tests seemed encouraging, but he wouldn't really know for sure until he tested it at full power.

That was approaching sooner than he was ready for it.

He shook that worry away and went back to work testing the water flow.

It had occurred to him, late in the design phase, that with the fuel tanks in the wings and the ballast tank at the thruster, he could dynamically balance the weight of the plane by pumping water forward or backward. That meant a little electrical pump at the very rear of the cockpit that could work in forward or reverse.

"Juan, bring me more water bottles."

His assistant ran over to the van and loaded the cart with four more gallon jugs of distilled water that Luke had purchased at the market. Probably tap water would have worked just fine, but he really wanted everything to work perfectly and he didn't want to have to worry about what kind of minerals were in the pipes, possibly clogging up the tubes. He was just glad he could afford to purchase what he needed.

. . .

Anna sat at the table and read. She sighed. "It doesn't sound like much."

Luke brought some sliced fruit to the table. "That's the point. I don't want the preliminary patent to set off a bunch of red flags. I had a dream a few nights ago that I filed the patent and then a bunch of federal agents showed up and claimed the thruster technology for the military and that I was barred from selling it or using it commercially."

Anna frowned. "Can that happen?"

"Yes, it can. I'm sure the feds have people who look over the new patents, checking for dangerous new tech. It just makes the idea of having a big viral demo all that much more important. If a huge number of people are aware of the zero-point energy thruster, then it makes it less likely the military would try to keep it a secret."

Anna nodded. "We have to go big right from the start."

"That's what I think. And now that the plane is 99% complete, then I think it's time to file for the preliminary patent."

"What's left to be done?"

Luke shrugged. "Installing the last of the radios, the navigation instruments, and getting the oxygen mask."

She nodded. "You want to go for an altitude record, right?"

"I hope. Once I get the plane certified to fly, I'll try to see what kind of envelope the *Celeste* can handle. The standard Long-EZ was rated to 27,000 feet altitude, but ours has had so many modifications, I don't really know."

"And you'll need oxygen for that?"

"Oh, yes! The regulations say I'll need it if I get to 10,000 feet."

Anna thought. "Don't people get to Mt. Everest without oxygen? That's what? 25,000 feet high."

"Something like that, but only trained climbers. Many people faint at Pikes Peak, which is like 14,000 feet. You don't want a pilot to faint."

"And if the *Celeste* isn't really a high altitude plane? What'll we do then?"

Luke shrugged. "A long-distance flight? Someone flew over 4,000 miles in a Long-EZ with an extra gas tank in the back seat. Since I don't need fuel, I'm sure I could fly all the way around the world. I'd have to pack a picnic basket to take along."

She giggled. "I'd need a bathroom break."

He tilted his head. "Um. There's a tube for ... liquid waste, but I expect it'd be ... complex ... in any case."

She giggled again. "I'm glad you're the one doing the flying."

To the Airport

Luke was reminded of those puzzle squares, where you slide the fifteen tiles around in the sixteen spots to make a picture. His first step was to ease the *Enchantress* on her trailer out of the warehouse and position her at the northwest corner of his property next to the fence.

After he cranked the nose gear into place, the plane wasn't all that hard to pull by hand, but it's 26-foot wingspan couldn't fit through the big doors. He had to pull the nose through the gap and then, once the forward canard wing was outside, he began moving the plane back and forth, edging the fuselage closer to the door frame.

"¡Hola! ¡Espera un minuto! Puedo ayudar." The man's voice called out.

Luke looked across the street and Juan and a man who looked like a much older version of him came running.

Juan said, "Este es mi padre."

Luke held out his hand. "Hola. Sr. Rivera. Gracias."

Hernando introduced himself.

He pointed. "I need to get the left wing out first."

The man nodded.

With the two of them, and Juan helping, they could lift the wing and soon it was clear. Then after more juggling back and forth, they had the entire plane clear.

Rivera asked, "How will you get it to the airport?"

Luke waved his hand. "Not a problem. I'll deal with it when the day comes. The wings can be removed for trailering."

Which was true, but it wasn't something he really wanted to do. Now that he had his wiring harnesses and air channels in place inside the wings, removing the wings and replacing them would be a much more difficult task than in the original design.

The three of them pulled the plane around behind the warehouse. Luke cranked the nose gear back into the fuselage, leaving the nose resting on its rubber bumper. After that, he covered the plane with a couple of tarps and staked them to the ground.

Luke invited father and son inside for drinks and chips. Juan tugged his father around the place, showing off the 3D printers and the kinds of toys that Luke had made with them.

Hernando fingered the fidget spinner from the bin. "You made the plane with this?"

Luke shook his head. "Only pieces of it. Nurse Anna Bushnell's father built most of it. I finished it." He nodded toward the boy. "Juan helped."

He explained the next step. "The government has to inspect the plane and I have to prove it works. That happens in a few days."

Hernando frowned, "They come here?"

"No, at the airport. I'll move it shortly."

It was plain Rivera was glad the inspection would be elsewhere. Even hispanics who could prove their ancestors had been citizens for generations had reason to be cautious of government agents.

...

It was two in the morning, with the quarter moon providing the only light. Luke removed the tarps from the plane and cranked the nose gear into place. He climbed into the cockpit and listened closely for any sound. Off to the north, across the valley, he could hear a heavy truck on the interstate, but that was nearly a mile away.

He strapped himself in, and then flipped a switch on the instrument panel.

Lights came on, but he resisted the impulse to turn on the plane's navigation lights. He definitely didn't want to be seen.

The GPS map display quickly showed his position and he tapped in his target destination—the tie-down area at Hatch Municipal Airport. It wasn't far.

He pulled out the game controller and turned on the vertical thrusters. Eyes locked to the little three inch display that was connected to the drone software, he slowly increased the thrust. The canopy was still open and he could hear the hissing noise climb. His inner ears told him when the plane lifted off the ground.

He'd flown the little Y-shaped drone for hours, to get familiar with the software, but riding the plane was a different experience altogether. He quickly increased his altitude to ten feet above the ground. The software was doing its job, holding the plane level and steady. With the thumb control, he eased the plane over the back fence and out into the undeveloped land behind his property.

I can't delay now. Maybe I haven't woken anyone up, but there's no guarantee.

He increased his altitude to twenty-five feet and with a tap on the yaw thruster pointed the nose around away from the warehouse.

He flew at that altitude for a few hundred yards before circling the housing development and aiming the plane toward the airport.

Luke wasn't even tempted to throttle up the main thrusters. He was content to fly quad-copter style all the way there.

He kept his eyes on the land ahead of him. Moonlight was bright enough to show him any hills or trees, but he didn't want to get much higher than this. Likely the vertical thrusters were visible to the frightened rabbits below, but he didn't want to make a spectacle of himself to anyone awake in the small hours.

The GPS told him he was traveling eight miles per hour, certainly not enough that he needed to close the canopy, so he just enjoyed the morning air in his hair. It was like taxiing a plane on the runway, although this runway was a couple of dozen feet high in the air.

When he saw the railroad tracks and then the arroyo, he knew he was getting close. He slowed down a little, and quickly passed over the corner of the cemetery.

Highway 26 was next and he should be over the airport land. He was grateful for the GPS, because without a tower and landing lights, it just looked like any other flat land.

He was nearly over the airstrip itself before he saw a flash of light—moonlight reflecting from the retroreflective markers. Any proper airplane with landing lights on could have seen it plainly, but he was being stealthy.

Lowering down to less than ten feet above ground level, he steered around the deserted airfield until he settled down at the tie-down area.

When he killed the thrusters, he realized his heart was pounding. There had been no danger, not really, but it was new, and untested.

It worked!

Headlights came on, and a car's engine. He tensed against the straps holding him in his seat.

That had better be Anna!

He saw the shape of the Buick and began unfastening himself. He powered everything down and climbed out. Reaching down to the crank, he retracted the nose gear and pulled out the tie-down straps.

Anna came up. "I saw you come in! It looked so spooky! The three lights made you look like a UFO."

He shook his head. "I never even saw the Buick. You were here early."

"I couldn't wait. It really flies, doesn't it."

He had a big grin. "Yes it does! At least in hover mode. Tomorrow, I mean in the morning, that'll be the real test."

"I know you'll do fine. I wish I could be here to watch."

"Oh, it'll be hours and hours of boring stuff. I'll be doing test flights for days."

"I guess I'd better get you back home then. You'll need your beauty sleep."

"Just a minute." He reached down beside the seat and unplugged a USB memory card. Without the software on that card, the thruster control circuitry would never start up. It was his key. He fastened the canopy down and secured the tie-down straps. Short of a severe storm, the *Celeste* should be secure.

. . .

When Luke got the phone call from Peter Kushner, the Designated Airworthiness Representative, he said he'd meet him at the airport's gate. The DAR was just a few minutes late, but Luke had the jitters. Today could make or break the whole project.

Kushner drove up in a Suburban and got out to shake hands.

He nodded. "I can see your Long-EZ from here. The place looks nice and deserted."

Luke chuckled. "Yes, when I called the Village Trustee to get permission to use the field, he was happy to have another plane to use it."

Kushner asked, "I've read over your documentation thus far. You purchased the plane from a homebuilder?"

"From his daughter. Mr. Bushnell has passed on. He was never able to finish the construction."

"But you've taken over the job. I'd like to look over your logs in a bit, but I'd like to get a closer look at the plane first. This is the third Long-EZ I've inspected."

Luke nodded. "Do you want to take my van?"

"Oh, I'll just follow you. It looks like we don't have a crowding problem."

Luke led the way.

Peter Kushner's face was entirely different when he stepped out of his vehicle.

"Where's the engine? I don't see an engine. Have you finished construction?"

And there it was. Luke forced a smile.

Certifying Celeste

Luke said, "Oh, it certainly has an engine. I've been taxiing up and down the airstrip since dawn, getting the feel for it.

"But I admit it doesn't look like what you were expecting. This is an experimental engine. I'm hoping to get a 21.191(a) experimental research and development certification."

The DAR walked over to the rear of the plane and stared at the white plastic surrounded by the metal ring. "Is this a jet engine? Or a rocket?"

Luke sighed, "It can't be classified as a turbine jet, since there's no turbine. In fact, there are no moving parts. It's a totally new kind of thruster, it's an air-breather, kinda-sorta jet engine, but really, nothing but 21.191(a) applies here. I've got a preliminary patent on it already, but I need to do a lot more research flying this plane before I can finish filing for the utility patent."

Kushner ran his fingers through his hair. "This is the first time I've had to deal with something like this. The airframe—the Long-EZ—is type certified, but not the engine."

Luke nodded. "I've read that this plane was a testbed for several types of experiments—NASA and everyone else trying out new engines."

The inspector nodded. "I'm familiar." He sighed. "Can you explain how it works?"

Luke hesitated. "I can describe it loosely, but anything more than that risks hurting my intellectual property rights to the invention. I have a non-disclosure document written up if you want to go that way."

The man nodded. "I understand. Let's hold off on that for now. I guess what I need first is to see it in action. Can you taxi to the end of the runway and back for me?"

"Certainly. Be advised that the exhaust is very hot, so keep to the side."

When the hissing started and the plane accelerated rapidly down the runway, Kushner made some notes on his clipboard. Then Luke returned, killed the thrust and coasted to a stop.

They discussed how much power the engine had and the inspector asked Luke to estimate how much horsepower it had, but Luke had to shrug. That was one of the things he'd need to discover, after he was able to get the certification and fly some more.

They talked about how Luke had no intention of taking the plane into controlled airspace, other than into class A if he exceeded 18,000 feet. He wanted to stay strictly in class E airspace if at all possible.

"I see that you're instrumented for IFR, and you have your license. Relatively recently, too."

Luke nodded. "I became a pilot to fly this plane."

"I see."

They spent some time, going over the modifications Luke had made to the original plane.

"What kind of fuel do you have in those tanks?"

"That's not fuel. It's just water I've added for weight trim."

"But... what do you use?"

Luke timidly mentioned the non-disclosure option.

Kushner winced. "I get the feeling I might not want to know. Have you contacted the military about this engine?"

"Not yet. I really need to understand it better before I touch that."

The inspector had a similar reaction when Luke got into the pitch and yaw thrusters on the nose. "Just how high are you going to take this?"

Luke gave a big sigh. "I really don't know yet. I haven't taken off from this runway. Not without your blessing."

He wanted to avoid discussing the hover mode as long as he could. He wanted the *Celeste* certified as an airworthy nearly-normal airplane, not as some totally new class of airship.

Late in the day, before the light faded, Luke was given the okay to take off, fly a pattern loop and come back in for a landing.

When he looked over the airstrip on the return leg, he saw Anna's Buick parked nearby.

After the DAR made his checkmarks and had scheduled the appointment to meet again the next day, he left, commuting from his home in Las Cruces.

Anna drove up. He tied the plane down and they went into town to celebrate.

"Have you told him about the thrusters?"

"He doesn't want to know. I really think he's afraid the military will walk in and take it over. He doesn't want to be caught up in the process."

"We don't want that to happen, or do we?"

Luke shook his head. "I'm sure the military would pay for the thruster, but if it went majorly public, then who knows what the limits of the zero-point energy technology might be. I still think we need to make a big splash—something everyone will talk about. Something that can't be put back into the box.

"I mean I got into ion tubes in the first place to try make a dent in climate change, tapping into zero-point energy on a large scale—using that instead of fossil fuels—that could change everything."

She nodded. "You're right. But I'd better double-down on making a great viral video."

...

The DAR was willing to bend on the experimental R&D classification and to keep his nose out of the details of how the thruster worked, but he was a stickler for the rest of the paperwork. It took a full forty hours of flight testing before he signed off on the airworthiness certificate.

Anna took video of his maneuvers. She even attempted to interview Kushner, but he shook his head. He did not give permission to be included in the videos. She smiled, didn't take it personally, and even showed up with burritos when they worked late getting the test flights done.

But then, Peter Kushner signed off on everything and headed back to Las Cruces.

Anna asked, "So, we're done?"

"Everything but the N-numbers. I've even got a little metal plate I have to install that identifies the plane if I end up a crumpled pile on the rocks."

"Don't say that!"

He chuckled. "But yes, it's all done and we can start doing real flights to test out the real capabilities of the *Celeste*."

She smiled. "I've got something for you."

"What?"

She pulled out a mailing tube and extracted the nose art decal.

He looked over the line-art drawing of a Sailor Moon style head and shoulders image. The girl was decorated with stars, rather than the crescent moon. *Celeste* was written below.

Luke said, "Were you the model for this? It looks like you."

Anna giggled. "Not officially, but Victoria, the artist knows me. Maybe she had me in mind."

Luke fingered the decal plastic. "This should lay down smooth if I heat treat it."

She gave him a swat on the shoulder. "You should be admiring the artistic elegance of the image, not worrying about construction details!"

He shrugged. "It is nice."

She sighed.

...

Anna: **You moved the Celeste back to the warehouse last night?**

Luke: **Yes, about 3am.**

Anna: **You were seen. I've heard tales of a UFO three times today at the hospital.**

Luke: **Well, as long as they don't point to me.**

Anna: **Don't count on it. Lots of people saw you on your test flights last week. It's common knowledge that Luke Moore has a fancy white airplane that looks like a spaceship.**

Luke: **We need our demo pretty soon. Certainly before guys in uniform come knocking at my door.**

Anna: **Dinner at my house tonight. You need to review all the videos I've prepared. Maybe record a couple of voiceovers.**

...

Anna looked over his shoulder. "If those are maps, I can't make sense of them."

Luke slid one sheet out from under the others. "Look at this one. It's the VFR chart—visual flight rules. It's the way most private planes fly in daytime and clear weather. It's got the most detail. Roads, lakes, mountains and such."

She nodded. "And those others?"

"IFR maps—instrument flight rules. If you can't see out the window, because it's night or bad weather, then you can still fly with these routes. It gives you all the compass bearings and the radio frequencies you need. The ATC, the air traffic controllers, will see you on their radar and give you the instructions you need to avoid other airplanes."

She frowned. "Do you need all that?"

"As long as I stay in this area, clear of the restricted areas and heavy traffic, and maintain my altitude under 18,000 feet, I'm pretty free to guide myself."

Anna nodded. "But above that—"

"Above that, I have to use these IFR maps to maintain contact with the ATC and make sure I dodge all the jet traffic."

"So we can't do this high altitude stuff in secret."

"Not really. Not as long as I want to keep my pilot's license."

She looked frustrated. "It's harder to spring a big surprise if you've got to ask permission each step."

He nodded. "Yeah. But if I advertise my new invention by committing a crime, it wouldn't go well trying to commercialize it afterward."

"Could they deny you the access to high altitude?"

Luke remembered the stories he was told at flight school. "I think the ATC are mostly concerned about keeping everyone safe. I doubt they'd turn me away just on a whim. But if they thought there was a danger, they might suggest an alternate course."

He shrugged. "The *Celeste* is already in the system as a research plane. ATC in this neighborhood is already familiar with Spaceport America's flights and the military restricted areas. I guess we just cross our fingers and go for it."

FL300

Luke glanced at the VFR map displayed on his iPad. He'd overlaid it with the major jet flyways from the high altitude IFR maps. In spite of the wide open skies that looked empty of any other planes, it had taken him a some juggling to identify a location that rarely saw other traffic.

He adjusted his radio and keyed the mike. "Experimental aircraft 8892 at flight level 130 flying a pattern above Lake Valley. Request clearance to flight level 300 for performance testing." Speaking into the microphones built into the oxygen mask made everything sound different, but the air was thin, and it would soon get even thinner.

"Albuquerque control, 8892, squawk 4000. Flight level 300." The voice was even clearer in his earphones than when he'd flown the Cessna. His thrusters were much quieter than the prop engine.

"Squawk 4000, climbing to 300, experimental 8892," he replied.

Luke changed the code on his transponder to 4000, confident that ATC had him on their radar. They hadn't warned him of any other traffic, so he could start now.

He increased the thrust and pulled back on the stick, climbing at an increasing angle until he was pretty close to standing the plane on its tail. There was nothing to see out the window except the sky above. He concentrated on the instruments, flicking his gaze between the original air-pressure airspeed and elevation gauges originally installed by Jase Bushnell decades ago and the digital GPS panel. They were roughly in agreement.

There as a deep satisfaction that the thruster was pushing him hard enough that his airspeed was increasing even at this attitude. He adjusted the thrust to keep the plane near 200 miles per hour. Even if he could theoretically crack the sound barrier, the plane was never designed for that. He didn't want the plane to fall apart around him.

The altitude crept ever higher and he eased the plane down to fly level, holding at 30,000 feet. With the ailerons, he flew a circular path in the sky to keep him at the same location.

A propeller-driven Long-EZ had gotten to 27,000 feet according to the operator's manual. Considering the plane had been built with so many other types of engines in its long history, Luke was sure that others had achieved flight level 300 before, but it was a personal triumph that his plane had come this far.

He was seeing no evident loss of thruster power either. The plane could certainly climb higher, and he was tempted to call ATC for permission to try, but that wasn't what he'd discussed with Anna.

The cabin wasn't pressurized and the air was just as thin inside as it was outside.

This caused two problems. One was that it was getting very cold. He'd worn his winter jacket and his gloves for this very reason. It would certainly get colder the higher he climbed.

The other issue was that an oxygen mask only helped protect him from hypoxia. Not too much higher was the Armstrong limit at about 63,000 feet. Even breathing pure oxygen wouldn't protect him then. The air pressure was so low that the water in his blood and tissues would boil, leading to quick death.

No, flight level 300 was his target for this flight. He'd need a pressure suit of some kind if he wanted to go higher, and that was more expense than he really wanted to deal with.

He called ATC again and let them know that he was descending back below 18,000 feet, back where he'd be under VFR conditions again and no longer of concern to the controllers.

When he got the go-ahead, Luke cut the throttle to next to nothing and began a slow glide in his circle, dropping in altitude. He wondered if he could glide all the way back to Hatch.

He glanced at the camera mounted on the instrument panel and gave it a thumbs-up for Anna's video. He just hoped the camera didn't show his frowns.

He had so much to worry about.

...

Anna met him at the airport.

He handed her the memory card from the camera. "I hope you can use this."

"You reached 30,000?"

"Yes. It was easy. I could have gone higher."

She nodded. "Why did you land here? I thought you didn't want to use the airport anymore."

He tied down the plane. "Well, there's a problem."

"Uh, oh. What happened?"

"I lifted off well before dawn, like I planned, but no sooner had I climbed to about twenty feet than someone aimed a flashlight at me."

"Oh, no! Who was it?"

"I couldn't tell. All I could see was the glare of the light. I pulled away and went on the flight as planned, but it's either one of my neighbors or maybe a policeman." He sighed. "It could be anyone. But the result is that I'd better not land the *Celeste* in my back yard anymore."

Anna frowned. "If it's someone looking for the plane, then they know it's a VTOL and they'd certainly come look at the airport again if you don't take it home."

"Have you heard any more UFO reports?"

"Not this morning."

"Sorry for calling you to pick me up. Do you need to get back to the hospital?"

"In a few hours. I'll be doing a late shift. I guess I'd better get you home."

He nodded.

She said, "You look glum."

"Well, the flight was great. The plane is great. But it feels like it's homeless. *Celeste* is stuck out on the tie-downs. I'm wondering if I should count my nickels and purchase a shack somewhere away from town to use as a hangar."

She shook her head. "I don't know." She chuckled. "I don't even have enough space in my back yard to park the plane."

They went to the warehouse and Luke invited her in so they could review the video card.

Anna frowned. "You're not very photogenic in that oxygen mask. Plus you don't talk much. I'll probably not be able to use more than a minute or so of this."

He smiled. "We should get you an oxygen mask so you could come along and do all the talking."

"Maybe. It looks like it would mess up my hair."

There was a knock on the door.

Mr. and Mrs. Rivera were there.

Luke invited them in.

Hernando looked very uncomfortable. "Your plane is gone?"

Luke nodded. "Did you see me leave this morning?"

"You went straight up."

Anna said, "It's a VTOL plane. Like a Harrier."

Hernando nodded. "My brother is a marine."

Luke sighed. "I apologize for hiding it that way. I really don't want people to know all about the plane until I'm ready to reveal it."

Delores said, "We understand, but is it safe, this close to the house?"

Luke said, "The plane is pretty safe. No more dangerous than a car on the road, really. But for me, the danger is having too many people know about it.

"Still, it is my fault for operating a new kind of airplane this close to a residential neighborhood. I think I realized that the moment you aimed your flashlight at me this morning. I've parked the plane at the airport for now and I won't be bringing it back here to the warehouse without letting everyone know about it in advance. Either that, or bring it back on a trailer."

Delores said, "It can't explode, can it?"

Luke smiled. "No. No gasoline. It can't explode like that. Still, it's not something I should have landed this close to your house."

Hernando said, "Juan has asked, many times, if he could fly in your plane. Did you invite him?"

Luke smiled. "Juan asked me, and I said his mother would probably object. I haven't invited him, and now that the plane is officially certified for research, I don't think I should carry passengers. It might violate the terms of the license."

Hernando nodded. "Probably a good idea, although Juan will be disappointed."

The Riveras went home and promised to tell Juan the bad news.

Anna said, once they were out of sight. "Does that mean I can't ride as a passenger either?"

Luke chuckled. "Oh, no. You'd be documenting the flights. That's a perfectly defensible reason for carrying you along."

...

Once he was alone with his thoughts, Luke updated his records and then got on the internet, looking for ideas on where to hide the plane.

Local news led him to a recent story he hadn't seen before. Starshine Space, one of the companies based at Spaceport America, was having financial difficulties. According to the article, the billionaire owner, Roger Wilson, was not denying that the space tourism business that Starshine hoped to ride had turned out less than profitable. There was some worry that bankruptcy was on the horizon.

Luke was intrigued. It was the same sort of story that had led him to purchase all the equipment that stocked his warehouse.

His fingers starting typing searches and clicking links. Three hours later, he was digging quite deeply into all the public info on Starshine Space and Roger Wilson.

Borrow a Spacesuit?

Luke was embarrassed to be stalking Wilson. He parked across the hot springs resort right next to the Rio Grande. One of the reporters that was trying to cover the Starshine launches several months ago mentioned that Wilson liked to stay at this resort. A more recent report mentioned that Wilson was staying in Truth or Consequences while the final decisions about the company were being made.

Anna told him to try to contact the man. "All they can do is slam the door in your face. Trying to talk isn't a crime."

Luke was less convinced. A billionaire obviously had lots of security.

It was 10 AM when he blinked as the man walked up to a silver SUV with another man and got in. The other man was driving—probably an assistant of some kind. When they pulled away, Luke followed, keeping his distance. It wasn't like the local traffic was packing the roads.

Luke had already decided that if Wilson drove off toward Spaceport America, then he'd give up on trying to make contact. He already knew that the place had security gates to keep casual tourists out. And, of course, trying to make contact with the SUV while driving would raise all kinds of alarms and likely get him arrested.

His only hope was that Wilson was going to an office here in the city. His spirits spiked when the car made no effort to head toward Highway 91 but instead went to an office building on Broadway in the middle of town.

Luke found a parking space for his van and walked up to the office building.

The same man who drove the SUV was sitting at the reception desk. "Hello, can I help you?"

Luke tried to slow his heart rate. He smiled. "My name is Luke Moore and I was hoping for a few minutes to talk with Mr. Wilson."

"Do you have an appointment?"

Luke shook his head. "No. To be honest, I don't know how to go about setting up an appointment with him in the first place."

"Well…" It was plain he was going to be brushed off.

From the other side of the door, a voice said, "Oh, Kurt, let him in for a minute."

Kurt got up and opened the door to the nicely appointed office. The walls were covered with images of the Starshine spaceplane and its booster, often with celebrities and politicians posing in the foreground.

"Have a seat Mr. Moore. That is unless you're a reporter. I doubt I have any more to say that hasn't been rehashed endlessly over the past couple of weeks."

Luke shook his head. "I'm not a reporter. I wish to discuss a business offer."

Luke could almost read the billionaire's mind as those tired eyes scanned his work clothes. He knew he didn't look like any kind of businessman.

Wilson said, "Okay, make your pitch."

Luke knew he only had a minute. "My company has developed a new technology thruster that will make a world-wide impact when we demonstrate it in a month or so."

"A 'thruster'?"

"An air-breathing ion engine with unprecedented fuel economy. I've already flown it to 30,000 feet with no noticeable fuel consumption. The weak link in my system is the pilot, and my oxygen mask. I could have easily gone a lot higher, past the Armstrong limit, past the Kármán line perhaps, but I don't have a space suit."

Wilson reacted. The Kármán line was the holy grail for space tourism. Above 100 km, their customers could claim astronaut status.

But he frowned. "That high, with an air-breathing engine? I don't think so."

Luke was ready. "My ground-based tests show the thruster works well with water vapor as well, and there's no difficulty getting vacuum-distilled water vapor at that altitude.

"I know it can work, if I had a spacesuit. And according to what I've read, you currently have six suits that you aren't planning to use. If one of them could fit me, I'd like to borrow it for a bit."

Wilson gave a short laugh. "What are you going to demonstrate?"

Luke tried to look confident. "A number of things. I'll break a few world records, all on live streaming video. And I'm sure that, without saying a word, people will instantly recognize that starburst-decorated spacesuit of yours."

Wilson frowned. "So I get advertising in exchange for a spacesuit rental? Is that it?"

Luke tilted his head. "There's a little more than that. My two person company has no capability to commercialize this thruster. We'll definitely need an experienced partner for that. If we can pull this off, Starshine will get first crack at it."

Wilson snorted. "So I get nothing but advertising up front, with nothing but promises if it works. What if you fail?"

Luke shrugged. "It's a risk. I can't offer more. I have no money that you'd even notice. But if I succeed and you're on board, the demand for this technology could make a big difference for any space tech company."

He reached across Wilson's desk and left his recently printed business card.

"Forty miles down south at Hatch Municipal Airport, my plane is sitting beside the landing strip, waiting to give you a private demonstration. If you are interested, give me a call."

Wilson nodded. "I'll have to think about it."

. . .

Luke purchased a couple of 30-inch monitors so that Anna could have a good video editing setup at the warehouse. Most hours that she wasn't at the hospital and not home sleeping, she was there tweaking her *Anna and the Fantastic* sequences. She'd already released two videos focused on 3D printing and all the things it was capable of doing. One didn't even mention Luke, but was more a general background of the technology from a variety of sources.

In each show, she hinted heavily that something really fantastic was coming and that everyone should subscribe and get all their friends to subscribe so that they wouldn't miss it.

Luke watched as she reworked the Elephant Butte Lake episode. He waited until she finished her drone video edits.

"Anna?"

"Yes, what's up?"

"I've got an idea for changes to the *Enchantress*."

"What kind of changes?"

Just then, Luke's phone rang. "Wait a sec."

He pulled out his phone and when he saw the caller ID, he gestured to her to pause her video.

He put it on speakerphone.

"Hello, Mr. Wilson. Nice to hear from you."

Anna leaned closer to hear every word.

"Mr. Moore, I was wondering if your plane was still there at Hatch."

"Yes, it is. Would you care for a look?"

"I probably have some time this afternoon. In an hour?"

Luke said, "That will work fine for me. I'll be there."

Anna was gesturing. Luke nodded and told Wilson the gate code necessary to enter.

When he tapped the phone off, Anna asked. "I need to be there, to take video."

"Make sure he gives you permission. Let's pack up and get there early."

...

Wilson frowned, "That looks like a Long-EZ."

Luke nodded. "Yes, we used a nearly-completed homebuilt plane built by Anna Bushnell's father. I've added several alterations to take advantage of the new thrusters instead of a traditional engine."

Anna introduced herself. "Luke is the inventor. I'm the PR department."

Luke showed off the plane, allowing Wilson to peer into the cockpit and puzzle over the very non-standard engine. "It doesn't make sense to me."

"Would you like to see it in action?"

Anna escorted Wilson back to the car as Luke climbed in and folded the canopy into place.

She held up her phone and started recording. "Watch closely. He's not going to taxi out onto the runway."

"What?"

Just then, the hissing noise began and the *Celeste* lifted straight up.

Anna said, "Since the ion thrusters are modular and can be built in a variety of sizes, Luke took open source drone software and used it to give the *Celeste* VTOL capabilities. The plane really has multiple sets of thrusters."

Just then the rear thrusters lit up and the plane accelerated down the runway, only a dozen feet above the pavement. The plane tilted up and gained altitude rapidly.

Anna said, "The main thrusters are more than capable of pushing the plane straight up in a tail-standing configuration. Luke took it up to flight level 300 a few days ago that way, and he still had to limit the throttle so that he didn't go too fast. The plane was never meant to go supersonic."

She had practiced a lot of her narration while making her videos. It was great to see the billionaire watching the climbing dot in the sky with his mouth open.

"Um. How high is he going this time?"

"Just a few thousand feet. He wanted to demonstrate the power of the main thruster. You can see that he's already on his way back."

The *Celeste* circled down, taking much longer to get down than it had in going up. Luke made one pass over the field and then settled down as a VTOL back at the tie-downs.

Anna and Wilson approached the plane once the hissing stopped.

The man circled the plane, peering closer at the thruster array.

Luke watched, with the canopy opened up. "Do you have any questions?"

"Many. What's it use for fuel?"

Luke scratched his chin. "No fuel."

"Batteries?"

"The only battery is a large lithium unit designed to keep the instruments and radios running for a day. I'm thinking of adding a hand-crank generator for emergencies."

"But...."

Anna said, "My job is to make a spectacular viral video when we first demonstrate the plane for the public. It has to be that way because no one will believe us without proof that the thrusters work as claimed."

Luke said, "Most people won't believe a video even then. We'll have to get independent confirmation as well."

Wilson shook his head. "A homebuilt plane that can climb all the way to space without fuel? You'll put me, Virgin Galactic, and Blue Origin out of business."

"Not if you're part of this."

"Is this patented?"

"I've got the preliminary patent in hand. We file the utility patent right before the demo."

"I could purchase the patent now."

Luke smiled. "I might ask for a very large sum. Why don't you wait until after the demo? I might just crash and burn."

Anna said, "Luke! I told you not to say that."

Wilson said, "It's a two-seater. Take me for a ride."

Luke nodded. "I could do that."

Breaking Ties

Anna cried and he couldn't do much more than hold her and pat her back.

"I didn't think it would be that hard."

Luke said, "Did Dr. Easton say anything?"

She took a deep breath. "He was sad, but not surprised. He said that he would be happy to have me back, but if I were going to take an indefinite time off, he really had to hire a full time replacement nurse."

"I'm sorry."

She shook her head. "I knew this was coming. From the first time we discussed taking the *Enchantress* to Hawaii, I realized that I'd have to walk away from the hospital, at least for a while. This isn't something we can do over the weekend."

He didn't know quite what to say. She had to work it out in her own mind.

Still, he asked, "So, what is your schedule?"

"Half days for the next two weeks. Dr. Easton would have liked full time, but I convinced him that it just wouldn't work for me."

She looked at Luke. "I've got a full time job here, getting ready for the demo. I just can't do it while putting in long hours at the hospital."

She took a deep breath. "And that's what I should be doing right now. I need to take some glamour shots of you in your spacesuit."

He chuckled. "That's not something I ever expected to hear."

She pushed his arm. "I want shots here with lights, but I really need some sunlit shots with you standing next to the *Celeste*. It's a good day for it."

She reached for his shirt button. "So ... let's get you ready."

"Hey! Remember the pact. I can get myself dressed."

"Oh, I don't know," she said in a coy voice. "I've seen those pictures of astronauts needing help getting into their suits."

"This is a modern LEA suit, not one of those bulky moon suits."

"I am a nurse. I've helped lots of people change clothes."

Luke nodded patiently. "Just let me change into the underalls in peace."

She sniffed. "Okay, but what's an LEA suit?"

"Landing, Entry, and Abort. It's the lightweight suit they use during takeoff and landing. There's an entirely different suit they use for bouncing around on the moon or doing spacewalks."

He opened the crate that had arrived from Starshine Space and pulled out the neck-to-toe undersuit. He retired to the bathroom.

Anna took hundreds of pictures, including the times he got into and out of the colorful outersuit with its built-in hood and transparent mask. They even connected the air hose and inflated the suit to test how flexible it was under pressure.

Then he stripped off the outersuit, packed it back up and loaded everything into the van.

As usual, the airstrip was deserted—mostly. There was a Cessna Skyhawk parked at the other corner of the tie-down area. He wasn't the only person who used the airstrip, but since it didn't even have a fuel pump, hardly any planes visited the place except during special events, such as the Hatch Chili Festival.

Just having the Cessna nearby made the *Celeste* look tiny. But Luke knew he could outfly the bigger plane easily.

But, just for the glamour shot, Luke removed the tie-down straps, raised the nose of the plane and climbed back into the spacesuit. Anna even perched on a stepladder to have a good angle taking shots of him sitting in the cockpit.

After he changed back into more practical clothes, he spent the rest of the afternoon installing the air tanks, rebreather controller, and hoses into the plane. The passenger seat was no longer usable to carry people. Luke had an extra air tank on order, hopefully arriving in another couple of days. The air system had been designed with tourist launches in mind. Luke wasn't confident his flight could be completed in the same length of time. Better to have a backup.

...

They stopped by Anna's house and knocked on the door of the house to the left.

Race Gonzales gave them a smile and invited them in.

"What are you two up to?"

Anna said, "Don't look at me like that. If something personal was going on, you'd hear it first from Tía Margarette, wouldn't you?"

He gave her a fond pout. "Probably, so what's the real story."

Anna leaned forward, "Well, you've probably heard about Luke's airplane?"

He nodded. "He finished Jase's plane, I heard. Some people have seen it in the air."

She nodded. "Only, it's a much bigger deal than that."

"Oh?"

"Luke and I have formed a company to promote and sell the engine that Luke created."

Gonzales blinked. "So it's some kind of invention?"

She nodded. "A really important one. And to make the biggest splash we can, we need to take the plane and my boat to California."

Luke said, "We could do that ourselves, but since I need to fly the plane and someone needs to trailer the boat; it's going to be complicated."

Anna said, "Tío, what are the chances you could help me haul the boat to San Diego while Luke flies the plane?"

...

The last minute changes to the boat and the plane took all their available time, and Luke often woke up in the middle of the night from dreams that military spies had come and stolen the plane. Twice he got into the van and drove to the airfield in the dead of night just to make sure it was still there.

Too many people knew about the thrusters. Word would get to the wrong ears sooner or later. But he made a list of people who knew; the man who had certified the plane, the air traffic controllers who must have noticed how fast he had climbed to flight level 300, and now Wilson the billionaire who called him every couple of days asking how soon his demo was scheduled.

Add to that the neighbors and the other residents of the town who had seen the plane or who had talked about the UFO, and there were just too many chances for a bad leak.

···

But the day came. Anna was dressed up in a stylish blazer over travel clothes and had a tripod for her cell phone. There was a special edition of *Anna and the Fantastic*, streamed live as they eased the *Enchantress*, draped in her protective cover, out onto the road.

Anna spoke to her followers.

"It's starting! All of you who've been following know that I've been hinting at something really big. Well, today, it's starting.

"Behind me is the *Enchantress*, a 32-foot cruiser that has been living in Elephant Butte Reservoir for a number of years. Over the course of the next two days I'll be traveling Interstate 10, taking it to San Diego where it'll settle into it's true native environment, the Pacific Ocean.

"Just to let you know how important this is, I want you to know that I've quit my important, well-paying job just so that I can be part of the event coming up on this channel. And I intend to bring you along for the ride.

"And to let you know what to expect—tonight, we'll stop over in Tucson, and then on to San Diego tomorrow. There, I'll meet up with Luke Moore, that clever maker guy I've talked about before. Together, we'll put the *Enchantress* into the water and start out on a most extraordinary journey."

Anna gave an evil grin. "And I'm *still* not going to tell you the most exciting part—not until it happens. Out in the ocean, the day after tomorrow, we're going to make history. People will be joining this channel in droves! You'll be hearing about it on the news. Make sure you've subscribed and tell your friends. You'll want to see it yourself live, as it happens."

Race called out, "Anna? Are you ready?"

She grinned, "Yes, Tío Race. I'm coming."

She pressed the button on her phone and collected her gear.

···

Luke had very mixed feelings watching her drive off in Race's heavy duty truck, towing the trailer. If he didn't have so many last-minute tasks of his own to deal with, he'd go watch her video again.

He double checked his stack of logbooks and the hard drive that contained a backup of all of his design files. He drove into town and locked them up in the safety deposit box he'd just rented at the Wells Fargo Bank.

A copy of everything was on the laptop he'd be taking with him, but just in case there was a problem, he wanted the discovery preserved.

His main computer at the warehouse was still sitting there, but all the important files were on an encrypted, hidden volume. If he were really paranoid, he'd have removed the files permanently, but part of him didn't really believe the warehouse would be raided by spies.

He added another check to his todo list when he purchased a pair of mirrored sunglasses. He had one pair, but if he broke it mid-flight, it would be better to have a backup.

He was up past midnight, making use of the computer he was going to leave behind.

He looked at the clock, drummed his fingers on the desk, and then went to the patent office website.

Off to California

Hernando and Juan were at the door at dawn.

Luke shook hands. "Gracias. I appreciate the help."

They all got into the van and drove to the airport. Luke prepared the *Celeste* for flight while Juan watched with wide eyes.

Then Luke had a few words with Hernando.

"I don't expect anyone to break into the warehouse, but if you see something suspicious, then feel free to call the police."

He then handed over an envelope with a key in it. "Should anything really bad happen, there's instructions inside. You'll probably never need it."

He waved them back. "I'll be taking off now. Just park the van in my yard as usual."

Luke could see Juan jumping and yelling excitedly at his father as the *Celeste* lifted and took off.

...

It was just thirty minutes into the flight when his cell phone chimed in the earphones.

"Luke here."

It was Anna. "I just wanted to let you know we're back on the road. Leaving Tucson."

"I'm over the interstate as well, at least for a little bit. My flight will be dodging controlled airspace and restricted areas as much as possible. I'm at about two thousand feet above ground level."

"Race says 'Hi!'"

Luke scanned the skies ahead of him. Talking on the phone was no excuse for distraction.

"For your information, the utility patent has been filed."

She giggled, "So I'm no longer under a gag order?"

He laughed. "You've been very good at hinting. I caught up with your latest video before I left this morning."

Anna was suddenly somber. "Luke, you're okay with releasing the videos now?"

"You're the PR department. It's your call. What are you going to release?"

He eased back on the throttle. Flying VFR was all about the landmarks and he was approaching the time when he had to avoid Cochise County Airport's controlled airspace. The rest of his trip was going to be complex, with lots of restricted airspace to fly around.

"I'm going to lead with the mystery story—the strange phone call, discovering you hurt in your accident, and the puzzling gadget spinning on the floor."

He nodded. "Sounds good. We've got to get the audience puzzled before blowing their minds. Demo time is fast approaching."

"Okay then."

"Sorry, but I'm going to lose cell signal. Gotta make a course correction."

"Oh! See you soon!"

...

Luke was there, later in the day at the Dana Landing parking lot north of the San Diego skyline and waved them to a preparation pull-thru slot.

Anna climbed down from the cab and gave him an impulsive hug. "You said you'd get here before us. How was your flight?"

He smiled. "The flight was smooth. The Uber ride here from Ramona Airport was nerve wracking. I'd forgotten what California traffic was like."

Anna nodded, "I know! Race was grumbling the whole way here."

The driver nodded. They shook hands. "Ready to unload?"

Luke glanced at his watch and frowned.

Anna asked, "Plan B?"

He nodded. "We should have time. And if not …." He shrugged. They had discussed several scheduling possibilities.

They removed the cover and all the tie down clamps. Then Race, with the skill of a lifetime trucker, eased the boat trailer down into the water. Anna idled the diesel until Luke yelled that the bow hook was free. She backed the cruiser away from the boat ramp and brought it over to the nearby dock.

Over the next few minutes, Luke folded out the new aluminum platforms and ran the thruster control system through its self-tests.

"Hey, I've got sandwiches from the deli."

"Oh, Tío Race, you're so good to me!" She grabbed a sandwich. "I'm starved!"

Race looked at all the additions to the cruiser that Luke had added since the last lake party he had attended. "I hope you kids know what you're doing."

Luke put his weight onto the platform he'd secured and nodded. "I hope so, too."

But then it was time to go. Anna gave her tío a big hug and promised that she'd be a good girl. "You've got the link to my channel, so make sure you keep watching and make sure everyone in town knows about it, too."

Luke held her hand and they shared a wordless moment. The next day or so was going to be stressful, and they could only hope that everything went according to schedule.

Then, they tossed the lines and Anna rumbled out into Mission Bay alone.

Race shook his head. "I hope she'll be safe."

...

Race said, as they wound their way through California traffic back to the Ramona Airport, "Do you really have an engine that doesn't need fuel? I could use something like that. The diesel costs are killing me."

Luke frowned, "I'll certainly cover your costs for this trip."

Race waved his hand. "Oh, Anna already wrote me a check. That's no issue. Just in general, this beast is thirsty."

Luke nodded. "In general, it's true my thruster doesn't use fuel, but that's no guarantee that it'll suddenly take over the world.

"I can make jets that can push my plane and push her cruiser, but I'm not sure how I could make a replacement for your big Cummings diesel."

Race frowned, "But you're flying that plane at hundreds of miles per hour. Anna said you hope to climb up into space with it. Surely that takes a lot of juice?"

"A lot less than you think. The standard engine for a plane like this is only 125 hp. For one thing, the plane is really lightweight. It's made of styrofoam and fiberglass, basically. Those rockets are all made of metal and weigh a lot more. But the real problem is that most of their rocket power is used to lift all that rocket fuel.

"A NASA rocket or a SpaceX has to lift tons of weight and accelerate it to supersonic speeds in a hurry to reach orbital velocity before running out of gas. The longer they take to get up to speed, the more fuel they need to burn, and thus the heavier the rocket."

Luke smiled, "But my cheat is that I don't use fuel and I can take my time. Instead of cracking the sound barrier, I can go to space at a snail's pace and I don't have to carry along millions of gallons of fuel to do so."

He shrugged. "If I tried to go supersonic, the plane would fall apart around me. I have to take it slow."

They pulled into the airport and Race parked his truck.

Luke said, "It'll be a while before I take off. I have to check the weather reports and file my flight plan."

Race shook his head. "I'll wait. I'd like to see the thing fly."

Luke nodded, thanked him again for his help and went over to his plane.

There were two men standing nearby chatting.

"Is that your Long-EZ?" one of them asked.

Luke nodded. "Yes, just passing through."

"The thing is," the man said, "I don't see a prop under that tarp. Is it a jet?"

Luke smiled. "I'll be taking off shortly. You can see for yourself. Let's just say it's called an experimental aircraft for a good reason."

Then he went inside to take care of his paperwork. The denser the population, the more important the paperwork, and San Diego County was a lot more densely populated than Hatch, New Mexico. Luke was in constant fear that some air traffic controller would see something irregular and call a halt to his flight.

But he checked the weather, filled out his flight plan with true, but innocuous details, and went back to his plane. He was watched as he removed the cloth that hid the details of the thruster and stuffed it into the back seat.

He waved to Race in the parking lot, and made his final preparations. Quickly enough, he got his clearance for takeoff and let the spectators make their guesses about his jet as he took off in traditional fashion down the runway.

Lifting Off

Anna's smiling face appeared on the screen. She was dressed in a sailor style blouse and shorts, but without the Sailor Moon wig.

"Hello, all of you. Long time followers will see instantly that I'm not broadcasting from my phone this time. I have a different studio set up for now."

She stood up and the camera tracked her motions, showing the interior of the boat and the Pacific Ocean in the background.

"I am currently several miles west of San Diego, on a heading toward Hawaii." She grinned. "And I'm sure some of you are more familiar with boats than others, and you'll be saying to yourself 'There's no way she can reach Hawaii on that cruiser.' And you'd be right, if I were going to rely on the diesel engine.

"The tank holds about two hundred and forty gallons of diesel, and gets a little over a mile per gallon. Hawaii is off that way, over twenty-five hundred miles distant. As you can see, the numbers don't work."

She gestured toward the aft of the boat and the camera followed her. "But I'm not using diesel. I'll only be using it to keep my batteries charged. Right now, the *Enchantress* is cruising along under ion thrusters powered by zero-point energy."

She chuckled, waving her hands down. "I can see your comments, you know. Yes, zero-point energy is only common in science fiction and quantum physics texts. Jeromy, you say it's not real, but tell that to the physicists, and we'll have this discussion when I show up at Hilo Bay on the Big Island, after having crossed twenty-five hundred miles in a boat that only has diesel for three hundred miles at best.

"You see, Luke Moore, the inventor of this thruster, told me when he first made the discovery that he was reluctant to go public with it because people who claimed perpetual motion machines were either crooks or delusional. What he said stuck with me. 'Extraordinary claims require extraordinary proof.' I looked it up and it's a variant of a quote by Carl Sagan. It's okay to be skeptical. Just keep your eyes open for the next couple of days."

She held up a clicker and pressed the button. The image shifted. She turned to face the new camera. "But just for now, let me show you around the *Enchantress*. Item one, I've got a satellite dish for internet support since I'll be well out of cell phone range."

She led the way across the deck showing off the four remote cameras and the computer she'd be using to originate her streams. She went down below and showed her fully stocked pantry and all the preparations she'd made for the trip.

A few minutes after the grand tour, she was showing off her ability to do split-screen in real time when the radio blared.

"*Enchantress*, this is *Celeste*, approaching from the east. Please confirm your coordinates."

Anna almost fell out of her chair as she reached over to grab the microphone.

"This is the *Enchantress*." She put her finger on the GPS display. "I'm at 32.58° north and 118.31° west. About fifteen miles south of San Clemente Island. I'm making 15 knots heading due west."

"Roger, *Enchantress*, 32.58 by 118.31. What's the wind speed?"

She read the gauge.

Luke said, "Roger. Turn into the wind and maintain five knots. I'll be there within five minutes."

Anna worked over her controls, narrating as she made her adjustments.

"Luke made me an autopilot, which is really great, since it allows me to get up and walk around the deck while the *Enchantress* maintains course and speed. It works by adjusting the ion thrusters, rather than worrying about the rudder.

"Right now, I've got the course adjusted and we've slowed down and I can trust the autopilot to keep everything stable while I set up the cameras. Nobody should look away from the screen or take a potty break for the next few minutes. You really don't want to miss this."

It was nearly five minutes later when the radio blared. "This is the *Celeste*, I see you, *Enchantress*. Please confirm that you're in the safe zone."

"I'm at the chair, I can see you in the aft camera view. You're clear to land."

"Approaching."

The white plane, only a couple of dozen feet above the waves approached slowly.

Anna narrated for the audience. "One of the major alterations Luke did to my father's Long-EZ airplane was to add vertical ion thrusters at the nose and on the rear wings. With open source software originally designed for quad-copter drones, he customized it, giving the *Celeste* VTOL capabilities— Vertical Take-Off and Landing. From the pilot's seat, he can fly his plane just like my camera drone."

Anna giggled. "I'm as nervous as a cat near a rocking chair. It's coming straight towards me!"

It was ten feet, then five, and then hovering right over the rear deck of the *Enchantress*. Carefully, Luke eased the plane down on a set of aluminum plates, carefully aligned so that the heated plasma from the thrusters splashed on the metal, rather than on the boat's deck.

The two rear wheels settled down on another metal plate and rolled back an inch. Spring-loaded clamps swung into place and clamped the wheels in place.

Luke didn't bother to lower the nose gear, settling the nose down onto its own metal plate.

"I'm down. Killing the thrusters."

Anna dashed out of her protected space and grabbed up a wide strap and tossed it over the nose of the plane. She grabbed the free end and tightened it.

"You're secure!" she yelled. The plane looked ungainly large, with the wings extending well out over the water.

Luke opened the canopy. "Ah! The ocean breeze smells great."

Anna grabbed her clicker and aimed the remote camera as she held out her hand as he climbed down to the deck of the *Enchantress*.

Luke grinned. "When I was filing my flight plan, back at the Ramona Airport, the guy at the desk asked me where I was heading. I said I was going out to join an aircraft carrier." He shook his head. "The guy thought I was joking."

Anna turned to face the camera. "I hope you saw all that. Not only are the zero-point powered thrusters driving the *Enchantress* to Hawaii, but also powering this unique aircraft, the *Celeste*. Not only is it a VTOL, but its main engines are capable of pushing the craft to extraordinary heights."

Luke watched fondly as she explained a few things to her audience. Then she turned to him. "Are we still on schedule for the record-breaking flight?"

Luke glanced at his watch. "Yes, I think so. I need to get dressed for it."

Anna turned to her camera again. "You heard it. In just about thirty minutes, the *Celeste* will be taking off in an attempt to break an altitude record. I'm going to be switching to a pre-recorded segment showing the history of the *Enchantress* and our early experiments for the ion thruster drive. Make sure you stay on this channel and let all your friends know that some truly breathtaking events will be happening shortly. See you in thirty minutes."

She clicked her control.

Luke shook his head. "Now, you've done it. You promised them."

She smiled. "Yes, I did. But you've got to deliver. This is our demo. I've already given them the 'extraordinary claims' speech."

Anna reached for his shirt button. "Time for you to get changed."

He sighed. "You never change."

...

Anna brought up her camera. "And I'm back live. I hope you enjoyed that look into the development of the thruster system for the *Enchantress*. And didn't Luke look great in a bathing suit!

"There will be more historical background videos when things get a little slow, and you can watch them again on the timeline sidebar. I've been recording video since this whole thing started and I've made many extra features for you, all in preparation for today.

"Just reminding you again. Spam all your friends right now to come watch what's happening on *Anna and the Fantastic* because this is history happening right now."

She looked up. "I think I hear him. Let's go look."

She walked over to the door to the cabin area and opened it a crack. "Luke, are you decent?"

"Yes. I'm coming." He came out into the daylight, and the starburst-decorated spacesuit was a dramatic change from his jeans and shirt earlier. He was carrying a canvas bag with a hose connected to the suit. He had the hood pulled back.

"I was just checking to make sure that the suit pressurized properly. If there is a hole, I didn't want to discover that mid-flight."

Anna beamed. "You look great! As our viewers can probably guess, this is a real spacesuit that Luke managed to borrow. It's handy that our home base in Hatch, New Mexico is so close to Spaceport America, where there are so many other companies working in the space industry. When you're going for a new altitude record, you have to be dressed for the occasion."

Luke nodded. "Anna, if you could help me?"

"Sure." She tapped twice on her controller and the camera followed them over to the cockpit. Anna supplied a footstool that helped Luke manage getting into place even when wearing the suit. He pulled the hose and the bag in with him.

"Oh! I almost forgot. Anna could you get the picnic basket?"

She laughed. "Yes, you can't forget that!" She rushed down into the cabin and brought the flexible, woven basket with her. Luke took it and stuffed it into one of the storage areas on the side.

"I'll be working down my checklist, now."

"Okay, plug in your microphone so we can follow along."

He made the connection between the suit and the radio on the control panel. "Can you hear me?"

She dashed over to her seat. "Yes! We're streaming you."

"Okay. I'm going to leave the helmet open until I get to ten thousand feet, but I'm switching the air supply from the portable tank over to the back-seat tank. I don't want to have to deal with that while flying."

He continued down his checklist until he said to Anna, "Give me a wind reading. It's time to remove the latches and free up the plane."

"Wind has picked up a little. Eight to twelve knots. Still minor."

"That's good. Unlatch the plane."

Anna dashed over and removed the nose strap and pushed the wheel latches back to their triggering positions. She yelled. "You're free."

"Get clear."

She dashed back into her protected area and brought up all the cameras, focused on the plane. "I'm clear. You're free to take off."

On the screen, the VTOL thrusters lit up and although they weren't very bright in the daylight, the heat shimmer was quite noticeable. The *Celeste* lifted clear, and Anna was quite pleased that one of her cameras had gotten a great shot of Victoria's logo image on the nose of the plane.

Luke quickly gained altitude and the main thruster lit up.

"I'm changing channels now. I've got to talk my way through this Air Defense Identification Zone with the ATC."

"I'll be following your transponder."

"Good. Later."

Anna waited a moment, but he had already switched frequencies.

She turned to face the camera at her computer.

"Well, until this is over, Luke won't be paying any attention to my stream, so I'd better just get this out there." She rested her head on her hand.

"Mary024 and JessicaL, yes, it's true. I've got a crush on the guy. I have since we first started this. But the thing is, we made a pact early on, when we joined forces to make something of this zero-point thruster business. Nothing personal is permitted until we go viral on this demonstration of the technology. We didn't want to sabotage the business with mis-steps in the more personal side of things.

"So today is the make or break. We've got to go viral on this stream. So please, any of you who've been making those snide comments, it's time to help a girl out. Call your friends and have them subscribe. If we succeed, you just might get something juicy. If there's a problem, well then I might need a friend to come pick up the pieces when I fall apart."

She straightened up. "Okay. Enough of that. Back to business.

"I'm putting up on the side screen a website some of you are familiar with, Planefinder.net. It tracks planes based on the transponder on board the plane. Let me show how to connect to *Celeste*'s transponder and we can all watch where it goes and how high it gets!"

High Altitude Glitch

Luke switched to the *Enchantress* private channel.

"Anna, do you read?"

"Luke! Yes, I hear you."

"Good. I'm above 10,000 feet and the spacesuit is working fine. I only have a moment before I've got to switch back to the ATC to notify them that I'm climbing up into class A airspace and let them watch out for passing airliners. I hope I'm in a clear area, but I need to rely on the towers and their radar."

She replied, "Be safe. I'm tracking your transponder. And I think that at least a few hundred of our viewers have pulled up their own copies of Planefinder. I get the feeling some of them don't trust my copy."

He chuckled. "The more independent eyes on us, the better. I'm going to request that the ATC track me as well. But, as you can see, I'm climbing pretty fast. Gotta go."

"Later."

Things were going well. He'd filed a flight plan over the internet while still on the boat declaring that he was taking off from the "ocean platform *Enchantress*", climbing to an undermined altitude and returning to the same platform. While that was his intention, the ATC who responded to his initial contacts had obviously seen his flight plan and questioned him about the altitude.

"Experimental aircraft 8892 has never reached its flight ceiling on previous test flights. That's the purpose of this test."

The ATC agreed to monitor his flight and gave him clearance to climb through class A airspace. Luke was supposed to confirm when he had reached his peak.

He took a moment to call Anna and give her the frequency he was using to talk to the controllers. She promised to listen in.

Luke checked his altitude on his GPS. At 48,000 feet, he no longer had to keep the throttle at reduced levels. At 55,000 feet, ATC contacted him for a status update.

"Still climbing," he reported. "Grateful for ITAR free GPS."

The International Traffic in Arms Regulation, designed to keep companies from selling sensitive technology to potential enemies was the source of the restriction on GPS that had caused his model rocket failure. He'd made sure the GPS for his plane was free of that limit.

"Roger that. You're cleared for class E airspace if you get there."

"Thanks."

The class A airspace, where all the commercial airliner traffic flew, topped out at 60,000 feet and above that it reverted to the less restrictive class E.

A moment later, Luke spoke into the microphone. "Flight level 601." He had made it clear of class A space.

Luke wasn't really sure how high he could reach. As long as he could still climb, balanced on his rear thruster, he'd keep going. The problem was that the air had gotten very thin. His wings weren't likely to provide enough lift in a normal flight attitude.

He glanced at the air-pressure based altitude gauge, almost resting on the pin. He was above the Armstrong limit and his spacesuit was fully pressurized, keeping him alive.

"Flight Level 700."

The plane's controls were feeling mushy and he was having difficulty keeping the nose pointed straight up. He had to use the nose-mounted pitch and yaw thrusters to help, but even those were weak.

"It's time." He was talking to himself and realized that he needed to turn on the flight recorder. Anna would be upset if he said something significant and forgot to record it.

He told the ATC, "Flight level 800. Switching over to water vapor for reaction mass."

"Experimental 8892, repeat."

"Flight level 800, switching from air thrust to water vapor."

He flipped a switch closing his air scoop. He could feel the thrust against his seat fade as the little bit of air pressure feeding the thrusters was consumed.

He turned the valve that connected the fuel tanks, filled with distilled water, to the thruster's air channel. Now exposed to vacuum, water started to boil in the tanks, venting water vapor to the thrusters.

He felt the pressure climb. He corrected his nose-up attitude with the pitch and yaw thrusters, and those were much more responsive with the water vapor as well.

The GPS said he was climbing rapidly. He was sure that he was feeling more power than he'd felt before. He adjusted the water valve downward. He didn't want to waste any of the water vapor. He didn't have real flight experience running on water vapor, and he wasn't ready to totally trust the lab experiments.

"Flight Level 900, water vapor thrust responding well."

. . .

Anna was chewing on her thumb, staring at the numbers on her screen. The comments on a side bar caught her eye.

"Yes, I'm nervous. Who wouldn't be? When Luke explained the flight to me, he was so confident that I just soaked that up. I made my objections about how dangerous this is and he had answers for everything.

"But it's a different in real life! Luke is up there in an airplane that was never designed for flying that high. He's three times higher than the design limit. He's so high that he has to wear a spacesuit!"

Just a moment later the numbers on the screen flicked up to 100,000 feet and kept climbing.

Anna winced every time Luke's voice broke up into static as he reported his altitude.

Anna said, "I've got a good antenna for the VHF radio on the *Enchantress*, but the plane can't get too fancy with antennas. I hope his signal lasts."

At about 200,000 feet the transponder numbers glitched.

Anna swallowed. "I expected this. Luke said the transponder's code failed after a certain altitude. It's designed for airplanes, not spaceships. We can't count on the Planefinder's numbers anymore.

Luke's voice was breaking up as he called out, excitedly. "Flight L…
3300. Passed the Kármán…."

Anna gasped. "He did it!" She put her hand on her chest, and swallowed.

"People, let me explain something. Luke Moore, in his homebuilt experimental airplane, something he cobbled together from my father's first efforts back at the time I was born, has climbed up past the Kármán line—a hundred kilometers, over sixty-two miles high. And that, my friends, is the official boundary line that marks the beginning of space!"

She had tears in her eyes. "Listen to me. A self-taught inventor, working in his garage, basically, has built himself a spaceship and made himself an astronaut!"

…

Luke was seeing some of his instruments go inactive, either from the lack of atmosphere or getting out of the range of navigation beacons on the ground. But his GPS was still giving him readouts.

The original gas tanks, two tanks holding twenty-six gallons each, had a clever low-tech "gas gauge". They had transparent plates that let the pilot look inside the tank and see how much fuel was left.

What he could see now was bubbles forming in the water. It wasn't a roiling boil like a pot on the stove, but it was obvious that the water was boiling at low temperature. When the pressure got lower it boiled more, until the vapor pressure climbed and quenched the process. He was having to eyeball it, rather than have numbers he could plug into his calculator, but he felt confident that he had quite a bit of reaction mass available.

He pressed the transmit button. "Going for plan B."

There was no reply from the ATC.

To his flight recorder he said, "I don't know if Anna heard me, and the ATC probably has no idea what plan B is, but in essence, I'm going to see if I can accelerate up to orbital velocity.

"Now that I am above the atmosphere, I don't have to worry about the wind forces damaging the plane. I can turn the thrust up to the limit and as long as I have enough reaction mass to slow myself down later, I can go as fast as I want.

"I know it's untried and dangerous, but I also believe that I'll never get another chance at this. The ATC let me get above controlled airspace because they really didn't know what I was doing. Next time, I'll probably be faced with a mountain of paperwork before I'd be permitted to try it again.

"The whole reason for taking off from a floating platform off the coast in international waters was that I was dead sure I'd never afford all the paperwork to get permission for a space launch from Hatch, New Mexico. I'm trying to be as legal as I can, but there are limits for a private individual without a fortune to spend.

"This is one of those situations where it's easier to ask forgiveness than get permission. Let's just hope I survive it."

. . .

Anna shook her head, staring at the camera. "People, I don't know. Our plan was that if he had plenty of oxygen for his spacesuit and if the water vapor from his water tanks worked well with the thrusters, he'd take a stab at trying to go into orbit. The idea was to take pictures from orbit and then to turn the plane around and slow himself down and re-enter the atmosphere at a safe pace.

"But the transponder failed, I guess. First, the altitude numbers froze up when he got too high, but the latitude and longitude worked, for a bit. At first, he was plainly traveling toward the northeast as he sped up, but something is wrong and the transponder decoding just looks wonky. On Planefinder, his little icon started jumping around and I can't trust anything it says."

She took a deep breath. "But... if there was a real disaster, there wouldn't be any signal at all, right? All I can do is cross my fingers and hope. I'm going to keep watching and pray that he starts coming back down safely."

She looked at the comments streaming on her screen.

"John9999, thank you. I'd appreciate someone watching the NASA channel, just in case anyone sees something."

. . .

Luke fussed with his gloved fingers, adjusting the options on his GPS display. Whoever designed the display had never expected the plane to be this high and once he crossed FL1000, the altitude display started displaying nonsense. But, he remembered in the manual that there was a way to make it display altitude in miles, and after a few false trials, he found it.

He'd heard the term "flying by the seat of your pants" and had always thought it was just a colorful bit of nonsense, but he had more respect for it now. None of his instruments were really designed for this environment and he was getting the feel for his acceleration mainly by how firmly he was being pressed into his seat. It was hardly digitally precise, but he had a feeling that he was accelerating upward and forward at a fairly constant rate.

He wanted a circular orbit roughly 250 miles high and to get there he had to bring the nose down with the pitch thruster ever so slightly from time to time. He wanted gravity to slow down his vertical climb even as his forward velocity increased.

There were a few numbers he'd memorized in advance. Since his thruster was powerful enough to climb in a tail-standing mode, then it could do more than one gravity's worth of thrust and so he should be able to reach orbital velocity in under fifteen minutes if he weren't climbing. Sadly, he was having to wing it all, guessing how much thrust to apply at what climb angle, and then checking the numbers on the GPS to see if he was getting close to what he wanted.

Luke sighed. Trial and error wasn't the way to go into space when error could kill you. Still, he didn't feel like backing out now.

He adjusted the climb angle down another notch.

...

Anna closed her eyes and looked away from the screen. PolloFarn was ranting on the comments that Anna was a horrible person for sending her boyfriend to his death just to go viral and make her name famous.

She had her own doubts. Second thoughts had been climbing higher than the *Celeste* as she went minute by minute with no firm contact. There was no transponder data now and Luke's icon had vanished off the map.

He's just out of range. That's all. He's too smart to get into trouble.

She tried to keep her sweaty hands out of the camera view. There wasn't anything she could do right now, other than recommend the viewers check out her historical videos showing how they'd gotten themselves this far.

Bragging Rights

The surge in thrust made him grab for the stick, although there wasn't a thing the elevators or ailerons could do right now.

It's the thrusters.

It took him half a second to look down at the water tanks. As he approached orbital velocity, the effects of gravity were being cancelled out, and he could see it in the water. The fluid was sloshing with hardly any gravity to keep it down at the bottom of the tank.

"I've got a problem," he spoke into his flight recorder. "With no gravity, the water is splashing in the tank and water droplets are being sucked along with the water vapor and reaching the thruster intake.

"It's just like the rain problem on the *Enchantress*. When a water droplet gets sucked into an ion tube, the thrust is very irregular. I've got to find a way to keep liquid water in the tank, away from the hose."

He throttled down lower, but cutting power abruptly was what had caused the thrusters on the boat to crack. He couldn't risk that now.

No gravity. Gravity had been holding the water down, away from the hose.

To the recorder, he said, "I need to find a way to keep the water away from the venting hose. Gravity won't do it anymore, so maybe centrifugal force?

"I'm going to spin the plane along its axis, just a little. That should force the water away from the center of mass. Since the vent hose leads close to that center line, the liquid water should stay away.

"At least I hope so. Cross your fingers."

Luke tapped on the right wing VTOL thruster, using it as a roll control. Just the one tap and the curved, night time horizon of the Earth below began to tilt. Instinct demanded he grab the stick and correct it, but once again, this was a spaceship, not an aircraft right now.

He forced his eyes to look at the water sloshing in the tank. It was still chaotic, but the water was mostly avoiding the vent hole he'd installed.

Starting the roll had thrown the plane slightly off his preferred course, so he carefully made adjustments with the nose thrusters. He had to keep it under control. If the plane started flipping end over end, he might never recover.

Taking a moment to make sure everything was still aligned properly, he added more thrust, resuming his attempt to reach orbital velocity.

"I think that did it. The *Celeste* is in a slight roll, maybe a little more than one RPM. The water is under control. I have resumed thrust."

His eyes were drawn to the nighttime lights of North America as the globe passed overhead.

He reached for the cell phone stuffed in a little side pouch on his suit. Grateful that the spacesuit gloves were designed with touchscreens in mind, he switched to video mode and recorded. He'd need to keep it short. In the vacuum, the phone could overheat quickly.

"Anna, I never wanted you to come along on this trip because it is just too dangerous, but for the first time, I really wish you were here to see this. I'm taking a video of the North American night outside the canopy and it's just breathtaking."

He recorded the lights and the thunderstorms over the northeast and then got back to the important business of flying a spaceship by the seat of his pants and a GPS that never thought it would be in space.

I miss you Anna. I hope I return in one piece.

. . .

He was just over the Atlantic when a flicker of light caught his eye. He turned his shoulders to get a better look.

I thought I missed it.

He keyed the recorder. "I have just caught a glimpse of the space station. It's right on schedule, but I thought for sure I had missed the chance to see it.

"We're both in the night shadow, but I caught some moonlight off its solar panels. According to my readings, I'm about thirty miles below it and just a little slower.

"I'm going to try to get closer."

. . .

Plan B had been a joke, hatched over Anna's enchiladas shortly after they got the word that Roger Wilson had approved the spacesuit loan.

She'd said, "Reaching that magic space line—"

"The Kármán line."

"Yes, that one. It isn't enough. That's just numbers on the screen. People won't *believe* it. You need pictures from space—something a little more dramatic than those weather balloon shots. Maybe like those from the space station."

He chuckled. "Maybe I'll just go up there and say 'Hi!'"

"Oh? Could you? That'd be great."

He chuckled. "Let's make that Plan B. I need to concentrate on reaching that boring line first."

"The 'Astronaut Line'. Can we call it that?"

"We're already going to be in trouble for using sci-fi technobabble. Let's not make up new terms on the fly."

Through the planning stages, Plan B retreated to just the chance to reach orbit, but Anna, with a grin, kept making plans—including the picnic basket.

. . .

Moving a few dozen miles in three dimensions wasn't hard in theory, but both the station and the *Celeste* were now in orbital paths and any change in velocity or altitude had side effects.

Flying by sight and making minor tweaks was the only way to go, but it did take longer than some pre-calculated course correction like NASA used.

I messed up.

Getting to the space station was relatively easy, but Luke had totally neglected to design a braking thruster. With an airplane that wasn't a problem because there was always drag from wind resistance to deal with.

The vacuum of space was a different problem. He had a rough idea how to get back out of orbit, but carefully slowing down as he approached the station was a different issue.

He couldn't fly backwards and use the main thruster to slow down because he couldn't see in that direction. He had the same visibility problem using the VTOL system.

He really hoped no one was watching as he used the pitch thruster on the nose to tilt the *Celeste* up ninety degrees for just a moment—long enough to fire the wing units, then tilted back down to see if he was still aimed correctly.

It seemed to work, so he repeated the process, keeping an eye on how fast he was approaching.

I must look silly, bobbing up and down like this.

But the alternative, just flipping over and over, might make him sick.

Ridiculous as it seemed, the bobbing trick gradually worked, leaving him drifting at a snail's pace just a dozen yards from the solar panels.

He pulled out his phone and unlatched the canopy, taking a dozen videos and stills of the space station from a totally unique viewpoint.

"Anna, you're going to love these shots. Nobody has anything like them."

He could see the cluster of windows called the cupola and the motion of some astronaut working inside, but nobody was looking his way.

Luke shrugged. Why should they notice? It wasn't like they spent all their waking hours staring out the window.

He could make a little adjustment with his thrusters and be gone with no one knowing he had been there.

But that's not the point of this demo.

He slid the phone into his suit pouch and took a deep breath.

The spacesuit was designed so that the air hose could be swapped in vacuum. That's what inspired him to 3D print a second hose fixture and buy that spare air tank.

He twisted the hose free that connected to the plane's air tank and hooked up the portable one. The bag that contained the tank and its controller had Velcro straps he could secure to his leg.

This LEA spacesuit was never designed for floating around outside of space stations, but as far as Luke could see, it ought to work in a pinch.

He just couldn't turn down this chance. He'd never get another.

"Anna, I'm unplugging from the recorder now. I'm trying for a full Plan B. Talk to you later."

Only once before had Luke been this frightened—when he'd jumped off a cliff into the ocean on his one and only trip to the coast as a teenager.

This could go so badly.

He unfastened his straps and unplugged the microphone cord. He gripped the side of the fuselage tightly as he began to drift free of his seat.

Better not lose contact.

With his other hand he fished out one of the tie down straps and knotted it to the seatbelt. Holding the other end, he climbed free of the cockpit.

The solar panels were too close. He did *not* want to have to pay for damage to the station.

Reaching out, he gripped the structure and killed any remaining drift with a little muscle power. He fished the strap through a gap and tied it off.

I can now claim I docked with the space station! Bragging rights.

He pulled out the picnic basket. With it looped over his arm, he began climbing toward the cupola on the center structure, never releasing one hand without his other hand already tight on a new grip.

The trapezoidal windows of the cupola were soon in front of him. Inside was an astronaut he recognized. June... somebody, a mission specialist. He was embarrassed he couldn't remember her last name. He'd looked them all up, just in case, but the names hadn't stuck.

He tried to knock on the glass, but either his glove was too soft or the glass was too hard. She didn't look up from her work.

Luke frowned, then pulled out his phone and one-handed, he took a flash picture through the window.

She turned, startled. Her mouth moved, saying something.

He smiled and waved. She yelled something down the passageway.

Luke stuffed his phone away and pulled a pre-printed card from the picnic basket.

In large, bold print, it said: **"May I come in for a minute? I have cookies!"**

Cookies

"Thank you, John9999! I'll bring up the NASA channel in a sub window."

As Anna moused and tapped, she told her audience, "I have a report that the NASA channel has interrupted their regularly scheduled program for a special announcement. Pray that it's good news about Luke!"

...

Luke unfastened the hood of his spacesuit the moment the inner hatch opened and helpful hands reached out to help him navigate the tight quarters inside. One of the men had a small hand-held camera recording everything.

He smiled at June Masters, grateful her name was stitched on her clothes. "Sorry for the snapshot. I was just trying to get your attention. "

She grinned. "No problem. You mentioned cookies?"

He laughed and handed her the picnic basket. She hurriedly pulled out the eight bricks tightly bundled together in plastic wrap. The package looked a little bloated from the pressure inside during the vacuum exposure.

"Girl Scout cookies! I claim the shortbreads."

Greg Anders looked at his suit and asked, "Is this a Starshine mission?"

Luke shook his head. "No, just a borrowed spacesuit. I'm Luke Moore—just a garage inventor in a home-built plane. A two-person company out of Hatch, New Mexico."

Anders frowned, "I saw the plane, but how?"

Luke nodded. "Impossible, I know, but I've got an ion thruster powered by zero-point energy. I'd explain more, but that's Africa outside the window and I've got to leave almost immediately if I'm to hit my landing zone.

"I just wanted to pop in, say hello, and drop off the cookies."

Masters was carefully chewing on her cookie to keep crumbs from drifting off. She said, "And thanks for these, I've missed them." The cookies were being handed around to the other astronauts.

Luke shrugged. "It was Anna Bushnell's idea. She's my partner in this project."

He shrugged, "And sorry I didn't call ahead. I looked for the station frequency and didn't find it."

Anders nodded. "Probably not. But are you sure you can make it down safely? Your plane doesn't look like it can handle re-entry."

Luke shrugged, "I can't do a ballistic return, I'll just fly back slowly. Don't worry, I've got it covered."

Anders didn't look convinced. "You should probably wait here for a return capsule. It's too dangerous in an untried craft."

Luke smiled. "Acceptable risk is what this is all about. But I've really got to be going. Deadlines."

He started adjusting the hood.

Masters said, "I see Anna Bushell's card in here. Do you want me to call her?"

Luke nodded. "I'd appreciate it."

...

Anna watched, glued to the screen, not even able to comment, as the astronaut's camera watched Luke climbing through the solar panels, reaching the *Celeste* and climbing in.

She couldn't help but grin when the image zoomed in on the nose art she had commissioned. Victoria would be thrilled at that shot.

Then there was the image of Luke pushing away by hand, and a minute or so later, the nose jets were slightly visible as the *Celeste* reoriented.

The VTOL thrusters were plainly visible as Luke pulled away from the station and quickly vanished from the camera's view.

Anna was grateful for the low-key narration from the NASA channel, but her own comment stream was out of control. She could barely follow what was being said. Some were amazed. Others were critical of *everything* from the style of the spacesuit to the direction of Luke's flight.

Anna didn't try to reply. Much of the technical stuff was beyond her. She just had confidence Luke knew what he was doing.

...

Something was definitely wrong with the thrusters. Luke glanced at the water tanks and his stomach turned.

He'd noticed that the water had some icy slush when he had docked with the space station, but in the brief time the *Celeste* had been idle, much more of the water had turned to ice. Much of it had formed into clumps with a surface skin.

If the fluid water in those clumps was trapped behind an icy skin, then the vacuum couldn't pull out the water vapor his engines needed.

Sitting idle in the shade. I should have anticipated this. Install heaters next to the tanks?

Power was fading rapidly as the ion tubes were starved for molecules to split and accelerate.

If I had just realized it earlier.

He had already killed part of his orbital velocity and without thrust to slow himself down and manage a slow descent, he'd burn up in that ballistic re-entry Greg Anders warned him about.

And there was no way he could even make his way back to the space station. They were separating rapidly.

He kicked at the water tank, but there was nothing more than a slight increase in thrust.

When it stops, I'm dead.

...

"What Luke told me is that normal spaceships use heat shields because using wind resistance to slow down from orbit is a *lot* cheaper than firing retro-rockets all the way down and—"

Anna stopped mid-sentence as she saw the notice pop up on her screen. "Sorry, I've got a call from NASA. I've gotta take this."

She tapped the button.

"Hello, this is Anna Bushnell."

"Hello, Anna. This is June Masters on the International Space Station."

"Oh, wow! Thanks for calling. I'm live on my stream, is that okay?"

"Sure. No problem. I just wanted to let you know that Luke Moore arrived and left on schedule. He seemed to want to get back to his targeted landing zone on time."

Anna laughed. "Yes, we'd planned it so that he could get back here relatively soon. I'm so glad he made it. Visiting the station was a stretch-goal. We were certain he could get into space, and maybe make it to orbit, but reaching the station was just an extra."

"Well, I personally am grateful for the cookies."

They laughed.

June said, "And I am very grateful for the shortbreads. I sold Girl Scout cookies myself back when."

"So did I! But these were purchased from a little girl named Sonia Olguin who had a table at the local market in Hatch, New Mexico. She'll be overjoyed to know her cookies made it to the space station."

Masters laughed. "Yes, I think I can hear her squealing all the way up here!"

"Probably! I've been told everyone in Hatch is watching my stream."

. . .

Luke kept trying to rub his scalp, trying to figure out a solution, and instead hitting the space suit hood with his gloved hand.

There was absolutely no way he could survive a ballistic re-entry. Other space planes—like the space shuttle and the military's X-37B—had very strong, short stubby wings. The Long-EZ's 26-foot fiberglass and foam wings might take a little more than 3-G's of force, but add to that the atmospheric friction heating, and the *Celeste* would be falling apart around him shortly.

Luke remembered something he'd said to Anna. "I don't really know what I'm doing."

It was when he was finalizing the design of the *Celeste*. She asked why the shape had bulbs front and rear.

About the rear bulb, he'd said, "That's a ballast tank. I don't really know how the plane will be balanced with the light-weight thruster instead of the engine and prop, so I can adjust it that way."

His eyes lit on the simple, unlabeled switch, almost out of sight at the rear of the cockpit. He flipped it and a small stream of water from the rear ballast tank squirted into the main tanks. Almost immediately, the thrusters began pushing harder.

Thank you for ignorance! Luke felt a hint of relief.

That wasn't what it was designed for, but it just might save his life—if the water in the rear ballast tank wasn't frozen as well.

From what he could see through the gas tank window, ice was melting when it came in contact with the ballast water. That made sense. The ballast water was wrapped around the main rear thruster. When he'd examined the *Enchantress* thrusters, they had shown some evidence of heating. The ballast tank was like a little water heater.

I may survive this—if it works.

His first order of business was to use the re-activated nose thrusters to get the plane back into the proper attitude and continue slowing down his near-orbital velocity before he got low enough to hit the thicker atmosphere. Falling too fast was deadly.

He put the *Celeste* into a belly-first attitude, using the VTOL thrusters to slow his orbital velocity. At the same time, he used the main engine aimed at the ground to slow his fall.

It was an elaborate balancing act, sometimes with all the thrusters working in order to keep the plane oriented properly.

He still had to keep juggling the water flow. The instant the ballast water emptied into the main tanks, he flipped the water pump into reverse, pumping the now cool, but no longer frozen, water back into the ballast tank to be reheated. He'd keep the water circulating the whole trip if he had to—at least until he had air to feed into the thrusters.

. . .

Luke had ten minutes of relief, feeling like he had his reentry under control, when he started feeling anxious again. He noticed himself breathing rapidly, as if he was having a panic attack.

No! It's my air supply!

He reached down to the bag strapped against his leg. He pulled the velcro open and glanced at the pressure gauge. The secondary tank had gone empty. It should have lasted a lot longer than that! The carbon dioxide in his suit was climbing and his body was reacting to that.

My 3D-printed connector! It's defective.

He'd never really done a full safety check on it. He didn't have time, while getting ready for the trip to San Diego. It looked good and seemed to hold pressure, but probably something had been off—maybe a bad seal or something.

I really am an idiot.

He swapped back to the factory original air supply and checked how much air was left.

Not really enough.

His original plan was to slow down to a reasonable velocity while still above the bulk of the atmosphere and use the water vapor thrust to fly at what would normally be supersonic speeds back to the area above the *Enchantress* and then descend at normal flying speeds back to the boat.

There was no time for that. He needed to get back to breathable air as soon as possible.

He fumbled for his spare maps and data sheets. He really needed to know where he was.

West of Baja

Anna was almost in tears. "People, people, people! Check your planefinders! I'm getting reports that Luke's plane is showing up briefly on the map—somewhere just south of Baja California. Some reports say his transponder is squawking the emergency code. I thought I saw it once, but it vanished on me. I need to find out where he is. Please help!"

...

Luke was sweating, and not from fear. The *Celeste* was getting warm, too warm. He needed to slow down a little more. He couldn't afford to get any hotter from the air friction. There had been a comment in the construction notes for the plane that it should be painted white, since sunlight on a dark painted surface might cause damage to the skin if it overheated.

He adjusted the plane's attitude a little more. He was almost down in a normal flying attitude, but using the VTOL thrusters to give him the lift that the air on the wings was too thin to supply.

He checked his speed and position again, then switched the radio to the frequency used by the air traffic controllers at the Cabo San Lucas International Airport.

"Experimental Aircraft 8892 at flight level 650 calling CSL tower. Request."

The reply came a few seconds later, and Luke was very grateful that international aviation had standardized on English.

"CSL tower. I see your 7700 squawk. What is your status, 8892?"

"Experimental 8892 is coming down fast. I'm very low on breathable oxygen and need to get down to flight level 100 as fast as I can. I'd like to stay on bearing 325 to get back to home base, and I have limited maneuverability while descending."

"Roger 8892, maintain course at your discretion. Will watch for traffic. Monitor this frequency. Squawk 4000 when at flight level 100."

"Thanks CSL tower. Monitoring. Maintaining course, squawk 4000 at 100. 8892"

...

Getting down fast was harder than it seemed. Even as Luke entered class A airspace, he was having to fight how slippery the *Celeste* was. The plane was too good at gliding. The Long-EZ was a very streamlined design, so much so that it had an airbrake—a flap that's sole purpose was to make the plane *less* streamlined. It had been necessary to allow the plane to land on shorter runways.

Luke had been faced with the problem of getting lower without speeding up too much. Once again, he wished for a braking thruster. He'd never really used the airbrake except at slow speeds during a landing, so he wasn't really sure how safe it was to use at high speeds.

...

The word spread that the *Celeste* was coming down. Anna watched the transponder numbers as the plane dropped, and dropped, and dropped. She knew that Luke had planned to stay at a higher altitude until he got closer and worried what was wrong.

"Oh! Thank you KevinPearce!

"People, I've just gotten a report that Luke has contacted Cabo San Lucas airport reporting that he's low on his spacesuit's oxygen. He's getting lower faster than anticipated so that he can breathe without the tanks. I think that's 10,000 feet for those who are tracking his transponder. Pray that he can hold out until he gets to that safe altitude!"

...

When Anna got a call on her VOIP phone over the satellite internet, there was a pop-up window with the caller-ID. When she saw Luke's name, she almost stubbed her fingers, accepting the call.

"Luke! You're back!"

"Yes, and flying at a safe and steady pace for once. It was a little anxious there for a little bit."

"Yes, I heard. An oxygen problem?"

"Yes, and other things. All past now. I've only got one bar of cell signal and it'll drop out quickly, I'm sure. I just wanted to tell you I'm okay."

"Great. Hang on one second."

She said, for her audience. "I'm going silent for a moment. Nothing too mushy, I promise." And she muted her feed.

"Luke, are you still there."

He chuckled. "Yes, and I assume you have something to say?"

"Yes, but nothing personal yet. I've gotten a call from Roger Wilson and he's desperate to talk with you immediately."

"Probably wants his space suit back."

"Maybe. But I'm sure he wants a signature on a contract before someone else tries to poach our little arrangement."

Luke sighed. "It'll still be four or five hours before I can get there because I had to come back to the lower altitude sooner than planned. You already know all the issues we discussed. You can negotiate our deal. I have confidence you're better at person-to-person things than I am anyway."

"Hmm. Maybe. But one thing he mentioned was that he wants to buy the *Celeste* outright, in addition to getting the patent rights."

Luke hesitated. "You have a lot of sentimental value in this plane. So do I, actually. But I'll leave it up to you."

"Okay but...." Anna blinked as the VOIP call ended with a dropped-call message. Luke had flown out of range of the cell tower.

...

His stomach growled, but Luke ignored it. If he hadn't made it to the space station, his backup plan was to raid the cookies for himself, but missing a meal was hardly the worst thing in the world. He was just grateful to be breathing, watching the waves below, glistening under the moonlight. Mexico was just a haze in the distance off his right wing.

He adjusted his speed a notch slower. There was no need to rush, and he hoped to meet up with the *Enchantress* when there was at least dawn light to assist. He'd never added special landing lights to the "aircraft carrier" upgrade.

One more oversight. He should write a book about all the mistakes he'd made.

For one thing, he wished he had an autopilot. He'd had very little sleep over the past two days and flying the *Celeste* meant his hand on the stick at all times. He could also use some caffeine.

But he couldn't doze off. So, he did what he usually did at times like these, work through the details of his next project, whatever that happened to be.

Forget about his past mistakes, forget about the urgent tasks in the next few hours. Just imagine he was back at the warehouse, tinkering with a new idea.

He blinked, seeing lights up ahead.

There were two planes, each had both red and green lights, heading toward him, maybe two miles out. He dropped his speed a little and angled a few degrees to the starboard.

Both planes moved as one, steering the opposite direction.

He had a hunch and switched his radio to 122.75, the fixed wing air-to-air channel.

"Experimental aircraft 8892."

"Greetings, *Celeste*. We're 5693 and 5982 out of San Diego, come to escort you to the *Enchantress*."

Luke laughed. "You've been watching Anna's channel?"

"Everyone is watching. We just thought you deserved an honor guard."

Luke could see the two planes passing to his port.

"You're both Long-EZs."

"Yes, and we're honored that the one of our own took the high road and showed just what a garage inventor could do."

Luke felt a surge of emotion as the two planes moved into position to the right and left.

On Deck

"Sorry, JosephUnderTheTable, gotta go!" Responding to the commenters kept her awake all night, but there were priorities when the radio called her name.

She grabbed the microphone. "Luke! Wonderful to hear your voice."

"Great to hear you, too. I'm just a few miles out."

"Yes, I've been watching you on the planefinder screen. Did you know you reached the top of the most-watched-planes list?"

"That's nice, I guess. I gather that you went viral."

"Of course we did. It dropped off during the night, but now that you're coming in for a landing, the numbers are growing again."

"Well, it won't be long. I slowed down a bit so we'd have sunlight. How are the seas?"

"Not too bad. Winds are five to ten knots out of the southeast. I've drifted a little, but I've been circling the place, less than a mile from where I was when you took off."

"Can you do five knots into the wind like last time?"

She clicked her teeth. "That may be a little difficult. I have guests."

"Oh, I think I can see them. A seaplane and a helicopter."

"Yes, Wilson arrived on the plane. The helicopter on pontoons is a San Diego news crew."

"Well, I have guests as well—a couple of pilots escorted me in. Nice guys. Kept me awake. But I need you pointed into the wind. Tell your guests it's important."

She chuckled. "They already know."

"Oh, your show mike is live."

"Well, of course! Who do you think I am?"

"You're my Anna. And I can't wait to be there."

She smiled, her heart beating rapidly.

Off to the side the news crew on board the helicopter were moving their cameras into position. When her guests had arrived, she gave them the wifi password but told them they couldn't come on board. They were probably following the show.

She eased the boat into the wind, making just a knot or two.

Up above, the trio of planes came into view and circled the area while she got ready.

Anna spoke. "The landing hooks are ready. I'm in the safe zone."

"Okay. Seeing my buddies off."

The *Celeste* wagged its wings and the two other planes broke away and circled at a distance. Then the *Celeste* slowed to a crawl with the VTOL engines lit up and came in to dock on the aluminum plates as before.

As Anna rushed out and secured the nose, Luke opened the canopy and waved up to the planes in the sky. They wagged their wings and headed back toward land.

The news crew was filming the whole thing. The two men from Starshine Space were standing on their seaplane's sponsons.

Luke whispered. "I'll talk to people, but after I get out of this suit and take a bathroom break. I'm also starving."

She helped him down the stepladder. "Do you need any help with the suit?"

He shook his head. "Just normal stiffness from sitting in the cockpit too long. I'll be right out."

Once he went below, Anna waved to the guests. She'd need to ease up closer to let them come aboard.

. . .

Luke's hair was still wet from his quick shower and he brushed at it with his hand as John Jacobs, the news man set up his camera on a tripod. Luke was just grateful to be back in his jeans and shirt.

Anna brought him a sandwich and Coke and sat down beside him. Roger Wilson and his assistant sat across from them on the other benches.

Jacobs held his microphone and asked, "Personally, I'm a little overwhelmed by the fact that if I stand up straight, I'll hit my head on an airplane that just a few hours ago was in orbit, tied to the space station."

Luke chuckled. "Go ahead and touch it. It's sturdy."

The reporter gave the wing surface a feel. "I guess this is real. I absolutely wouldn't have believed a story like this a week ago."

Luke nodded. "And when it first happened to me, when I first saw the ion thrust right in front of me, I didn't believe it either. It took a lot of experiments and a lot of evidence to convince me."

Anna chuckled, "And you can see a lot of that on my *Anna and the Fantastic* channel. It was just luck that I was there when it happened, ready to record it all."

Luke took her hand. "Now Anna, let the nice man tell his own story. People aren't going to forget your stuff."

She pouted. "Just say'n." But she squeezed his hand back.

Jacobs said, "Perhaps we should all introduce ourselves. Everyone knows Anna Bushnell, the bright face that greeted everyone as you produced your live coverage."

She waved her hand.

"I've been told you're a nurse?"

"Yes, until recently a Registered Nurse at Hatch Municipal Hospital. I had to step away from that for a bit, but nursing is my profession."

Jacobs said, "And you are Luke Moore, the self-made astronaut."

Luke chuckled. "Hmm. I wonder if there's a lapel pin for that. If not, I guess I should make myself one."

"And from what I've been told, that's what you do—make things."

Luke smiled. "That's my hobby. I've sold art and trinkets through my 3D-printing company, Maker Products, for a while. I've also dabbled in salvage sales and even worked in plant operations at the hospital."

"Oh, is that where you two met?"

Luke and Anna shared a look. She said, "That's where I met him. He didn't remember me until later. He was a bit timid. Putting this whole space project together has really made him more social."

"Maybe," Luke said.

Jacobs turned to face the two businessmen. "And I believe I recognize your face, Mr. Wilson?"

He nodded. "Yes, Roger Wilson of Starshine Space. This is Kurt Simpson, my assistant."

Jacobs nodded. "And Starshine Space is involved, how?"

Luke interrupted. "I'd like to take this opportunity to publicly thank Roger Wilson for the loan of the spacesuit. Without that, I'd never have been able to pull off such a high altitude flight, much less getting into orbit.

"Due to this support, we've had talks—our little two-person operation and his much larger enterprise—and shortly we'll be finalizing an arrangement.

"You see, I'm a garage tinkerer. It'll take a billionaire businessman to really make something of the patent I've filed."

Jacobs pushed for details but Luke shook his head. "Anna did all the negotiation and I'm sure there will be a suitable press conference explaining all the details later."

Wilson chuckled. "I don't have much to say right now. You should be interviewing these two. It's their day."

Jacobs asked, "So what are your plans now?"

Luke leaned over and whispered into Anna's ear. She leaned back and looked him in the eye. "You're serious."

He nodded.

Anna pulled out her phone. "Sorry, I have to make this call."

Jacobs said, "There's no cell coverage."

She waved her hand, her ear to the phone. "Working over the internet."

"Tía Margarette? It's me, Anna.

"Sí, en el océano. I just needed to call and make sure you'd be okay if Luke Moore and I went to have a Las Vegas wedding. No, there won't be time to come back home first."

She nodded to Luke.

"Yes, Luke and I are going to take the boat to Hawaii and I'm sure you'd be happier if I had the wedding *before* the honeymoon. We'll come back home and have a big family celebration afterwards, but … yes, I promise. Gracias, Tía."

She looked up at Luke's face and beamed.

...

Even after the reporter got his interview and Anna gave the good news to her followers on the stream, there was a lot to be done.

In addition to the patent rights, Anna had negotiated to lease the *Celeste* to Starshine, but it would stay in their name. Luke had to fly it to Boulder City Municipal Airport in Nevada where he could give one of the Starshine pilots a tutorial on how to fly it and use the VTOL features. Wilson brought Anna on his seaplane while Kurt Simpson stayed behind to babysit the *Enchantress*.

They had a Las Vegas wedding in rented finery with photos for the family back in Hatch and then spent the first night at a casino hotel before Wilson's people flew them back to the *Enchantress* the next day.

Then, they were alone, blasting away from annoying well wishers as fast as the thrusters on the boat would push them.

Anna drove the boat while Luke pulled weather charts over the internet. "I'd rather dodge any storms if possible."

She chuckled. "I don't care how long it takes us, as long as the food holds out." She looked at her husband. "What are your plans?"

"When we go back to Hatch?"

"Yes."

He shrugged. "I've had a few ideas. How would you like an electric car with a little zero-point generator in the trunk that keeps the batteries topped up? No gas, no charging plugs. Just a car that could drive forever?"

"Oh, I'd put the Buick out to pasture for that!"

He nodded. "I got into this with the idea to help the climate. Maybe something like that could make a dent."

He stretched back in the chair and said, "But no hurry. I intend to enjoy every minute of this trip."

She chuckled. "That's a good idea. How about you take a break from inventing and I'll take a break from streaming?"

He considered the idea, nodding. "Mostly."

She laughed, "Mostly."

END

If you want more books like this, consider leaving a review on your favorite online bookstore or review service.

Other books by Henry Melton include a number of young adult adventures, mainly science fiction. A few recommendations to start with are:
Emperor Dad
Extreme Makeover
Falling Bakward
Golden Girl
and many others.

In addition, there is the Project Saga, a multi-generation future epic spanning centuries.
Begin with: Star Time

https://henrymelton.net/2/quick-list-of-my-books/